I'M ON WHATEVER YOU ON

A.C. TAYLOR

Copyright © 2023 by A.C. TAYLOR

All rights reserved.

No part of this book may be reproduced in any form or by any electronic or mechanical means, including information storage and retrieval systems, without written permission from the author, except for the use of brief quotations in a book review.

Trigger Warning: Please note that this book contains the mention of sexual assault and may be triggering to survivors of assault or those sensitive to the subject matter. Reader discretion is advised.

1

SIMONE

"What's the damage?"

I placed my mother on speaker, then lifted the phone closer to my lips as I paced back and forth on the sidewalk. "Depends. Are we talking about my car? Or me?"

"My concern is you, Simone."

"Well, I'm fine," I replied before looking out into the intersection as a police officer directed the traffic that was quickly piling up. I shot my eyes back over to my car. From its flawless midnight paint job to the pristine dark leather interior, my Audi was my baby, and it always looked like new money. But right now, it looked like shit. Just the sight of it made me cringe. Forcing myself to look away, I whined, "Mama, the whole front end of my car is on the other side of the damn road, and there's a massive dent on the passenger's side. It's going to take days to get it fixed. Hell, maybe even weeks."

"Don't worry about all that. It will get handled. I'm just glad you're okay."

Taking a deep breath, I dropped my head back, forcing my hair to fall behind my shoulders. As soon as I closed my eyes, I was hit with the memory of rushing through the green light, and seconds later, my body slammed against the driver's side door.

As quickly as I could, I forced my eyes back open and shook my head until I was no longer plagued with the devastating reminder.

Feeling a twinge of pain, I lifted my arm and looked at the back of my hand. My deep brown skin was slowly turning purple, which didn't come as much of a surprise since I'd banged it against the window while trying to protect my head.

Still staring at my bruised flesh, I let out a deep sigh. "Yeah, I'm glad I'm okay too. It could've been a lot worse, and before you ask," I said, knowing that my mother wouldn't be able to resist trying to get more details, "It wasn't my fault, I got the other driver's insurance information, and I'll explain what happened later."

"Really, Simone?"

"Yes, *really*," I replied. "I'm tired, and I just want to go home."

"Okay, fine. Do you want me to send my driver to pick you up? Matter of fact, I'll just come myself."

"No, Mama. I'm fine. My assistant is on her way."

"Are you sure?"

"Yes. Oh, and please tell Legend I'm sorry that I'm not going to make it to his show tonight and that I promise to make it up to him." I placed my hand on my hip. "You know what? Just tell him his upcoming appointment is on me."

"Okay, but—"

"Mama, please get off this phone. You have more important things to be doing right now."

"Sweetheart, nothing's more important than my girls."

Knowing that was true, I nodded. "Okay, but you still have an artist to look after. This is Legend's first solo show at home, I'm sure he's probably looking for you. Go support him."

There was a moment of silence, then she finally said,

"Alright. But call me as soon as you get home. Even if I don't pick up, leave me a message. I want to know that you made it home safe."

"Will do."

"Alright, baby. I love you."

"Love you too." Ending the call, I turned toward the tow truck driver as he pulled up and parked in front of my car.

I can't believe this, I thought. *How did I let this happen?*

But I knew exactly how. Although it wasn't my fault that the other driver ran the red light, I probably would've seen him coming had my mind not been elsewhere.

"Hey, are you okay?" my assistant, Nitra, said as she hurried to meet me on the sidewalk.

"Yeah, I'm fine."

She darted her eyes over to the street. "Damn, is that your car?"

"Yes, and my feelings are too hurt."

Wrapping her arms around me, she said, "I'm so glad you're okay. As soon as I get you home, I'll make sure your rental car is ready to be picked up first thing in the morning."

"Thank you."

"Come on, let me get you home." She grabbed my hand and led me toward her car. "I'm sure you're still a little shaken up."

"That's an understatement. I just can't believe I let this happen. I should've been paying more attention. I shouldn't have allowed my mind to be bombarded with bullshit."

"Didn't you say the man ran the light?"

"Yeah, but I always double check before going. Thanks to my lack of focus, I didn't do that this time, and look where it got me." I dropped my shoulders, then opened the passenger's side door, and fell into the seat.

Easing behind the wheel, Nitra looked over at me, her doe eyes softening at the sight of my defeated expression. "It's okay,

Simone. The important thing is that you're not hurt, and the one thing that was damaged can easily be replaced."

Forcing myself to find the good in what she'd said, I nodded, then pulled down the sun visor and looked myself over in the mirror. Although I felt like a complete wreck, my appearance didn't show it. My wavy hair was still in place, my lips were effortlessly glossed to perfection, and my eyeliner hadn't made a mockery of my face despite how much crying I'd been doing.

Closing the visor, I said, "Well, at least the guy had decent insurance. I would've been in the middle of the street in tears if he hadn't."

She chuckled. "Why? It's not like you couldn't afford it if he didn't."

"Yeah, but that's not the point. I didn't start my own business just so I could take what I earn and throw it away because of stupid mistakes."

"I know, I know."

I slammed my head back against the seat. "You know what? Let's just talk about something else. How was your night at the club? I heard there were some heavy hitters in there. Did you make some good money?"

She swallowed hard, then squeezed the wheel. "I actually didn't go last night."

"Why? I thought that was something you were looking forward to?"

"I was, but I've decided to stop dancing."

Shocked, I jerked my head back. "Since when?"

"Since about three days ago."

"Really? Well, that seems abrupt. What changed?"

She shrugged. "It was just time."

"Nitra, I've been trying to talk you into leaving the strip club for a minute. But every time I mention it, you blow me off and insist that you will one day. I lowkey think you enjoy it," I said with a chuckle.

She scoffed. "I enjoy the dancing, and sometimes I enjoy the attention. But dealing with the drunk fools that feel like they can do whatever the hell they want...that's the shit I don't enjoy."

"Of course," I replied, then paused for a moment to look her over. Her face had become somewhat pale, which was saying a lot since her skin was already light. "Did something happen?"

"Huh?"

"I said, did something happen?"

Staying focused on the road, she quickly shook her head. "Something like what?"

"I don't know. You just seem a little fed up, which is the only reason I could see you making such a quick decision."

"I mean, I am. I'm ready to put the stripping life behind me and focus on my son. He deserves better, and I want to give him that."

Happy to hear her say that, I smiled. "Well, good for you. I'm proud of you, and I'm keeping my fingers crossed that you stay out of there for good this time."

"Oh, I will. I refuse to die in that place."

Laughing, I said, "Girl, not die in that place."

"Yes. It's just so easy to get addicted to the bright lights and all the attention. Not to mention, dancing is how I met EJ's father."

I sighed. "Of course."

"I don't know, I guess I keep doing it in hopes that one day I'll come across someone just like him."

"Nitra, Eric was one of a kind. I'm not sure if there's another one out there like him."

"I know, and it hurts me every time I think about it."

I turned toward the window, trying not to allow my tears to make their way to the surface. Eric was the father of Nitra's three-year-old son, and he was one of the kindest men I knew. He wasn't your typical guy who was at the strip club trying to get his rocks off while staring at naked women. He was just the mail guy making a delivery, and the day he came to the club, Nitra just so happened to be on stage. According to him, the moment he laid eyes on her, it was love at first sight. But he didn't talk to her then. It wasn't until weeks later, when he started delivering mail to my spa that he decided to shoot his shot. From that moment on, they were inseparable, and three months later, Nitra told me that she was pregnant.

Their love was like something you saw in the movies. It was sweet, beautiful, and so genuine. Despite her being a stripper, Eric treated Nitra like she was a queen, and he protected her like that was the only thing he was put on earth to do.

I blinked a few times, trying again to push back the tears. As great as he was, it pained me to think about Eric. I hated being reminded of how short life really was, and just how careless other people could be. A little over a year ago, Eric was shot and killed by a man that was robbing a gas station.

Forcing my eyes away from the window, I placed my hand on Nitra's back. "Are you okay?"

"Yeah, I'm fine." She sniffled, then quickly changed the subject. "Did you call Wiz and tell him about the accident?"

Wishing my boyfriend was the last person she had brought up, I rolled my eyes. "No."

"Why not?"

"Because his ass is the reason I'm in this mess in the first place."

"What? How?"

Damn it, Simone, I scolded myself. "Nothing. I shouldn't have said that."

"But it sounds like you meant it."

"I didn't. I'm just in my feelings right now."

"Apparently for good reason. What's going on?"

"A lot. But I can't talk about it right now. I'm still trying to wrap my mind around it."

Keeping her eyes straight ahead, she pulled into my driveway, put the car in park, and then looked at me. "You know you can tell me anything, right?"

"Of course, and once I have a clear understanding, I promise I will."

"Okay. Well, go in there and get some rest. I know you're exhausted."

"I sure am," I replied. "Oh, please don't forget—"

"You don't have to remind me. I'll make sure your rental is ready to go before your appointment with Legend tomorrow."

"Thank you. I already feel some type of way about missing his concert tonight. I would hate to have to reschedule his appointment because of transportation issues."

She belted out a laugh. "Girl, please, I don't even know why you're playing. You and I both know that you're going to make sure that man gets taken care of. Even if your ass has to call *his* driver to pick you up."

"Whatever."

"Don't *whatever* me. Legend is one of your top three clients, and he's the only male who has the luxury of being serviced at his home, which he pays you graciously for. Trust me, you're not missing those funds for anything."

Giving her a playful glare, I tilted my head to the side. "Yeah, I guess you're right about that."

"Oh, I know I'm right. Although I think your reasoning isn't just because he pays good..."

"Alright, I'm getting out of the car now."

"What? Was it something I said?" she teased.

"You already know, and I'm not sticking around to entertain it."

She shrugged. "I'm just saying, not all of us have the luxury of having a fine ass friend that just so happens to be in a top-selling music group while also being a client that we get to see partially naked from time to time."

Waving her off, I hopped out of the car. "Bye, Nitra. Thanks again for picking me up."

"Mmhmm...no problem." She waited for me to close the door, then backed out of the driveway.

I turned toward my home. On the outside, it presented the perfect image. A modern style home with gorgeous potted plants leading to the door, a two-car garage, and dark green manicured grass that anyone in the neighborhood would kill for. How did I know? Because on more than one occasion, I'd been stopped by several of my neighbors just to find out the name of my lawn guy. Unfortunately, there was no guy to tell them about. The immaculate lawn they saw was a labor of love done with my own two hands. Working on my yard made me happy, and it always gave me a sense of peace once the job was done. Too bad that peace didn't make it any further than the front yard.

Sliding my key into the lock, I let out a deep sigh and then pushed the door open. As soon as I made it in, I saw Wiz sitting in one of the chairs near the couch. I looked down, immediately noticing his shoes as they rested on my lavish white rug.

Noticing where my eyes landed, he quickly pulled them off and scooted them behind the chair.

"Too late," I said. "Looks like I'll be taking *that* shit to the cleaners."

"Sorry, I forgot to take my shoes off. I was just so worried about you, and I wasn't expecting you to be home so soon. I thought you were going to a concert."

"I was, but I got into an accident." I eased my feet out of my heels and slid into my furry white slippers.

"An accident? Are you okay?"

"I'm fine."

"You sure? How did you get home? Why didn't you call me?"

"I had Nitra bring me home," I replied, purposely ignoring the rest of his questions.

"Okay, well let her know that I appreciate it. How's your car? Do I need to take you to get a rental?"

"It's taken care of," I placed my keys on the key holder, then walked toward the stairs.

"Simone, we need to talk."

I stopped. "Oh, do we?"

"Yes, we do, and you know why."

"Nah, I *don't* know why."

But I did know why. I just didn't have the energy to talk about it. At least not right now. The only thing on my mind was getting in the shower, cozying up in my bed, and pretending like tonight had never happened.

"Yes, you do."

"Okay, fine," I blurted as I spun around. "Let's talk about it then. Why the fuck did you tell your boys that you want a hall pass?"

2

LEGEND

"Hey, boss man, they said you're on in thirty," my guard, Cade, called out from the other side of the dressing room door.

"Mmhmm," I lowered my gaze, making sure I didn't miss a second of the cute little redbone taking my dick further into her mouth.

"Do I need to stop?" she asked.

"Nah, keep going."

Still on her knees, she smiled, then tilted her head to the side. "So, will we be going back to your place after the show?"

I frowned.

Why is she still talking?

"I really don't have much time for conversation, so..."

"Oh, right." She wrapped her hand around my dick, then stroked it slowly, allowing me to return to the headspace that I needed to be in before a show. The mood was just right until I felt a sharp pinch at the tip of my shit.

"What the fuck was that?" I reached down to grab her hand, my eyes widening when I saw what damn near ripped off my skin. "Is this what I think it is?"

"Huh?"

"Don't play dumb. Is this a fucking wedding ring?"

Giving me a nonchalant shrug, she said, "Does it matter?"

"Hell yeah, it matters. I don't mess around with married women. I don't need that kind of karma in my life." Zipping my pants, I walked toward the door and then gave it a gentle tap.

Cade peeked inside. "Y'all all set?"

"Yeah, we're good here. Make sure she gets to the concert floor safely."

She sucked her teeth, then stood up. "You know this isn't a big deal, right?"

"It is to me. I don't get down like that, and neither should you."

"Are you really going to let a nigga you don't even know keep you from getting some good pussy?" She smiled and lowered her hand between her thighs.

I couldn't do anything but laugh. As tempted as I was to slide into what I could tell was top-notch, I knew it wasn't in my best interest. Nothing good could come from coming between someone and their vows.

Turning away from her, I said, "Enjoy the show," then motioned for Cade to take her out of the room.

Before the door could close, another pair of heels entered the room. But these were more expensive. I could tell just from the way they clicked against the dressing room floor that it was my stylist, Eden.

"What's up?" I said while pouring myself a drink, then turning to face her.

"Nothing. Just came to check on you before you hit the stage."

"Thanks. I'm good."

She looked me over with a lifted brow, then glanced over her shoulder. "You sure about that? I saw the girl that Cade just escorted out of here. She didn't look too happy. What happened? Did she not perform to your liking?"

"Ha, very funny."

"What? I'm just trying to see what happened. You don't look too happy either."

"I'm not. Her ass was married."

"Oh, for real?"

"Yeah, which I didn't find out until after she'd had a mouthful and damn near ripped the skin off my dick with her ring."

Eden laughed, then folded her arms over her chest and leaned against the wall. "Well, in the future, maybe you should issue some sort of documentation before whipping it out. You know, letting them know that although you have no problem fucking everything that moves, you draw the line at married women. Perhaps then you'll have the right selection of women waiting outside of your dressing room, and you won't have to worry about not getting off before a show."

"Kiss my ass, Eden."

"What? I'm just trying to help you out."

"Nah, you're trying to be funny. It's all good though. I hope you have one too many drinks with your baby daddy and slip up and let him hit again."

"Wow, that's a low blow."

I shrugged. "I'm just coming back at you the way you came at me."

"Well, you can keep that shit to yourself. You know damn well I wouldn't screw Teddy again if I was dying and his penis was the only source of survival."

I jerked my head back. "That's cold as hell. If he heard you say that he would lose his mind."

"Good thing he isn't here then."

"Whatever. You know his ass is still in love with you."

"Mmhmm...I can tell every time I watch a video of him slapping a stripper's ass on the internet, or every time he gets drunk and calls me every fucked up name he can think of. You know, *whore* is his favorite name for me these days."

I closed my eyes and lowered my head, quickly hating that I'd brought him up. "My bad, Eden. I shouldn't have—"

"It's all good, Legend. I'm not worried about Teddy." She waved me off, then looked me over from head to toe. "Let me make sure you don't have any cum on the outfit that I spent hours putting together." She moved in a little closer. "This black can hide a lot of things, but not that."

"Trust me. I'm good. We didn't even make it that far."

There was a loud knock on the door. "Hey, you dressed in there?"

Recognizing my manager's voice, I lifted my gaze. "Yes, Ms. Regina. You can come in."

"Good. I don't have time to be walking in on something I don't want to see."

I laughed. "I see you're coming in here with jokes too."

"Of course," she said while smiling and leaning in to hug me. Like always, she smelled like fresh strawberries and vanilla. A scent that I was all too familiar with since Simone was often covered in the same fragrance.

Ms. Regina was a strikingly beautiful woman, and she didn't look anything like she was knocking on fifty. She had straight dark hair that stopped at her shoulders, high cheekbones that accented her golden brown skin, and piercing hazel eyes that could see right through your soul if she stared at you long enough. As a teenager, I was mesmerized by her beauty. But as I got older, that childhood crush turned into admiration. Ms. Regina was a boss in every sense of the word. When it came to getting shit done, she did just that. She always knew the answers, and she always had the right connections to make things happen. People in the entertainment industry respected her, and she gave the same in return.

"How are you feeling?" she questioned, her hands resting against her hips while looking me over.

"I feel pretty good."

"Great. That's what I like to hear."

I glanced over her shoulder. Noticing that no one had come in behind her, I asked, "Did Simone come with you?"

She sighed. "No. She got into a car accident while trying to get here."

Eden gasped. "Oh my God."

"Is she okay?" I blurted.

"She said she's fine. She's more worried about her car than anything."

Damn, I thought as I searched for my phone.

"Don't worry about trying to call her. I need you to focus on the show."

"How do you expect me to do that after telling me that Simone was in an accident? I need to at least hear her voice and make sure she's okay."

Ms. Regina placed her hands on my shoulders. "Trust me, if I thought she was hurt bad, I wouldn't even be here right now," she said. "Oh, and she told me to tell you that she's sorry she couldn't be here, but your upcoming appointment is on her."

"Oh yeah?"

"Yep. Now, the fact that she was thinking about you should tell you that she's okay. She's probably resting right now anyway. I'm sure you don't want to disturb her."

Taking a deep breath, I shook my head. "Nah, I don't."

"Okay, good. Now, back to focusing on the show."

I closed my eyes and tried to get my head back in the game, which was a lot easier said than done since my mind kept wondering if Simone was truly okay. Not to mention, I was a little disappointed that she wouldn't be at my show. I was looking forward to seeing her in the crowd.

Snapping her fingers, Ms. Regina said, "Oh, did you talk to Teddy and Kendrick yet?"

"Um..."

"I'll take that as a no," she shot back.

"I just haven't gotten around to it yet."

"Mmhmm...well, you better get around to it before they hear the announcement through the press instead of you."

"Okay, okay. I just need a little more time."

"Your time is up. Take care of it before I do," she said before tapping on her phone screen to decline a call. "I know you're worried about how Teddy is going to react to the news, but there's nothing you can do about that. He's going to act a fool no matter what. That's part of the reason you're making this decision in the first place. You don't have time to keep dealing with his drunken outburst and temper tantrums. No one does."

"I agree with Ms. Regina," Eden chimed in. "Teddy's behavior has only gotten worse, and it doesn't look like it's going to get better anytime soon. Despite what you may think, you're doing the right thing, and it's not like its new information. You've been talking about going solo for a while, so they both should've known that it was coming."

"I think Kendrick is good," I said. "He's getting ready to fly out to Arizona and shoot some action film that's coming out next year."

"Oh, right. He mentioned that he had some auditions lined up."

"Yeah, acting has always been his first love."

Pleased, Ms. Regina returned to the conversation. "Good. I'm glad to hear that." She looked over at Eden. "Any idea what your baby daddy might have a love for?"

Eden shrugged. "As far as I know, strippers and the bottle."

"Hmph...well, that's not going to cut it once this group comes to an end. You better let him know that he needs to get it together before he ends up falling on his damn face."

"Ms. Regina, if I could get that man to listen to me, we wouldn't even be having this conversation."

"That's unfortunate," she replied. "I sure wish he would've gotten himself together a long time ago. Maybe then, Legend wouldn't have felt the need to go solo."

I shook my head. "Nah, I think I would've always gone solo eventually. I probably would've waited a little longer before leaving the group though."

Eden gave me a confused gaze. "Are you saying you would've tried to do both?"

"I mean, yeah. I want us all to be out here making money."

"I get that. But you don't think that would've been too much for you?"

I shrugged. "Maybe. But I would've been willing to at least do another album. I felt like we had one more in us."

"I don't know," Ms. Regina said. "The response after your debut has been phenomenal, and this is only the beginning. So, after tonight, I want you to enjoy your week off. Because once you finish up the remaining dates for this tour, you have to get back to preparing for the Rhythm City Festival, then get your butt into the studio so you can start working on new music."

"Speaking of the Rhythm City Festival...that's going to be my last performance with the group, huh?"

"Yep, which is why you need to handle things with Teddy so your fans can be aware of that too. But enough of all that. It's time to head to the stage," she said before patting my shoulder. "Have a good show."

"Thanks."

I watched as she walked out of my dressing room, then I looked over at Eden. "Yo, have you seen my phone?"

"No." She took a moment to glance around the room, then stopped once she made it to the couch. "Here it is," she said before kneeling and grabbing it.

"Thank God."

"Damn, your ass was about to have a heart attack, huh?"

"Shit, wouldn't you?"

"Yeah, you're right." She dropped it in my hand and then walked toward the door. "Let's go."

I was about to follow her out, then I stopped. "Oh shit, hold up."

"Legend, whatever it is can wait. You need to get to the stage."

"Nah, this can't wait. Just keep walking though. I'm right behind you." I hurried to pull up my grandmother's number. As soon as I heard her pick up, I said, "Hey pretty lady. You good?"

"Mmhmm...I'm sitting here on this website trying to figure out the damn word of the day. I'm on my third try."

"Well, if you get it this time, you'll tie with me."

"I don't want to tie with you."

I laughed, knowing how competitive she was. "Doesn't sound like you have much of a choice."

She sucked her teeth. "Damn it, I still didn't get it. Now I'm on my fourth try."

"Aw dang," I teased. "Well, think of it this way, you still have three more tries to get it right. If you manage to do that, you will have at least beat someone somewhere in the world. That's the luxury of playing a word game that's worldwide."

"Hush up with all that bragging."

"I'm not bragging. I'm just stating the facts. Lucky for you, tomorrow's a new day. Maybe it will go better for you."

"Look here, don't you keep getting smart with me. You're not too old for me to make you go pick out a switch."

I quickly straightened up just in case she wasn't joking. "Alright, I'm done messing with you."

"Mmhmm...that's what I thought."

Still somewhat amused, I shook my head, then said, "I just wanted to call and hear your voice before I hit the stage. I love you."

"I love you too, baby. Have a good show."

"Thank you." Smiling, I ended the call, then picked up the pace to catch up with Eden and my assistant, Mya.

Just as I was about to hand off my cell, I noticed I had a missed text.

"I'm sorry I'm missing the show. I know you're going to do awesome. Can't wait for you to tell me all about it tomorrow. Good luck." –Simone

That was all I needed to see.

Lowering my head, I took a moment to say a silent prayer, then I grabbed my mic, listened for my cue, and hopped on stage to give my hometown the show they'd been waiting for.

3

SIMONE

"Wow, so that's how we're starting this?" Wiz questioned as he stuffed his hands into his pants pockets.

"You acted like you were ready for the conversation, so let's get into it."

"I am ready for the conversation. But I was hoping we could be a little more adult about it."

"*Adult*?" I questioned, my head jerking back. "Boy, I'm twenty-seven years old. Don't come to me about being more adult about a damn thing. Hell, the fact that I haven't tried to take the heel of my shoe and shove it between your eyes is pretty damn adult if you ask me. Be grateful."

He took a hard swallow, then moved his hand toward the couch. "Can you please sit down?"

"I don't want to sit down, Wiz. I want an explanation about the bullshit I heard you say on the phone. Why do you feel like it's necessary to go screw another woman? Why am I not enough?"

"I didn't say you weren't enough."

"Maybe not in those exact words, but it was damn sure implied."

Lowering his gaze, he pressed his fist against his mouth. "Simone, please sit down. I want us to talk about things calmly."

"Fine." I let out a heavy sigh, then made my way over to the couch. "I'm sitting. Now explain." Silence filled the room, which quickly aggravated me. If there was one thing Wiz didn't have, it was time. Folding my arms over my chest, I tilted my head to the side. "Tick tock. I'm waiting."

He lifted his hands. "Look, I know hearing what I said was shocking for you, and I hate that you heard it that way. That was a conversation that I wanted us to sit down and have together."

I looked at him like he was crazy. "So, let me get this right...you think I would've responded better if you would've sat me down to talk about this?"

"I mean—"

"The answer is no, Wiz. I would've been just as pissed."

"But why?"

"What the hell do you mean, *why*? You're asking me for permission to fuck another woman. Why would I be okay with that? Are things so bad between us that you feel like you need to cheat just to get things back on track?"

"No, I'm not saying that. Look, I was just talking about it with my boys. A few of them have tried it to spice things up in their relationship. I just figured I would mention it to you and see how you felt about it."

"I don't see how sleeping with another woman spices things up."

He shrugged. "I don't know. Maybe it's the thrill of being with someone else, then realizing that you have it so much better at home."

Rolling my eyes, I belted out a laugh. "Boy, bye! Is that what your boys are telling their girlfriends?"

"I don't know what they're telling them. I was just trying to give some sort of reasoning."

"And that sounded legit to you?" I asked. "What if I told you that I wanted to go ride another niggas dick to spice things up? Would you be open to hearing that?"

"Stop trying to turn things around."

"No, Wiz, answer the question. What if I was the one that came to you about this shit? What would your response be?" I crossed one leg over the other and waited for his answer. But he didn't speak. Instead, he just gave me a smirk. It pissed me off, but I knew exactly why he was reacting that way. Wiz knew that I would never sleep with anyone else. I was too loyal for that. Not to mention, I couldn't even fathom the idea of allowing another man to get that close to me. Wiz was the only man I'd ever been with, and I was comfortable with him. Our sex life wasn't the best, but I just assumed that was to be expected after ten years of dating.

I paused for a moment.

Who am I kidding? It wasn't fireworks in the beginning either.

It was hard to think about, but it was true. Even in the early days of being together, our sex life was a struggle. Don't get me wrong, it wasn't that Wiz was a bad lover. He just didn't seem to care as much about pleasing me as I did him. It saddened me to say, but not much had changed. No matter how many times I'd addressed it in the past, the result was always the same. But because I'd fallen for the bright smile that matched his even brighter complexion at the age of seventeen, and the golden brown eyes that he made me believe were only for me, I just rolled with it.

Scooting to the edge of the couch, I said, "So, you're really not going to answer the question?"

He shook his head. "Let's just drop it, Simone. It's not even that big of a deal."

"Oh, it's a very big deal. How long have you been thinking about this?"

"I already told you, it's a conversation that me and the guys *just* had."

I eyed him for a moment. "So, you're telling me that it just crossed your mind today?"

"Yes."

Staring in suspicion, I shook my head. "Nah, I don't believe that."

"What?"

"You heard me. I'm not buying it. So, who is she?"

"Excuse me?"

"You heard me, Wiz. Who is she? Who's the chick that you want to fuck? Is it someone at one of the clubs you're working at?"

"Now you're talking crazy." He stood up then walked toward the back door and stared outside. "I knew I shouldn't have tried to have this conversation with you."

"You're right, you shouldn't have. The last thing I want to do is make plans for another woman to screw you." I shrugged. "Sorry, but that shit doesn't get me wet. Matter of fact, I would love it if we talked more about how *you* could put forth a better effort to get me wet."

Groaning, he slowly turned around. "Don't start."

"What? So, you can make suggestions and I can't?"

"You can make suggestions all you want, but most of your suggestions require me playing with your pussy for hours and you complaining about me not going down on you."

"First of all, you're being dramatic. I'm not asking you to play with anything for hours. But if you did it for more than ten seconds, it would be nice. Second, I don't think asking for a little foreplay should be seen as a problem. As far as you going down on me, I've come to grips with the fact that that's never going to happen." I tilted my head to the side and stared at him for a moment. "But since we're on the subject...what's the issue? Why are you so against it?"

"Really? We've been over this."

"Yeah, I know. But I was hoping I could get an answer that makes sense because what you've been telling me for the last ten years isn't adding up."

"I just don't think it's necessary in order to enjoy sex."

"For who?"

"For either of us."

"That's easy for you to say," I blurted. "I slob on your shit like it's a damn popsicle."

"And that's your choice. I don't ask for it."

"You don't have to. I do it because I know you like it," I said. "When we're having sex, I'm not just thinking about what pleases me. I want to please you too."

"So, just because I won't go down on you, I don't please you?"

"That's not what I'm saying. I just wish you would put a little more effort into—"

Turning away, he said, "I'm done talking about this. I'm not about to sit here and listen to you downplay me when it comes to our sex life. That's fucked up."

I frowned.

He can't be serious right now.

Less than five minutes ago, he was suggesting screwing someone else to add spice to our relationship. Meanwhile, I'm not the one lacking when it comes to turning things up. I'm willing to do anything in the bedroom. Toys, role play, different positions...hell, hang my ass from the ceiling and fuck me upside down. I'm all for it. But none of that is *his* thing. In fact, I'm usually told that I'm trying to do too much.

I shook my head. "You know what? That's not even the real issue here. Our problems go way beyond sex. You and I have been together since we were seniors in high school, and we're no closer to getting married than we were back then. That doesn't make sense to me. After all this time, we're still walking around playing house." I gave him a stern glare. "That doesn't seem ridiculous to you?"

"Simone, you already know how I feel about this subject. Now isn't the right time for that."

I rolled my eyes. "Why not? We're financially in a good space to get married and start a family."

"It's not about the money. You know how important my career is as a DJ, and shit is really taking off for me right now. I can't afford to slow down."

"Okay, fine. I understand wanting to hold off on having children. But what's the deal when it comes to making me your wife? Why are you so hesitant about that?"

He dropped his shoulders, then returned his gaze to mine. "We're still young, Simone. Since high school, you're the only woman I've ever been with."

"And *you're* the only man I've ever been with...so?"

"As much as that is a good thing, it may also be a bad thing," he said. "So many people marry their high school sweethearts and end up divorced two years later because they realized that's not the person they're truly meant to be with."

A little stunned to hear his reasoning, I frowned. "So, is that what you think? You think that if you marry me, you're going to realize that you don't want to be with me?"

He paused for a moment, then shrugged. "I...I don't know."

"Oh, wow."

"Simone—"

I lifted my hand. "Don't say anything else, Wiz."

"But—"

"Please. I need a moment." I pressed my hand against my mouth, then walked toward the staircase.

I'd heard enough.

Of all the things I expected him to say, the words he shared today never crossed my mind. Sure, our relationship wasn't perfect, but I thought the love we had for each other overshadowed everything. I thought that our future together was sealed. After today, I wasn't sure if any of that was true, and to make matters worse, I had no idea what to do about it.

4

SIMONE

I wanted to breathe a little lighter.

I wanted last night's conversation with Wiz to be so far in the back of my mind that it was as though it never happened. But it did happen, and every reminder of it was driving me crazy. So crazy that I left the house while he was still taking his morning shower. I knew if I stuck around, he would just find a way to stir up the conversation again.

I wasn't ready for that.

I was still struggling to understand why he felt the way he did and then chose to keep it from me. For years he'd been giving me the same excuse about it not being the right time for us to get married and start a family. Although it never made much sense to me, I kept accepting it because I figured eventually enough time would pass and he would come around.

I mean...why wouldn't he? I'm his first love...right?

I didn't bother pondering on the thought for too long. I didn't have time.

Reaching into the backseat, I grabbed my tote bag and prepared my mind to focus on the appointment I had with Legend. Just as I was about to step out of the car, my phone rang.

It was Wiz.

I hurried to hit the decline button, then stepped out of my car, and walked toward the house. On the outside, Legend's home screamed bachelor pad. The entire exterior was black with large floor-to-ceiling windows that allowed you to see directly inside. But since he didn't have a neighbor for miles, his landscape was covered with tall trees that obstructed outside viewers, and his property was heavily secured, someone seeing inside was the least of his concerns.

As soon as I made it to the front door, his assistant motioned for me to come inside. "Hello, Miss Simone. How are you?"

"I'm good." I hugged Mya, then took a step back while still looking at her. "One day I'm going to get you to stop putting *miss* in front of my name. We're the same age."

She laughed. "My bad. You know I can't help it. Mr. Legend gives me a hard time about doing it to him too. But I just tell him that since he's a year older than me, I have to respect my elders."

"Oh, damn."

"Mmhmm. But he knows I'm just teasing. I have to dish out a little something every now and then since he's always hitting me with a short joke."

"Well, that does sound pretty fair." I glanced around the room. "Speaking of the big man in charge...is he here?"

"Yeah. I told him you were here as soon as I let you through the gate. He should be down any minute now. Did you want something to drink while you wait?"

"Nah, I'm good. Thank you though."

"No problem," she said while smiling. "Let me know if you need anything."

"Will do. Thanks."

Nodding, she pulled her phone from her pocket and walked out of the living room. But I remained still, enjoying the peace that consumed Legend's space. Although the color scheme was just as dark on the inside as it was on the outside, the wood furniture that sat near the black couches did just enough to lighten the mood when needed.

Pushing my bag further onto my shoulder, I walked to the massage table that was sitting in the center of the room, then took a few deep breaths to regain focus once again.

I didn't need Legend to sense that there was something wrong with me. Although we were friends, I tried to keep my relationship troubles to myself. I didn't need another man looking at *my* man sideways every time they were in the same room, which was very likely to happen given their professions.

"Well, well, well, look who decided to show up," Legend teased as he strolled into the living room.

I sucked my teeth, then looked him up and down since he was a bit too overdressed for a massage. "Okay, before you start giving me the third degree, you want to explain why you're still wearing a shirt and basketball shorts instead of having a towel wrapped around your waist?"

He lowered his gaze, then shrugged. "My bad. I was upstairs looking over some footage from last night. I got a little sidetracked."

"Mmhmm...I bet. Anyway, I'm sorry that I didn't make it to your concert."

"It's all good. I'm just glad you're okay." He eased his arm around me and pulled me into a hug.

Like always, he smelled like he'd just stepped out of the shower. The freshness that leaped from his caramel colored skin spoke to every one of my senses. I wanted to linger in the warmth of his arms and forget about every irritating thing that I'd dealt with the day before. But I had to move. It was way too easy to get lost in him.

Holding me a little tighter, he said, "Is everything okay?"

"Um...yeah." I hurried out of his grasp and avoided looking

into his eyes. "I guess I'm still a little shaken up from the accident. What about you? How are you feeling?"

He slid his hand down the back of his head, then squeezed his neck. "I'm stressed."

"Stressed? Why?"

"I still haven't told Teddy that I've decided to go solo, and your mom has pretty much told me that my time is up."

I nodded my head slowly. "Oh, I see. Well, I can understand why you're stressed. Teddy's a ticking time bomb. You never know how he's going to respond to things."

"Right, which is what has me so worried. I don't have time to deal with whatever he decides to throw my way."

Folding my arms over my chest, I shrugged. "I get it, but there's nothing you can do about that. More than likely, he's going to act out anyway. I feel like you should just rip off the band-aid and get it over with."

"That's pretty much what Ms. Regina said."

"Trust me, my mother's right," I told him. "Besides, the sooner you get it over with, the sooner you can deal with Teddy's temper tantrum and move on. You guys were friends before starting a music group. He may be in his feelings at first, but he'll come around."

"Yeah, I know. I just wish he knew how to handle shit better."

I lifted my eyes to the ceiling. "I wish a *lot* of people knew how to handle shit better."

"What was that?"

Damn.

Lowering my gaze, I quickly shook my head and then cleared my throat. "Nothing, I was just agreeing with you."

"Nah, I saw the face you made. You were doing a lot more than just agreeing."

I forced out a giggle. "No, I wasn't."

"Hmm...now you're doing that fake ass giggle that you do when you're lying or trying to avoid something."

"Lying? I don't lie."

"When it comes to your personal life, yes you do."

"No, I don't."

"Yes, you do. But just know, I always know when shit's going on with you. I just don't press the issue."

"Whatever. I promise you I'm fine."

"You're not, but okay," he said before lifting his t-shirt over his head and grabbing the towel that was sitting on the massage table. "I'm going to go get changed."

"Okay, fine, I'll tell you," I blurted. "But what I'm about to say can't leave this room."

"Of course."

"And this has absolutely nothing to do with me. I'm just really concerned about a friend of mine."

"Okay. What's up?"

I took a hard swallow while trying to decide how much of my situation I wanted to share. "So, my homegirl has been in a relationship for a while, and out of the blue, her boyfriend told her that he wants a hall pass."

"A what?"

"A hall pass. You know, a one-time fling with—"

"I know what it is. I was just trying to make sure I heard you right. Why in the hell would he ask for that? Well, unless he's trying to end the relationship."

My eyes widened. "You think that's what he's trying to do?"

"I mean, it has to be. Either that, or he just wants an excuse to hold on to what he has and cheat without really labeling it as cheating."

"But what if it's not that? What if it's just an itch that he needs to scratch because neither of them has ever been with anyone else, and he just wants to have that one experience?"

Legend shrugged. "I mean, I can see that, I guess. How long have they been together?"

"Um...a while. Since college," I lied.

"Oh okay, and neither of them have been with anyone else?"

"Anyone else how? Like in a relationship?"

"No, sexually."

"Oh, no. They're high school sweethearts, so—"

"Wait...I thought you said they'd been together since college?"

"Yeah, that's what I meant," I said waving him off. "Anyway, my friend is freaking out about it. Especially since he's been so hesitant to marry her. She's wondering if maybe she should let him do it so he can get it out of his system and realize that she's the only woman he wants to spend the rest of his life with."

"But he should already know that."

"Yeah, he should, but what if this would really solidify it?"

Legend shrugged. "Shit, does she get a pass too?"

"I...I don't think she's interested in one."

"Maybe not. But I only think it's fair if she gets to have one. Who knows? She may want to experience someone different too."

I forced out a faint giggle. "Nah, I think she's good."

"How do you know?"

"I don't know. I'm just assuming."

"Well, I think you should ask her. If she's down for the experience herself, she should let him have it, and if she's looking for someone to have hers with, I'm down."

Belting out a laugh, I said, "Okay, now you're tripping. I'm not hooking my friend up with you."

"What? I'm just saying, clearly your girl needs to get it in just like her man wants to get it in. Why not let it be with someone that you know can handle things like they need to be handled."

"First of all, I don't know how you handle things. Second, this conversation is officially over."

"Damn, okay. I was just trying to be helpful."

"Mmhmm....a little too damn helpful," I said before giving him a playful shove in the chest. "Go get undressed. I'll be out here waiting."

"Okay." He shrugged and then walked toward the bathroom. Just as he made it to the door, he stopped and looked over his shoulder. "Hey, Simone."

"Yeah, what's up?"

"So, are you going to do it?"

"Do what?"

Eyeing me with a smirk, he said, "Take the hall pass."

Realizing that I'd failed at being discreet, my mouth dropped.

Shit!

5
LEGEND

With my hands shoved into my pockets, I stared out of my living room window. I couldn't stop thinking about Simone's story from earlier. When she was talking, it didn't take me long to figure out she was talking about herself and not her friend. I could tell that she was somewhat embarrassed by the fact that she was even dealing with such an issue. But in my eyes, she had nothing to be embarrassed about. If anyone should feel dumb as hell, it should've been Wiz's weak ass.

"Damn, this fool can't be on time to save his life," Kendrick said, pulling me from my thoughts. "His ass was supposed to be here thirty minutes ago, and I've texted him twice."

Shaking my head, I said, "Typical Teddy. He has no respect for people's time, which is why—"

"You're about to tell him you're leaving the group, huh?"

I shrugged. "Yeah, Ms. Regina has been on my ass about it. She said my time is up. It was either tell him today or have him read about it on the blogs. I figured the latter part probably wasn't the best way to go, so here we are."

"You did right. The internet is the last place Teddy needs to hear this."

I glanced down at my watch. "Hell, at the rate he's going, that might be the way he finds out."

"Let's give him five or ten more minutes."

"Five," I shot back. "My time is precious."

He nodded, then leaned back on my couch. "I have to give you props, bro. You've really been doing your solo thing. Your show was good as hell and the women were going crazy."

"Thanks, man. Even though you probably paid more attention to the women than the show."

"Come on now, don't play me like that. You know I was paying attention to what you had going on...*and* the women." He laughed. "I know how to multitask."

"Yeah, I bet."

"Speaking of multitasking...how about you share some of that ass you probably had thrown your way last night. Preferably, the cheeks you didn't smash. I'm not trying to have your sloppy seconds. Matter of fact, we can do a little swap. I ran into a few chicks myself last night."

Laughing, I shook my head. "Nah, bro. I'm good on the groupies that you and Teddy fool with. Since we got into this industry the two of you have chased all the fake asses and titties you could get your hands on. Y'all should be tired."

"Shit, I am. That's why I'm trying to swap," he shot back. "I won't even lie, the females you be messing with be bad as hell, and they all look natural too. I mean, they might have less ass than I'm accustomed to, but—"

"That's because you're so used to messing around with women that go to the same bargain basement plastic surgeon for their butt shots."

He lifted his shoulders. "What can I say? I'm an ass man."

"Yeah, okay."

"Whatever. But to be real with you, I am thinking about

chilling out on all of that. You know, finding me a good wholesome woman."

Once again, I couldn't resist breaking into laughter. "Now I'm convinced that you just want to hear yourself talk."

"Damn, man. That's cold. I'm pouring my heart out to you and—"

"Kendrick, shut the hell up, man. For you to even go that route, you would have to change the people you roll with."

"What do you mean?"

"You know exactly what I mean," I said. "Everybody you deal with is from this industry. Either they think like you, or they're fake as hell."

"Wow! That's funny coming from someone that is damn near surrounded by the same people as me."

I scoffed. "Nah, that's where you're wrong. The only industry person we have in common is Ms. Regina. Other than that, my circle is small as hell with genuine ass people."

Waving me off, he said, "Speaking of your circle, I saw Wiz and Simone while I was out a few nights ago. She was looking fine as hell."

"Um...okay." I gave him a confused glare. "That shouldn't be much of a surprise. She always looks good. What are you telling me for?"

"Yeah, you right, she does," he replied as he rubbed his hands together and licked his lips. "Anyway, how much longer do you think the two of them are going to be together?"

"What?"

"You heard what I said. Wiz has been hogging Simone's fine ass since we were kids. Don't you think it's about time that he let her go and give someone else a chance to see what's up."

Stepping away from the window, I looked at him like he was crazy. "Bro, you sound stupid as hell right now. Even if they did break up, I can guarantee you that she's not trying to fuck with you."

"Why? You don't think I'm her type?"

"Hell naw, you're not her type."

"Damn, why are you so heated?"

"I'm not heated."

Laughing, he stood up from the couch. "Yes, the fuck you are. You should see the fumes coming from your nose. Looks like a damn fire is about to start in here."

"You're exaggerating."

"Nah, I'm not exaggerating at all. You're responding like I stepped on your toes or some shit."

Moving a little closer to him, I looked him in the eyes. "To be honest with you, you did. Simone is good people, and the way you just talked about her rubbed me the wrong way. Shit, it almost got your ass beat."

He took a step back, then lifted his hands. "My bad. I was just saying—"

"I know what you were saying, and I'm telling you never to say it again. At the end of the day, Simone is a no nonsense type of woman. If her relationship ever ends, she needs a no nonsense type of man."

"And let me guess...that's you?"

"That's not what I said."

"But that's damn sure what you're implying," he said, then gave me a smirk. "It's all good though. Clearly, you've marked your territory."

I frowned. "Fool, I'm not no fucking dog, and she's not some light post on the sidewalk. But I will say this, if she ever becomes the one I choose or vice versa, you'll know it."

I couldn't lie and say that I hadn't had my eyes on Simone since the first day I saw her hanging around her mother's office when we were teenagers. My favorite times were when she would stick around a little longer to do her homework and listen to us sing, then give us feedback on how she felt about each of our voices. The way we hung on her every word, I'm pretty sure all three of us had a crush on her back then. Lucky for me, I was the one she felt more comfortable talking to and we eventually became close friends. I knew just about everything there was to know about Simone. From her favorite color, which was brown, to her love for comfy socks, fluffy slippers, and warm glazed donuts, which she could devour within seconds.

"Y'all ready to get this meeting started?" Teddy shouted as he strolled through the door and took off his shades.

Just as expected, his entire attitude was as if he didn't have a care in the world and the clock only started ticking when his ass arrived.

Looking at him like he was crazy, Kendrick said, "Fool we've been ready. Where the hell have you been?"

"Handling business."

"Try handling a watch. Maybe then you can be somewhere on time for once."

He plopped down on my couch. "I'm here now. What's up?"

"Your ass is about to be filing for unemployment is what's up."

"Kendrick, chill," I said.

"What? I'm just keeping it real."

Teddy leaned back, then looked at me while adjusting the gold chain that was around his neck. "Legend, what is this fool talking about?"

Still not letting up, Kendrick told him, "Exactly what I just said."

I stretched my arm in front of Kendrick's chest, trying again to get him to relax. Looking back at Teddy, I said, "After we do the Rhythm City Festival, I'm going to focus on my solo career."

He didn't respond. Instead, he just looked at me as if he was waiting for me to say that I was joking. But when I didn't, his eyes widened. "You're bullshitting me, right?"

"Nah, I'm not."

"Yeah, you got to be."

"He's not," Kendrick blurted. "He's leaving the group and going solo."

"What the fuck?" Teddy shot up from the couch and met me where I stood. "Damn, your little tour got you feeling yourself so much that you're ready to break up the group?"

Not feeling the way my nostrils were flaring from the liquor I could smell on his breath, I spoke to him through clenched teeth. "First off, you need to back the fuck up. I can smell the back of your throat right now, and if you want to keep that bitch intact, I suggest you let your feet take you back to the couch."

"Man, fuck you!"

"Alright, alright," Kendrick said as he stepped between us. "Let's not come to blows over some shit we all knew about a long time ago."

"Knew a long time ago?" Teddy jerked his head back.

"Yeah, fool. This isn't the first time Legend's mentioned potentially going solo. Your ass just chose not to listen to him."

"That's because I figured he just needed to get the idea out of his system. Isn't that why we agreed to let him do a solo album in the first place?"

I shook my head, once again reminded of how Teddy only heard what he wanted to hear. "I didn't say that. You said that."

"But you didn't correct me," he replied.

"I get tired of correcting you. It's a waste of time. You don't listen to anybody. Not me, not Kendrick, not Eden."

"Oh, don't bring my baby mama into this shit."

"I'm just saying. You're hardheaded us fuck, and—"

"No, you're arrogant as fuck! You always have been, and you let people get into your ear."

I frowned. "*Let people get into my ear*? What are you even talking about?"

"You know exactly what I'm talking about," he said. "People have been filling your head with the solo bullshit for the longest, and you finally bought into it."

I waved him off. "Nah, you're tripping. I'm doing this shit for me. I'm doing it because it feels right."

"No, you're doing it because you don't give a damn about anyone but yourself."

"Really? *I'm* the one that doesn't give a damn about anyone but myself?"

"That's what the fuck I said, didn't I?"

"Hmm...interesting. This is coming from the same person that's late for every damn meeting, studio session and rehearsal. Oh, and when you do show up, nine times out of ten you're drunk and don't have enough energy to work."

"Man, whatever." He waved me off as he stumbled forward. "You're tripping."

"Oh, really? I can't tell," I replied. "You're drunk as hell right now."

"Fool, please. I might be a little tipsy, but I'm not drunk."

"Yeah, okay. Anyway, we have two months to get ready for the Rhythm City Festival, and then I'm done."

Teddy looked back at Kendrick. "You're cool with this shit?"

"To be honest with you, I think it's time for us to go our separate ways anyway. We've outgrown each other, and I'm ready to explore other things. So...yeah...I'm cool with it."

"Oh, I see. So, both of you niggas have found your calling elsewhere and just said fuck me, huh?"

Sighing, I glanced down at my cell. "I'm done with this conversation. Y'all can continue if you want or see yourselves out. I have somewhere to be."

"Wow, okay," Teddy said while nodding. "Mr. Big Time has somewhere to be. Let's get the hell out of his house."

"Stop being extra," Kendrick said.

"Don't tell me what to do. Fuck both of you fools," he said as he stormed out of the house.

Looking back at me, Kendrick said, "That went exactly as expected."

"Damn sure did."

"How long do you think it's going to take for him to get out of his feelings?"

"I'm not sure," I replied. "But if that nigga ever gets that close to me again, I'll cave his fucking chest in…and that's a promise."

6

SIMONE

Sitting between my two sisters, I dipped my feet into the pool, then lifted my margarita glass to my lips. "Damn, I needed this."

"That makes two of us," Riah replied.

"Make it three."

Laughing, I looked at my little sister, "Nori, I know you must be going through something. I could tell by the way you walked in and fell on my couch when you first got here. What's got you so stressed?"

"My damn love life," she blurted. "Once again, I've finished filming another dating show, and I *still* don't have a man."

Riah rolled her eyes. "That's because you insist on trying to find love on reality TV. How many times do you plan on putting yourself through that mess?"

"Look, I'm just trying to find someone that cares about the same things I care about or at least understands it."

"Trust me, it's going to be hard to find a man that's comfortable living their life in front of the cameras."

"Exactly. That's why if I meet someone who's also in front of the cameras, there's no issue."

"I guess you have a point." I took another sip from my drink.

Nori was one of reality TV's finest and every inch of her proved it. It didn't matter the time or the day, she was always camera ready. In fact, even though it was late in the evening, and we were enjoying sister time, I was one hundred percent sure she had her glam team nearby.

No matter what, no one would ever catch Nori Baltimore looking a mess.

Wrapping my arm around her, I said, "Well, I'm going to keep hope alive. Keep doing your thing, you'll find true love one day."

"Or..." Riah chimed in as she slid her fingers through her slick bob. "You can stop looking and let love find you. That's how Owen and I found each other."

Unable to hold back the disgust from the mention of my sister's trash ass football player husband, I rolled my eyes. "Next subject please."

"Don't do that."

"What? I just feel like we should move on."

"Yeah, well, if I want to talk about my husband, that should be okay."

Placing my glass down behind me, I let out a deep sigh. "Riah, if you want to talk about your husband, that's completely fine. Just do it at someone else's house."

As close as we were, this was the one subject we always damn near came to blows over. Although I didn't naturally have the desire to get physical with my sister, the way she came to Owen's defense when he didn't deserve it made me see red. Especially if his punk ass was in the room.

Riah folded her arms over her chest and gave me a mean glare, which was even more intense because of her thinly arched eyebrows. But I didn't give a damn. She may have been good at intimidating others with those things, but that shit didn't fly with me.

"So, it's really like that?" she questioned.

"Yeah, it's like that, and you know why," I told her. "Did you have one too many drinks and forget that I don't like his ass?"

"Okay," Nori stepped in. "Let's leave it alone. In case you guys forgot, we're still sitting by this pool, and I know how y'all can get. I'm not trying to fuck up my silk press because y'all want to start acting a fool out here."

Completely ignoring her, I kept my eyes on Riah. "You know what? Since you want to talk about him so badly, please explain why you choose to stay with him. Not only has he cheated on you, but he's been accused of inappropriately touching women on several occasions."

"Being accused and *actually* being found guilty are two different things, Simone. You're smart. You should know that."

Frowning, Nori leaned forward. "Riah, you really think all of those women are lying on him?"

"First of all, stop saying *all*. It was only three."

"Yeah, and that's three too damn many," I blurted.

"Simone, every one of those claims was over a year ago. We've moved on from that. As far as him cheating, he's apologized and we're going to counseling. Our primary focus right now is raising our daughter and making the best life we can for her. I would appreciate it if you would stop bringing up negative things."

Knowing that I was beating a dead horse, I shrugged. "Fine. Just do me a favor and stop bringing him up in my home. If you do, I'm going to go in on his ass every time."

"Fine."

"Thank you."

Nori slid the back of her hand over her forehead in relief, then quickly changed the subject. "So, Simone, what's up with you? How are you feeling after the accident?"

"I don't feel too bad. More damage was done to my car than me."

"Well, that's a plus."

"Yeah. I'm grateful. I know it could've been much worse."

"Sure could have," Nori said. "What happened in the first place?"

"Wiz is what happened," I shot back.

They both eyed me in confusion.

"What did he do?" Riah questioned.

"He said something he had no business saying, which left me so damn distracted that I didn't notice a man run a red light while I was driving. The guy rammed right into me."

"Oh, wow," Nori replied in alarm. "That's terrible."

"Yeah, I know. I just wish I would've been paying more attention. All of this could've been avoided."

Riah sucked her teeth. "Girl, this isn't your fault."

"I know, but it damn sure feels like it. Well, partially anyway."

"So, what did Wiz do?" Nori asked.

"Long story short, he told his boys he would be interested in a hall pass, and I overheard him."

Riah leaned back and kicked her feet in the water. "What else did he say?"

"Does it matter?"

"Yeah, Simone, it does," she insisted. "Like, is it just something he needs to get out of his system because he wants to see what it's like with another woman? Is he trying to spice things up? Is he—"

"It doesn't fucking matter why he's talking about it," Nori spat. "He shouldn't be. The end."

"That's my exact thoughts," I said. "Like, why is this even a topic of discussion? You shouldn't have to be with another woman to figure out if you want to be with me."

"Did he say that though?" Riah asked.

"In a nutshell...yeah."

Waving me off, she said, "You're putting words in that man's mouth. He loves the hell out of you. You guys have been together since high school."

"Well, according to him, that's a part of the problem, and the number one reason why he hasn't asked me to marry him yet."

"Huh?"

I shot Nori a glare. "Mmhmm. Does it sound as crazy to you as it did to me when he said it last night?"

"He said that?" Riah asked.

"Since I know how much you want accuracy, let me make sure I tell you his exact words. He told me that so many people marry their high school sweetheart and end up divorced two years later because they realize that that's not the person they're truly meant to be with. Apparently, he doesn't want that to be the case with us."

"Wow!" Nori said. "That's some bullshit."

Riah lifted her finger. "Okay, wait a minute, he's not exactly wrong. I mean, not everyone that's high school sweethearts are meant to be together as adults."

"And that's fine," Nori replied. "But he shouldn't keep telling Simone that his career is the reason he's not ready to get married when it's something else."

"That's the same thing I told him," I said. "Not only that, don't dangle screwing someone else in my face and talk to me like that's going to fix things."

Riah shrugged. "Maybe it will though."

Per usual, my sister's relationship advice made me want to scream.

Doing everything I could to maintain my composure, I crossed one leg over the other and said, "You're not being serious, right?"

"I am," she replied. "Look, sometimes men just have to go out and do their thing just so they can realize how much better they got it at home."

Nori scoffed. "Damn, Owen really has your ass brainwashed, huh?"

"Whatever. I'm just saying, don't be so quick to turn the idea down. Besides, take it as your opportunity to see what else the world has to offer."

"What do you mean?" I asked.

"I mean, if he wants a hall pass, then you get to have one too. This isn't a one-sided opportunity. He's not the only one that gets to go play in the sandbox."

"Wait a minute," Nori said while staring at Riah. "Have you and Owen done it?"

She smiled. "Sure have, and it was an amazing experience."

"Oh, no wonder you don't give a damn about how many other women his ass is sleeping with. You're out here fucking too."

"Okay, hold up little sis, you're making it sound like I'm just out here going crazy," Riah said. "Just to be clear, it was a one-time thing, and it happened months ago. Which is one of the reasons his ass doesn't cheat now."

"Really?"

Riah lifted her hand to admire her nails. "Let's just say that he didn't like the idea of me being so freaky with another man. It drove his ass crazy. A week later, he was vowing to never be with another woman again, begging me not to cheat on him and agreeing to do whatever I wanted to do to make things work."

"So that's how you got his ass to get it together?" Nori asked.

"Look, something had to be done. Desperate times call for desperate measures."

I shook my head. "But I shouldn't have to do all that just for a man to fully commit to me. Either he wants me, or he doesn't."

"Trust me, he wants you," Riah said. "He just needs to be pushed in the direction of certainty. The moment he comes to grips with how freaky you probably were with someone else, he's going to fall on his damn knees and beg you to be his wife. Mark my words. He's not going to want someone else to have you like that ever again."

"This sounds dumb as hell," Nori blurted. "Just dump his ass and call it a day."

"I wish it was that simple," I told her. "Wiz and I have been together for ten years."

"And yet, here we are?" she shot back.

"Don't listen to her, Simone. Isn't there a man you want to knock off one good time?"

My eyes widened. "What? No!"

"Girl, bye. Quit lying. I know there has to be someone you want to test the waters with."

I tucked my bottom lip between my teeth, then looked away as thoughts of Legend's proposition entered my mind. Clearly, he was down for whatever, and he wasn't a bad option either.

But I couldn't.

Shaking my head, I said, "Regardless of whether there's someone or not, there are several reasons why I can't."

"Why?"

Choosing to say as little as possible, I said, "Because he's a client, and you know I don't get down with my clients like that. If word got out—"

Riah sucked her teeth. "Girl, please. Make his ass sign an NDA and keep it moving. No one else has to know what went down between you two. That's the fun of it all."

"I don't know. That sounds like a lot for some shit that I don't even feel the need to do."

"When it's all said and done, you'll be glad you did it, trust me," Riah said. "Oh, and make sure that you and Wiz have an understanding. Neither of you is allowed to talk about who the pass was with. It keeps down the drama."

"Hold up, so you're telling me that I can end up being in the same room as the woman that he screwed and not even know it?"

"Yep. But it's better that way," she said before letting out a little chuckle. "Honey, if Owen knew who my pass was with, he would kill my ass."

"Really? Who was it with?" Nori asked.

"His best friend."

"I know you fucking lying!"

"Nope." She shrugged. "I felt like it was only fair since he couldn't stop slanging his dick in every other city his team played in."

"Wow! That's lowdown."

"Yeah, I know. But it is what it is," she told Nori before looking back at me. "So, what's up? Are you going to take the pass or what?"

"I...I don't know. I need to think."

"Fine, but don't think too long. This is the perfect opportunity to have a little fun. You've been locked down for ten years. Go see what it's like to experience something new. Hell, you might even get your pussy ate." She rolled her eyes. "We know damn well Wiz isn't doing that shit."

Laughing, I tapped my glass against hers. "I know that's right."

"Mmhmm...so, if you can't think of any other reason, do it for that one. Because I can almost guarantee there's a man out there just waiting to feast on your pretty kitty." She turned up her nose. "Wiz is a fucking alien."

Laughing even harder, I said, "I can't lie, you make one compelling ass argument."

"I know I do."

Nori sucked her teeth. "Damn, I hate to admit it, but it

doesn't sound all that bad. I mean, I still think you should dump Wiz's ass though." She gave me a playful nudge. "But I also want you to get some good tongue action in the meantime too. Every woman deserves to experience that kind of orgasm."

"Yes!" Riah lifted her hand to give Nori a high-five. "You better tell her."

"You two are a mess," I replied before scooting back and pulling my feet out of the pool. "I don't know what I'm going to do. I need to sleep on it."

"Fine by me," Riah said. "Just make sure you're dreaming about whose dick you plan to ride in the near future."

"Seriously?"

"What? I'm just trying to keep you on your toes," she said with a giggle. "You may not realize it now, but some shit like this will change your life."

"Mmhmm...I bet."

7

LEGEND

"What's this I hear about you and Teddy getting into it yesterday?" My grandmother questioned as I stepped onto her front porch and made my way to the rocking chair that was next to hers.

I sighed. "Dang, who told you?"

"Who do you think told me?"

Letting out a laugh and shaking my head, I said, "Wow, that fool called you to tell on me?"

"That's neither here nor there. Why didn't *you* tell me?"

"Because there wasn't much to tell."

She folded her arms over her chest and rocked even harder in her chair. "Hmm...not according to Teddy. Are you really leaving the group?"

"Grandma, I told you a long time ago that I was thinking about going solo. You don't remember me saying that?"

She paused for a moment, then sat her phone down in her lap. I quickly looked away since I could tell that she was working on the word of the day, which I hadn't started yet. If I even glimpsed at it, she would swear I cheated, and it was a requirement to win the game fair and square.

"Hmm...I guess I do remember you saying something at some point."

"Exactly, and I also mentioned it to them several times. Teddy is the only one upset. Kendrick knows what's up and he's ready to do his own thing."

Nodding slowly, she looked away from me. "Well, I hate that you're leaving. But I understand. You guys have been doing this group thing for a long time. I still remember when the three of you started hanging out together."

She laughed, which prompted me to do the same. "Yeah, I remember too. All because we wanted to impress these girls that were hosting the high school talent show."

"Mmhmm...I thought it was so cute. You three were some singing ass boys from the time you got home from school until it was time for dinner, and then y'all would go at it again before bed."

"I know. We did that for two weeks straight."

"Sure did," she said before getting quiet and staring into the yard. "You three were inseparable. It didn't surprise me at all when y'all decided to start a group."

"You always say that."

"That's because it's the truth, and thankfully, Ballman Hills is a place with endless opportunities for people who want to try and make it in the entertainment industry. It didn't take long for you boys to get noticed."

"Nope. Not long at all, thanks to you," I said. "The moment we came to you about it, you made sure we were entered into every talent show and music event this city had to offer."

"Yep. I had to. I couldn't let those good voices go to waste. Not to mention, I only did what your mother and father would've done had they been around to hear your voice."

I lowered my gaze, the mention of my parents quickly tugging on my heartstrings. I was two years old when they were killed in a car accident, so I don't remember much of anything about them. But my grandmother has always made sure to remind me of the beautiful people they were and how much they loved making music.

"Speaking of my parents, who do you think had the better voice? My mother or father?"

She patted her hands against her thighs, a giddy smile spreading across her face. My parents were her favorite topic of discussion. Unlike most people who struggled to talk about their deceased loved ones, my grandmother did it every chance she could. She believed in celebrating the lives of those who were no longer here, which is what she always taught me.

Touching my hand, she said, "So, I may be a little biased because she's my daughter, but your mother had the most amazing voice. Don't get me wrong, I loved your father's too. But my Rochelle always sounded like an angel, and I'm sure your father would agree. Although he enjoyed singing with her from time to time, playing the drums was his passion, and that's one of the reasons your mother fell in love with him. No one could come close to doing what Leon could do on the drums."

I smiled, quickly reminded of the countless videos my grandmother had shown me. She was practically a part of their recording crew. Whenever they were on stage, she was there to catch every moment, and I'm grateful that she did. Those videos made me feel like my parents were a part of my childhood.

Feeling myself getting emotional, I decided to switch subjects. "So, how was church this morning?"

"Church was great," she replied. "But let's get back to this situation with you and Teddy. I want you two to fix things. You've known each other way too long to be acting silly with each other."

"Yeah, I know. But I'm just going to give him some time to

cool off. We still have the Rhythm City Festival to do, so hopefully he pulls it together before then."

Her eyes lit up. "Wow, I can't believe it's time for Regina's festival again. It seems like it came fast this year."

"It really did. But everyone's pretty excited about it. Especially Ms. Regina. She's managing a lot of great new talent this year, so it's going to be quite the show."

"I bet. I can't wait to see it for myself. Is it still going to be in October?"

"Yeah. I'll be sure to get everything taken care of so you can be there."

"Okay, good. But in the meantime, you better make sure you get a handle on this Teddy situation. Don't let this thing linger on for too long."

"I'll do the best I can."

"I'm serious, Legend."

"I know, and I'm sure things will be back on track soon enough."

"Alright," she said before looking toward my car. "Did you get a new bodyguard? Where's Cade?"

I laughed as I pulled out my cell and pulled up the website to do the word of the day. "That's still Cade. He just shaved all his hair off."

She nodded in admiration. "Hmm...he looks good bald. Tell him I said if I was a few years younger—"

"No, I'm not telling him that," I replied with a frown, "and you're not allowed to finish that sentence...*ever*!"

"What? I may be old but I'm not dead. I still got eyes, and right now they like what they see."

"Grandmother!"

"Oh, hush. Stop acting like you've never heard a woman admire a man before." She turned to look at me. "Speaking of which, who's admiring you these days? I hope it's someone ready to give me some great-grandchildren."

I shook my head. "Not even close."

"Dang it, Legend...what is it going to take to get you to settle down long enough to have some great-grands running around here?"

"Well, first it's going to take me finding a woman that's even worth doing that with."

"I'm sure you could find one if you put as much energy into your love life as you did your music career."

"Grandmother, I'm only twenty-eight. I have plenty of time to do all that love stuff. Right now, I need to be focused on my solo career."

She shrugged, then lifted her lemonade glass to her mouth. "Well, I'm not getting any younger."

"Don't worry, I'm sure you'll be around to see me start my little family," I told her. "Hey, look on the bright side, at least you know that I still want one. I wish that could be said for all the boys you practically raised."

Knowing exactly who I was referring to, she shook her head. "I'll never understand why Teddy didn't make an honest woman out of Eden."

"Because he was too busy chasing strippers and groupies. I keep trying to tell you, Teddy has changed. The fame has really gotten to him."

"You keep saying that. But every time he comes by to visit, he seems like the same old Teddy to me."

"That's because he's putting on an act. You're the last person he wants to upset. He loves the hell out of you."

She lifted her shoulders. "I just find it so hard to believe that Teddy would become such a different person. The same boy that I would fix peanut butter and jelly sandwiches for after school."

"Trust me, I hate it too. It's hard to see someone who's been like a brother to me turn into a person that I barely even know. Some of the things he's done, you wouldn't even believe."

Waving me off, she stood up. "I don't even want to know."

"And I don't want to tell you," I replied. "But, on another note, I got today's word in five tries. How about you?"

"Three!" she blurted before holding up her phone and shoving it in my face.

"Damn it."

"Mmhmm...today is my day. Better luck tomorrow."

Amused, I looked down at my ringing cell. Noticing Ms. Regina's name flashing on the screen, I hurried to answer it. "Hey. What's up?"

"Where are you?"

"At my grandmother's. Why?"

"Because we need to talk."

"Right now?"

"Yes! Right now!"

The urgency in her voice put me on edge. "What's going on?"

"Nothing that I want to talk about over the phone," she answered. "I was on my way to Simone's. Meet me over there."

"Um...okay."

"Oh, and don't look at your messages or the blogs."

"Why not?"

"We'll talk about it when I see you. Just don't look. Understand?"

"Alright, got it." Frowning, I ended the call and then looked at my grandmother. "Well, I hate to leave so soon, but I've got to meet up with Ms. Regina."

"It sounds urgent. Is everything okay?"

"I have no idea. I was just instructed not to look at my phone."

"Well, that can't be good," my grandmother said as she wrapped her arms around me. "Call me later. Love you."

"Love you too." I slid my shades on and rushed to my car.

"You good boss?" Cade asked.

"I'm not sure. But I guess I'll know in a few minutes."

8

SIMONE

I strolled through my living room with my cell in one hand and a wineglass in the other. There was nothing better than being home alone in my fluffy slippers, a loose-fitting tank, and my favorite gray booty shorts. I was in comfort heaven.

"When did they say my car would be ready?" I asked Nitra.

"Tomorrow morning."

"Wow, that was fast."

"Mmhmm...that's what happens when your mother makes a phone call."

I laughed. "Of course, she did, and I'm sure she made sure they bumped my car to the top of their list."

"You already know," Nitra replied. "Anyway, how are you feeling? Are you sore at all?"

"No, I feel pretty good. I'm just ready to get back behind my own set of wheels."

"I completely understand."

Hearing a tiny voice talking to Nitra in the background, I said, "Is that EJ?"

"Yes. He's begging for the chips I have in my hand."

"Well, give him some," I demanded.

"No. He hasn't had dinner yet. I don't want to spoil his appetite."

"Girl, please. Give him the chips. He'll be fine."

She sucked her teeth. "See, this is why I have to give you strict instructions when I let him come over there to visit. You'll spoil this little boy rotten."

"Sure will, and in case you were wondering, I hardly ever follow your rules."

"Oh, wow! Seriously?"

"Mmhmm...we don't have time for rules when we're trying to have fun."

Nitra chuckled. "Oh, just wait until you have a kid. I can't wait to do all the things you tell me not to do, then send the child home with you."

Pleased by the mere thought of having a child, I said, "I look forward to it."

"Yeah, okay. You say that now, but we'll see."

Hearing a knock at the door, I placed my wineglass on the coffee table. "I gotta go. My mom's here. Oh, tell EJ that his godmother loves him."

"Will do."

As soon as I ended the call, I rushed to open the door.

Much to my surprise, it was Legend.

I glanced down at my skimpy attire, which left very little to the imagination, thanks to me not wearing a bra. "What are you doing here?" I asked. But he didn't respond. Instead, he remained still, his eyes looking me over. I snapped my fingers in his face. "I said, what are you doing here?"

"Oh, my bad." He ran his hand along his beard. "Um...your mother told me to meet her here. Did she not tell you?"

I looked back down at my phone to see if I'd received a text, but there was nothing. "No, she didn't. Did she say why?"

"No, but from the phone call, it sounded urgent. She said for me to come here, and she would be here shortly."

"Really?"

"Yep," he replied, then lifted his hands. "Hey, I'm not trying to intrude on whatever you've got going on. I can call your mom and tell her we need to meet up somewhere else if you need me to. I just assumed you already knew I was coming."

Shaking my head, I said, "No, it's fine. I just need to go change into some decent clothes."

He gave me another once over then licked his lips. "They look pretty decent to me."

"Whatever," I replied before moving over to let him in. "Just get in here and sit down."

"What? I'm just being honest."

"A little too honest."

"My bad. I don't want to step on any toes." He looked around the room.

"Wiz isn't here," I told him. "He's doing an event tonight."

"Oh okay. Good to know." He moved in a little closer to me and slid his thumb over my lip.

"What are you doing?"

"You had some icing on your lip."

I hurried to lick whatever was left of it off. "Sorry, I had a donut a few minutes ago."

"Hmm...wine and donuts. That's an interesting combination."

I giggled. "I didn't have them together. I just fixed this," I said as I went to grab my glass. "Would you like some? Or a donut?"

"I'll take the donut. I'm good on the wine. I need to keep a clear head for whatever your mother is about to tell me."

"I wonder what it is," I said as I strolled to the kitchen, allowing my hips to sway a little more than usual.

Legend let out a deep sigh, which could only mean one thing...

"Take your eyes off my ass," I spat.

He hurried to clear his throat. "Sorry, I'm just not used to seeing you so comfortable."

"Yeah, well, when I'm at home this is usually me. The less clothes, the better."

"Hmm...I see."

I tried not to smile too hard as I glanced over my shoulder, but I liked the way Legend was looking at me. It was a look that I hadn't seen in a long time, and it was one that I'd forgotten I needed.

Giggling, I pulled a donut from the glass cake stand and handed it to him. "Here, try to focus on this."

"I'll do my best." He grabbed the donut and looked around the kitchen. "You know, in all the years I've known you, I've never been inside of your house. It's nice."

"Thanks. I designed it myself."

"Even the glass balcony that looks over the living room?"

"Sure did," I replied. "That's one of my favorite parts. I love being able to see almost every room on the lower level as soon as I step out of my bedroom."

"Well, you did a damn good job."

"Thank you. I always had a vision of how I wanted my dream house to be. I love fresh, bright colors and natural lighting, which is why I have so many damn windows. It's almost similar to yours, but on the opposite end when it comes to brightness."

"Yeah, you got me beat on that, but it fits your vibe."

"Thanks. I'm just glad the builders were able to do things exactly the way I wanted them to," I told him. "Of course, Wiz wants to change it. He says it's way too white in here, which isn't manly enough."

Legend frowned. "It looks pretty neutral to me."

"That's what I said. But he wants to make this place look like a bachelor pad, which isn't happening. He should've thought about that before he decided to move in with me."

Leaning against the kitchen island, Legend said, "So, what's really up with you two? And before you try to avoid the question, just know that I'm fully aware that the little hall pass story was about you."

I rolled my eyes. "Okay, fine. But before I tell you anything, let me go and put on some clothes. I shouldn't even be standing here like this."

"Why? We're friends and two grown adults. We've seen body parts before. Shit, you've seen me in nothing but a towel while doing my massages."

"Yes, but that's normal," I said. "You're never supposed to see me like this."

Walking toward me, he said, "But what if I like seeing you like this?"

Immediately, my words got stuck in my throat, and I could feel my pussy growing wetter by the second.

Oh, this is bad, Simone.

"Legend, what are you doing?"

"Whatever you want me to do."

"But you can't do anything."

"Take the hall pass and I can."

Shaking my head, I said, "Please forget I ever told you that."

"I can't, and now I need to know more."

"There's nothing more to tell."

"But there is," he insisted.

Still, we were inches from each other. The crisp smell of him invaded my nostrils. The shit was intoxicating, and it made me want to open my legs for him.

But that couldn't be done.

Well, unless I agreed to the hall pass.

Stop it, Simone. You're not doing that.

Pressing my hand against his chest, which was firm as hell, I swallowed hard. "Legend, I know you're used to getting whatever you want when it comes to women, but that's not going to happen with me. I've only been with one man, and unless our relationship ends, that's not going to change."

Lifting his hands, he gave me a nod. "Understood. But for the record, I don't always get everything I want...trust me."

Confused by what he was implying, I said, "What do you mean?"

"Exactly what I said."

"But you made it sound like it was about me. As if—"

Before I could finish, my mother rushed through the door, which I'd mistakenly left unlocked. "Sorry it took me so long," she said while looking at Legend. "I've been on the phone trying to put out this damn fire your boy created."

"Fire? What fire?" Legend asked.

I lifted my finger to intervene. "Hold up, before the two of you get into your little meeting...Mama, why did you send him over here without telling me?"

"Oh, sorry. I was so focused on all this shit I'm trying to handle that I forgot to call you." She looked me over and smiled. "You look cute and comfortable. Doesn't she look cute, Legend?"

"Mama!" I spat.

"What? I'm just trying to get the man's opinion."

I shook my head. I knew exactly what she was doing.

When it came to Wiz, my mother only tolerated him, and she would do anything to get me away from him. Mostly because she knew I wasn't happy, and the things I wanted, Wiz wasn't anywhere near trying to provide. But she would never say that out loud. Supporting her children's decisions was very important to her...even if she didn't always agree.

Legend smiled and hugged my mother. "She looks *very* cute, Ms. Regina."

"Mmhmm...I know."

I rolled my eyes. "I'll let you two discuss whatever it is you need to discuss. I'm going to go change." Not sticking around to hear their response, I strolled out of the living room and up the stairs. As I made my way to my bedroom, I glanced over the balcony. My mother handed Legend her cell. I couldn't see what she was showing him, but from the way Legend's demeanor changed, I knew it couldn't be good.

He was pretty quiet as he examined whatever was on the screen, then all of a sudden, I heard him shout, "What the fuck?"

9
LEGEND

"I'm done fucking with your boy," I told Kendrick as I stood in Simone's backyard with my cell up to my ear, "and in case it wasn't obvious, I'm not doing the festival."

Kendrick blew out a heavy breath, then sucked his teeth. "Damn, I knew your ass was going to say that."

"Hell yeah, I'm saying that. Did you see what that fool accused me of?"

"Yeah, I did, and it's pretty fucked up. I just don't understand why he would take it there. He had to be drunk."

"Oh, I know he was. But that doesn't give him a pass to lie on me."

"Naw, it doesn't. That shit ain't cool at all," Kendrick said. "What's up? Do you need me to swing through and hit some weights with you? I know you need to blow off some steam."

"Yeah, I do. But I'm not at the house right now. I'm at Simone's."

"Oh really?"

Aware of the nonsense that was probably brewing in his mind, I said, "Before you start conjuring up the wrong ideas, the only reason I'm over here is because Ms. Regina had me meet her over here to tell me what was going on."

"Mmhmm."

"Man, whatever."

"Look, I can't blame you for wanting to calm your nerves with your fine ass friend after reading that shit. Is Wiz there?"

"No, he's not, and it's not like that."

"Yeah, I hear you. Anyway, I don't think you're wrong for wanting to knock a hole through Teddy's face. Shit, I want to do it for you," he said with a chuckle. "But as far as the festival, maybe you shouldn't rush to decide just yet. Think about the fans."

Turning toward the pool, I scoffed. "Oh, so *I'm* the one that needs to think about the fans? He damn sure didn't think about the fans when he sent that shit to the blogs...and of all the bloggers he could've chosen, he chose Keke. That chick lives to drag people on her ratchet ass website and podcast."

"Yeah, he definitely did it on purpose. But we both know it's because he's in his feelings about you leaving the group."

"That's fine. He can be in his feelings. But don't release some shit about our group splitting up, and then make it seem like one of the reasons is because I wanted your baby mama. Who does that?"

"Apparently, Teddy does." Kendrick laughed. "You know he's never been a fan of how cool you and Eden are. Especially since they broke up. He doesn't say it to you, but he loves whispering that shit to me."

Frowning, I put my cell on speaker. "Man, that fool is stupid. Eden's been my stylist for six years. I'm cool with all my staff. That's how I continue to have the same loyal people working for me. But he doesn't know what that's like since his silly ass can't control his mouth or his hands. He has to find a new assistant damn near every other week," I said. "And let's not forget that

I'm the one who introduced him to Eden in the first place, and they would still be together had he not spent the last two years of their four-year relationship fucking strippers."

Just saying that shit out loud pissed me off. Eden deserved so much better than what she got from Teddy. From day one, she was all about him, and at first, he was all about her. But shortly after she had their son, he began to recognize all the responsibility that came along with it, and he started focusing on everything but them. So many times, I tried to talk some sense into him. But my words fell on deaf ears, and eventually, Eden decided she'd had enough. She walked away from him, and he hasn't been right ever since.

Pulling me from my thoughts, Kendrick said, "I can't even imagine how Eden is feeling about all of this."

"She's probably livid," I replied as I rubbed my hand over my forehead. "I thought about calling her, but I can almost guarantee she's ignoring everyone's phone calls right now. You know how she is when it comes to Teddy and his outbursts."

"Yeah, I know. All I'm going to say is somebody better get his ass. He's spiraling out of control, and it's going to cost him big if he's not careful."

"It sure is, and I would hate to see him ruin the little bit of communication he still has with Eden and his son. She's not feeling that alcohol shit at all, and she's ready to cut all ties with him."

"Damn, he'll *really* lose it then."

"Most definitely."

Letting out a deep sigh, Kendrick said, "Let me see if I can talk some sense into his ass. He works my nerves, but I'm not trying to see him lose everything. In the meantime, please hold off on deciding about the festival. Now that everyone knows we're splitting up, they're going to be looking forward to our last performance. They deserve to have that moment."

I closed my eyes for a moment, then opened them slowly. "Alright, I'll try to hold off. But if he does anything else, I swear I'm done with his ass and the festival."

"Noted," Kendrick replied. "Well, I'll talk to you later. Try to chill for the rest of the night. Matter of fact, since Wiz isn't there—"

"Bye." I ended the call and shoved my cell into my back pocket.

I wasn't trying to hear whatever bullshit Kendrick was about to spew. I might have my wild thoughts when it came to Simone, but I wasn't entertaining those thoughts with him.

"Are you okay?"

I turned around to see Simone walking outside. Her hair was tossed into a messy bun on top of her head, and she'd changed into an oversized t-shirt and some biker shorts. Even with her change of attire, I could still see her nipples poking from beneath her shirt and her thighs were still just as visible.

Damn, she's gorgeous.

Clearing my throat, I looked her in the eyes. "I'm good."

"No, you're not," she said as she folded her arms over her chest and walked toward me. "My mother's been on the phone nonstop, so I heard what's going on. I can't believe Teddy did that, and of all the people to give that kind of information to, he chose my damn cousin."

"That's exactly what I said. Keke knows how to twist and turn some shit just to get views."

"Yeah," Simone replied. "But what would even make him think you want Eden? Did he catch you guys in a compromising situation or something?"

Immediately I frowned. "Hell no! Eden and I have never been close like that. First off, she's his baby mama, so I would never cross that line. Second, she works for me. I may fuck around, but I don't do it with my staff."

"Understood. I just had to ask."

"No, you really didn't," I snapped. "You should know me better than that."

"I mean, I feel like I do. But I couldn't help but wonder why he would go to that extreme and put that out into the public."

"Because his ass was probably drunk and still in his feelings. Not to mention, Eden probably got on to him about acting stupid over me going solo and he took it some kind of way."

"You think so?"

"I'm not for certain, but that's the only thing that makes sense. Why else would he bring Eden into this shit?" I said. "He's known for getting drunk and having his little temper tantrums. But this time he's gone too damn far."

"I agree," Simone replied. "I know this has to be burning Eden up. I saw some of the things people were saying in the comments on the blogs. A lot of people are blaming her for breaking up the group, calling her all kinds of names and even issuing death threats."

Hearing those last words, I looked at Simone with wide eyes. "Are you serious?"

"Yeah. It's pretty bad."

"Fuck!" Snatching my cell from my back pocket, I called my assistant. "Mya, I need you to pull one of my guys from the security team and get them over to Eden's."

"Okay. Will do. Do you want me to call her first?"

"You can, but no matter what she says, I want them wherever she is until I say otherwise."

"Got it."

I ended the call and returned my attention to Simone. "I would be devastated if something happened to her because of me."

"*Because of you*? This isn't your fault. This is about a grown ass man not being capable of handling his emotions."

"Yeah, but—"

Resting her hand on my shoulder, Simone said, "Nope. Don't even try to carry this. You have a right to do what's best for you, and him not being okay with that has absolutely nothing to do with you."

"I know. But the shit he said—"

"Is shit that my mother will make sure gets handled." Moving in closer to me, she placed her hands on my face. "You know my mother is the best. She has a team of people built to handle stuff like this."

"Yeah, I know."

"Okay, so stop worrying and relax your mind."

"That's a lot easier said than done."

"I know it is." Moving her hands away from my cheek, she eased her way to the back of my ears and then used her fingertips to caress them slowly. The shit felt good as hell, and for a second, I forgot that she was paid to do stuff like this. But right now, it felt a little more intimate than usual. So intimate that I caught myself closing my eyes and wrapping my arms around her waist. Much to my surprise, she didn't stop me. Instead, she kept massaging and making sweet humming sounds. "I don't want you leaving here in an uproar. I want your mind and spirit to be at peace. What Teddy said and did isn't a reflection of you. Don't let the blogs get into your head...understand?"

I nodded. "Okay."

"Don't respond to a single thing unless my mother tells you to, and most importantly, don't go anywhere near Teddy."

"Hmm...this is an interesting sight," Ms. Regina said as she stepped outside.

Simone eased back. "Relax, Mama, I was just trying to help him pull himself together."

"Is that right?"

"Yes." Simone pulled her shirt down, which had risen a bit while she was in my arms.

"Mmhmm," Ms. Regina replied. "Anyway, Legend, I want you to remain silent. I don't give a damn who approaches you, I need you to make sure you keep your cool. Just relax and stay focused on finishing up your tour."

I nodded in understanding. "Got it."

"I'm not playing, Legend. I know how you get when these people get you riled up. Especially my silly niece."

"I'm good. I'm going to take my ass home, blow off some steam in the gym and go to bed."

"Good, and as for the festival, I know you were talking about not doing it, but—"

"It's fine. I'm going to do it."

"Perfect. You guys have a photo shoot coming up. I'll make sure that everyone is instructed to keep you two separated as much as they can."

"Thank you."

Ms. Regina placed her hand on my arm. "Don't worry about any of this. I'll take care of it."

I nodded in understanding, then turned to look at Simone.

Smiling, she lifted her shoulders. "See, I told you my mama's got you."

"What about you?" I asked, unable to resist the moment. "Do you got me?"

"Of course, I do."

10

SIMONE

I sat at my desk, my mind in a bit of a fog after everything that had happened with Legend last night. The fact that someone he once called a friend had gone to such great links to hurt him, was beyond me. But I shouldn't have been surprised, Teddy was the kind of guy that you had no clue what personality you were going to get from one day to the next. Especially if alcohol was involved, which it usually was.

But Legend's issues weren't the only thing on my mind. My response to his reaction was heavy in my mind too. I couldn't explain why I felt the need to comfort him the way that I did. At first, I thought it was just the massage therapist in me. But when his arms ended up around my waist and I didn't move them, I knew that wasn't the case. I liked his arms there. They felt good to me, and I wanted more of what that felt like.

Tossing myself from my thoughts, I peeked out of my office door, which gave me a clear view of Nitra's desk. Oddly, she'd been quiet most of the day.

I stood up and walked toward her. "Hey, you got a sec?"
"Um...yeah...sure."

I motioned for her to come into my office and asked her to close the door behind her.

As soon as she sat down in front of my desk, I said, "Is everything okay?"

She didn't say anything right away, but when she finally did, she simply nodded. "Yeah...everything's fine."

"Come on, Nitra. You know I know you. You're not your usual bubbly self. What's going on?"

"Nothing...I'm fine...really."

"Well, you don't sound fine. You sound exhausted. Is everything okay with EJ? Is he sick or something?"

"No. He's fine," she replied. "I...um...I danced last night."

I jerked my head back. "You did what? Why? I thought you were done dancing."

"I am. Last night was kind of an unexpected thing. After we got off the phone yesterday, one of my girls called and asked me to attend this party at the club. I told her no, but she insisted that there was big money in it for me since I was requested."

"Really? By who?"

Clearing her throat, Nitra looked away from me. "I'd rather not say. Bottom line, I shouldn't have done it.

"What happened?"

Before she could respond, Wiz came barging into my office. "We need to talk."

"What's wrong?"

"What do you mean, *what's wrong*? We haven't talked since Friday. It's Monday, Simone. I'm tired of you giving me the cold shoulder and avoiding me."

I stood up and placed my hands on my desk. "So, you felt like barging into my office would make things better?"

"I'm going to let you two talk," Nitra said as she stood up and scurried out of the room.

"Wiz, how dare you bring our drama to my place of business?"

"Baby—"

"No, don't *baby* me," I spat. "You're wrong as hell right now."

"Okay, maybe I am wrong for showing up like this. But I couldn't take another day of the silent treatment. We need to talk about what was said. I know you're upset—"

"I'm not just upset, Wiz. I'm hurt. Never in a million years did I think you would question if I was the right woman for you."

"Look, I'm sorry, I shouldn't have said that shit. I was just tripping." He hurried over to me and grabbed my hand. "I guess I'm just scared about the marriage thing."

"But why?"

"It's a big commitment."

"I know, but if you know I'm the woman you want to be with then it shouldn't be that difficult to stomach."

He nodded, then kissed my lips. "You're right, I'm sorry."

I should've turned away from any affection that he tried to give, but I still loved him. He'd been my other half for so long.

Placing my hand on his cheek, I said, "I always want you to be sure about us and sure about me."

"I know, baby." He lowered his face to my neck and then pressed his body against mine. "I love you. I don't want anyone but you, and I'm sorry I put you through that." I could feel his dick against my thigh, then his hands against my waist as he tugged on my scrub pants. "Take them off."

I did as he asked while he lowered his jeans and slid on a condom.

My eyes were closed, and I should've been ready to take him in. But I wasn't.

My body wasn't.

Just as he was about to enter inside of me, I pressed my hand against his chest to stop him. "I think you should take the hall pass," I whispered.

He jerked his head back. "What?"

"I think you should take the hall pass."

Easing his dick back into his boxers, he said, "Are you serious?"

"Yeah. I am."

"But why? I told you I was just tripping."

"I know. But I get the feeling that you're not as sure as you want to be about things, and maybe being with someone else will help change that. Like you said, it could help you realize how good you got it at home."

He cleared his throat and turned away from me. "Wow. I wasn't expecting to hear this."

"I know. I wasn't expecting to say it," I told him. "But, when we walk down the aisle, I want you to be completely sure, which may be somewhat difficult since we've been together for so long."

"Yeah, that's true."

I tried not to roll my eyes at his response. But it was hard to hear him agree.

"Anyway, I think this will be good for us," I said. "A one-time opportunity for us to play outside with someone else, then get on with our lives together."

"Wait a minute...*us*? You're thinking about taking a pass too?"

"I mean...yeah. You're not the only one who's been with the same person for ten years," I replied with a chuckle.

He frowned. "You're not making any sense. Why would you need to take a hall pass? You're not the one with the uncertainty."

To get my pussy eaten for once, I thought then quickly shoved back the words.

I opened my mouth to say something else, but he stopped me. "No, Simone."

"Excuse me?"

"I said no. You're not sleeping with another man and then think I'm going to make you my wife."

Confused by his absurd response, I stepped forward. "Oh, but I'm supposed to let you sleep with another woman and allow you to become my husband?"

"I'm not asking to be your husband. That's all you."

Looking at him like he was crazy, I said, "Wow...just wow!"

He squeezed his eyes shut and pinched the bridge of his nose. "I didn't mean to say that."

"Oh, but I feel like you did."

"Look, all I'm saying is that I don't want another man's hands on you, and neither should you." He shrugged. "Where is this even coming from? What happened to you not being able to even think of another man touching you?"

"Honestly, Wiz, had you not said something about it in the first place, I wouldn't have even thought about it. But I just don't think it's fair that you get to do whatever the hell you want to do, and I'm supposed to just sit back to see if you choose me."

"It's not a competition."

"That's what it feels like though."

"Okay, fine. Then we're done with this conversation," he said. "The hall pass option is off the table for both of us."

"Fine."

"Fine," he said before storming out of my office and slamming the door behind him.

I hurried back to my seat and folded my arms over my chest.

The nerve of him. Shit was all good until I decided to have a little fun too.

Typical.

I snatched my phone from my desk and called Nori. "What are you doing?"

"Nothing much. Getting my nails done. Why?"

"We need an emergency sister night."

"When?"

"Tonight. You won't believe the shit I just had to deal with."

"Say no more. I'll text Riah."

"Cool. I'll see you in a few."

"Okay, sis. See you soon."

I ended the call and then dropped my head on the desk. As much as I shouldn't have been, I was somewhat disappointed that Wiz had decided against the hall pass. After my last few interactions with Legend, he was definitely on my mind to try things out with.

But maybe it was for the best. The last thing I needed was for things to end up being awkward between us. I mean, what if his dick wasn't even that good? What if he was one of those men that just talked a good game? I would hate to have to find him a new massage therapist and end our friendship because I couldn't erase the horrible images from my mind.

Sitting up, I shook my head. *You know what? It doesn't even matter. The decision has been made. Just move on, Simone.*

11

SIMONE

I stood in Riah's kitchen, patiently waiting for her to fill my margarita glass. "I wish you could've seen the look on Wiz's face," I said.

"He really acted a fool, huh?"

"Hell yeah. You would've thought that I was the one that came up with the idea to screw someone else."

Returning from the living room, Nori rolled her eyes. "Typical male bullshit. Everything was perfectly fine when he was talking about sleeping with another woman. But it's just outright ridiculous when you hit him with the same thing." She shook her head. "Men are so full of it."

Riah handed me my drink. "Well, I guess it was a fun idea while it lasted."

"Yeah...I guess."

Leaning into me, Nori said, "Is that disappointment I hear in your voice?"

I averted my gaze, trying to avoid the discussion of what I was truly feeling. But they were my sisters. I could talk to them about anything, and I never had to worry about it going any further than this room.

"Okay...so...maybe I was actually starting to look forward to the idea of trying things out with someone else," I said.

"Oh, really?" Riah said with a lifted brow. "With who?"

"Does it matter?"

"Not really. But I want to know anyway."

I took a sip of my drink, then sat it back down on the island. "Legend."

Nori's eyes widened. "Are you serious?"

"Oh, damn," Riah blurted before clapping her hands together in excitement. "You were really going to do it with him? I bet that would've been so fire."

"What makes you say that?" I asked

She shrugged. "Shit, I don't know. He just looks like the type of man that knows what he's doing. Not to mention, I've always felt like he was into you."

"Same." Nori chimed in.

I shook my head. "Okay, y'all are tripping."

"No, *you're* tripping," Riah shot back. "That man looks at you like he wants to drink your bath water...*all of it*."

"Whatever."

The sound of the front door opening caught our attention. As soon as Owen walked in, Riah rolled her eyes and gulped down every bit of liquor that was left in her glass.

Confused by her reaction, I said, "What's up with all that?"

"All of what?"

"Don't try to front. I saw the way you just responded when your husband walked in. What's going on?"

"We're not talking to each other right now. Well, *I'm* not talking to him."

"Why?"

"Because his silly ass thought it was okay to come in at damn near five o'clock in the morning."

"What? When?"

"This morning," Riah replied. "He claims he was at one of his boy's birthday parties, but I'm more than sure his ass was at the strip club."

"Shit, that's probably where his boy's party was," Nori said.

Riah folded her arms over her chest. "I bet it was. But either way, we had an agreement. No more coming in at all hours of the night or morning."

"So, what was his excuse for staying out so late?" I asked.

"According to him, he had too many drinks and fell asleep."

I rolled my eyes. "And you believe that?"

"It doesn't matter if I believe it or not. What matters is he shouldn't have allowed himself to get that drunk in the first place."

"Girl, I don't know why you always waste your time believing everything he says. He's full of shit. You know that, I know that...hell, the people across the street know that."

Giving me a stern glare, Riah spoke through clenched teeth. "Simone, lower your damn voice."

"Yeah, Simone, lower your voice," Owen said with a smirk as he made his way into the kitchen. "If you're going to talk shit about me in my own house, at least wait until I go upstairs."

"Now, why would I do that? It just makes more sense for me to say my piece loud enough so you can hear me."

"Simone, cut it out."

Owen looked at Riah. "No, let her say what she needs to say, so I can kick her ass out."

"You don't have to kick me out. I'll gladly leave."

"Hold up." Riah stood in front of him. "Ain't nobody kicking anyone out. This is just as much my home as it is yours, Owen."

"Well, you better get your sister in check before I check her myself."

Riah scoffed. "Nigga, please. You know damn well it's not

going down like that. Especially with the way I feel about you right now."

"Oh, really?"

"Yes, *really*?" she spat. "You don't bring your ass in here right before the damn sun comes up then decide you want to check my family for feeling some kind of way about it."

He frowned. "Shit, she wouldn't have to feel some kind of way if you would've kept our business between the two of us."

"Well, maybe I wouldn't feel the need to talk so damn much if you had kept your dick between just the two of us a long time ago."

He waved her off. "You need to let that shit go. We're supposed to be moving beyond that."

"How can we when you don't follow through on the things we agreed on?"

"Look, my bad. I know I shouldn't have come in as late as I did. But I told your ass that I was drunk. I wasn't with another bitch."

Grabbing her purse from the couch, Nori said, "This is too damn much. I'm leaving."

"I'm right behind you." I followed her out the door, then yelled back, "I'll call you tomorrow, Riah." But she didn't say anything. Instead, she gave me a wave and then continued going off on Owen.

After closing the door, I hurried to slide on my jacket and then met Nori in the driveway. "Well, I can tell that's about to get ugly."

"It sure is. I don't know why you even said anything to his ass."

"Because he gets on my fucking nerves," I told her. "He's an asshole, and I don't give a damn what he's saying, he's still cheating."

"You think so?"

"Hell yeah. Men like him don't stop doing dirt. Especially if they were able to get away with it."

Nori sighed. "Damn, I hate that. Riah deserves so much better."

"Yeah, she does. Unfortunately, she doesn't seem to think so."

"But why? Mama didn't raise us to look down on ourselves. Not to mention, she doesn't even act like she's less than."

"No, she doesn't. But between his money, them having a child together, and just the belief that he's the person she's supposed to be with, she can't walk away from him. She won't."

"God, I hope no man ever has a hold on me like that," Nori said before making it to her car and waiting for her driver to open the door. "Oh, before we go, I wanted to ask you more about this Legend thing. Were you really going to sleep with him?"

I shrugged. "Maybe."

"Wow. I can't believe you were considering being with someone besides Wiz."

"I know. Me either. I guess it was just a moment of weakness." I lifted my shoulders. "But it's neither here nor there. It's been called off."

"Yeah. It's probably for the best though. But you should still dump Wiz's ass."

I laughed. "You've made that very clear."

"Mmhmm...I'm dead ass serious."

"I know you are."

"Oh, and is all that stuff on the blogs true? Did Legend have something going on with Teddy's baby mama?"

"No, of course not." I stuck my hand in my purse and grabbed my cell. "That reminds me, I need to call Keke. She has some explaining to do."

"Girl, please, you know you're wasting your time. She's going to give you that whole speech about how reporting the news is her job, blah, blah, blah."

I rolled my eyes and sighed. "Yeah, I know. But I'm going to do it anyway. Probably not tonight though. I'm feeling a little tipsy."

"Well, good thing you decided to use one of Mama's drivers tonight. I know you didn't want to mess up your car after just getting it back."

"Damn right," I said while laughing and hugging her. "Have a good night, sis."

"You too. Love you."

"Love you too."

After saying our final goodbyes, I made my way to my car and waited for the driver to open the door to my backseat. Although my sister made it a regular thing to have someone drive her around day after day, I only did it when I felt like it might be necessary, and tonight felt like one of those nights.

As soon as the driver started the car, I let my head fall back against the seat. I couldn't stop thinking about what it would've been like had I been able to have a pass with Legend. Granted, that should've been the last thing on my mind. But I was intrigued, and the more I thought about it, the more I wondered if I should try talking Wiz back into it.

Shaking my head, I sighed. *Just focus on your relationship, Simone.*

12

LEGEND

"I'm proud of you," Ms. Regina said as she stood in the corner of my dressing room watching me assess my attire in the mirror.

"Oh yeah? Why is that?"

"Because you haven't made one attempt to break Teddy's neck during this photo shoot. Even though I know you've wanted to."

"I sure have." I lifted the hood of my sweatshirt onto my head just to see what it would look like. "But I have more important things to worry about, and kicking his ass isn't one of them. For the sake of the fans, I'm willing to put all bullshit aside."

"Good," she said while squeezing my shoulder. "And just remember, eventually, you won't have to deal with any of this. You'll be on your own."

"Yeah, I know."

"So, are you nervous about the big change?"

I shrugged. "I was at first. But now, I feel like I'm ready."

"Good. That's what I like to hear." She looked at her cell, then pressed her hand against her face while grinning.

"What's so funny?"

"Oh, nothing. Just Nori being Nori," she replied. "She just

sent me information about some new matchmaking experiment she wants me to look into for her."

Laughing, I shook my head. "That girl is determined to find the love of her life, huh?"

"Yes, and by any means necessary."

"Speaking of finding love...do you think it's possible to find love on reality TV?"

"Honestly, I think anything is possible. I'm not sure if I'm completely convinced when it comes to reality dating shows and matchmaking. But I do have a few clients that are big in the reality TV game, and I've heard of people falling in love while filming. But it's usually on accident."

"Hmm...interesting."

"Yeah, I know. It sounds crazy, but it happens."

"Do you think it will happen for Nori?"

"I'm not sure. But I'm hopeful. I want all my girls to find love."

"I feel you."

She moved closer while eyeing me in suspicion. "So...um...about the other night. You and my daughter were mighty comfortable in her backyard."

I cleared my throat. "That...that was just her looking out for me while trying to help me relax."

"Mmhmm...whatever you say."

"That's the truth, Ms. Regina. I promise."

She lifted her hands. "Don't worry. You don't have to keep trying to convince me. I'll take your word for it."

Intrigued by how giddy she seemed about the idea of us getting together, I asked, "How do you feel about Simone and Wiz's relationship?"

"Hmm...do you want my honest opinion, or do you want the one that I usually give as a supportive mother?"

I laughed. "I would like your honest opinion."

"Well, I think she could do much better. I'm sure you're aware that my daughter wants marriage and a family, right?"

"I am."

"Wiz isn't ready for that, and despite what she's hoping for, I don't think he ever will be."

"What do you think is holding him back?"

"I don't know. Maybe it's his fear of missing out," she replied with a shrug. "Him and Simone have been together since they were kids. For years, neither of them has experienced anyone outside of each other. Perhaps that reality is finally starting to hit him."

Tilting my head to the side, I said, "But I thought there was supposed to be something special about marrying your first love."

"There is. But how can you truly claim that someone is the one if you've had no other experience outside of them? Don't get me wrong, I believe in meeting your soulmate early in life. But experience is the best teacher. Simone feels that Wiz is the only man for her because he's the only man she's ever been with. But at the end of the day, they don't want the same things out of life, which is something they've learned over time. Deep down, I think Simone knows that Wiz isn't the man for her anymore, but she struggles to let go because she isn't sure if there's someone better for her."

I sighed. "Damn, that's crazy."

"Yeah, it is. But keep your mouth shut. You never heard any of this from me."

Amused, I nodded. "Don't worry, my lips are sealed. I do hope she realizes that she's worthy of more though, and there's someone out here that will give her everything that she desires."

"Me too."

Returning my gaze to the mirror, I took a moment to digest everything Ms. Regina had said. The fact that Simone could ever think that she was only deserving of one man to love her was crazy. Clearly, she didn't recognize just how amazing she was. I couldn't lie, there was a part of me that wished I could be the man to show her that. But women like her didn't just walk away from the only thing they'd ever known. Loyalty would keep her right where she was, which left me no other choice but to keep my eyes open for whenever he fucked up.

That was an opportunity I wasn't going to miss.

"They're ready for you," Ms. Regina said as she looked up from her phone.

"Okay, cool." I slid my shades on and strolled out of the dressing room.

As soon as I made it to the studio floor, Eden hurried over to me and pressed her hands against the front of my hoodie. "Make sure you do a few shots with the hood on."

"Will do."

"Alright guys," the photographer said as she lifted the camera closer to her eyes. "Let's take these first few shots with Legend in the front."

I glanced over at Teddy and Kendrick, who both nodded in understanding.

Surprisingly, this shoot had been a breeze. Granted, every now and then I would feel Teddy staring at me. But that was only when he saw Eden near me, which was crazy since nothing she did was out of the ordinary. Like always, she made sure everything I had on did exactly what it was supposed to do. If I felt like shades were necessary and she didn't, she made sure to take them off. She was all about getting the perfect shot.

As the lights flashed over and over, we switched up our positioning, making sure nothing ever looked the same. Although the agreement was for Teddy and I never to be close to each other, there were a few times that we ended up in the same space. But we kept it moving and didn't think anything of it.

Lifting her hand, the photographer said, "Alright, guys, let's take five. I want to switch up the backdrop."

"Okay. Cool." I stepped away and Mya handed me a bottle of water.

Changing my shades, Eden said, "So, how are you feeling?"

"I'm cool. But I should be asking about you. I wanted to call and check on you, but I figured you probably wouldn't want to talk."

"And you were right. I wasn't answering the phone for anybody."

"Damn, I'm sorry Eden."

She looked me over in confusion. "What do you have to be sorry for? You didn't put those things in the blogs. That was all Teddy."

I nodded. "I know, but I'm the reason he did it."

"No, *he's* the reason he did it. Teddy's responsible for his actions. No one else."

Even though I knew she was right, it still didn't feel good to know that she got caught up in our mess. "So, what did he say to you about everything?"

She scoffed. "Nothing."

"Really? He didn't apologize?"

"To apologize, he would have to have the opportunity to talk to me, which is something he doesn't have at the moment."

"Oh, so you're not speaking to him at all?"

"No."

As soon as she responded, I could feel Teddy's eyes burning a hole in the side of my forehead. "That explains so much."

"Mmhmm...I know he's feeling some kind of way. I haven't responded to his texts unless they involve our child, and even then, I keep it short and sweet. Several times he's asked me to meet up so we can talk, but I refuse. At this point, we have nothing to talk about. He chose to hurt me rather than protect me. I don't know when or if I'll ever forgive him for that."

"Looks like you two are having a deep conversation over here," Teddy said as he approached us. "Do you guys want to share what it's about?"

"Teddy, please don't start," Eden said. "Just focus on the shoot."

"I will once I know what the two of you are talking about, and why you seem to have no problem talking to him instead of me."

Turning toward him, Eden said, "What the hell do I need to say to you? You told the world some shit that isn't true just because you were in your feelings about Legend leaving the group. That should've been between the two of you. But no, you decided to put me in it."

"That's because you were defending him. I had every right to voice my opinion on why I felt like you were."

She looked at him like he was crazy. "Seriously, Teddy? It never crossed your mind that maybe I was defending him because he has the right to do what he wants, and it wasn't new information?"

"Nah, I just assumed that it was probably because the two of you had been fucking and he told you his decision way before he told me."

Eden's mouth dropped.

Staring at him, she shook her head slowly. "You know what? I'm not dealing with this shit."

I watched as she stormed off, then turned my attention to Teddy. "Bro, you need to chill. That's the mother of your children."

"Nigga fuck you."

"Oh, so we're going *there* again?"

"Yeah, we are," Teddy said as he got in my face.

I turned away as my hand balled into a fist. "I thought I warned you about getting this close to me."

"Alright, that's enough." Kendrick stepped in. "Let's just finish up this shoot, so we can go our separate ways."

Teddy shoved him to the side. "I'm not doing a damn thing until this nigga admits to wanting my bitch."

"*Your bitch*?" I shot back. "Have you lost your fucking mind? Don't you ever call that woman a bitch in my presence."

"I'm just calling it like I see it."

I could smell the liquor on his breath, which was odd since I knew he didn't show up that way. Then it hit me...there were plenty of drinks floating around the studio and probably even more in his dressing room.

Recognizing what I was dealing with, I decided to be the bigger person and diffuse the situation. "You know what? I'm going to take whatever minutes we have left and chill in my dressing room."

"You do that?" he shot back. "And while you're back there, try not to cry on my bitch's shoulder. Don't get beside yourself just because she let you fuck!"

Feeling the little bit of resolve that I had left disappear, I rushed toward him and planted my fist right into his nose. I watched as he fell to the ground, a loud grunt expelling from between his lips.

I squeezed my fist and hovered over him. "Be glad I only hit your punk ass once." I turned back toward the photographer who was standing just a few feet away in shock. "I'm sorry you wasted your time," I told her. "We're done here."

"It's fine. I think I got enough photos of you guys."

"Oh, it doesn't matter what you got." I looked over at Ms. Regina. "These photos will never see the light of day. I'm done with anything involving this group...and that includes the Rhythm City Festival."

13

SIMONE

I grabbed my backpack, and then took one last look around my office before heading to the front. I'd just finished going over some paperwork, so I was the one closing for the evening.

Glancing down at my watch, I contemplated if I had enough time to stop and get gas before heading to Legend's for a last-minute massage my mother insisted that he would need.

When she first mentioned it, I told her that it would have to wait until tomorrow. But after she filled me in on what went down at the photo shoot, I knew her request was probably necessary.

Snatching the keys from the side pocket of my bag, I decided I would just grab some gas on the way home and then I walked out the door. No sooner than I'd locked up, Legend appeared right behind me. "Oh my God," I said as I pressed my hand against my chest. "What are you doing here? I was on my way to you."

"Yeah, I know. But I was still out and about, so I figured I would just try to catch you here."

"Well, you barely did."

"I see," he said before looking around. "I don't like you being out here like this so late in the evening. Where's your security?"

"I don't have security."

He frowned. "Why not?"

"Because this is a nice area."

"Nice area or not, you shouldn't be out here alone at this time of night. None of your staff should." He pulled his cell from his pocket and took a moment to type up a text.

Tilting my head to the side, I said, "Please tell me you didn't pull someone from your security team to—"

"I sure did. There will be someone here every day from now on."

"Legend, you didn't have to do that. I'm fine."

"I know I didn't have to. But it would make me feel better if I knew you were safe at all times of the day."

"Okay, well, I'll talk to my mother about getting someone to be here in the evening. I don't want you to have people that are paid to take care of you looking after me."

"Too late. It's done, and it's not a problem."

"Fine. At least tell me how much it's going to cost, so I can add it to the budget."

He scoffed. "Quit playing. You know damn well I'm not going to make you pay for that."

"Why not?"

"Because I'm not. Now, can you unlock the door so we can go inside."

"Wait, so you want me to do your session here?"

"Yeah. I need to get some shit off my chest, and I can't wait until I get all the way home."

"Um...okay. Is this about what happened at the photo shoot?"

"Yeah, Ms. Regina told you?"

I nodded, then returned my key to the lock and pushed the door open. "What the hell happened?"

"The usual...Teddy had too much to drink and started acting stupid." Legend followed me inside and Cade remained near the entrance with his hands folded in front of him.

Leading Legend to one of the private rooms, I said, "He came to the shoot drunk?"

"Nah, I don't think he was at first. But I'm sure there was plenty to drink in his dressing room and I know there was stuff around the food area."

"Damn, I hate that. What do you think set him off?"

"For starters, he's pissed that Eden defended me about leaving the group and then he's even more pissed that she's talking to me while ignoring him. Things got ugly when he saw the two of us talking about the shit he put out in the blogs. One thing led to another, and I ended up knocking him on his ass."

"You hit him?"

"Sure did. He got too fucking close."

"Oh, wow. I can't believe it even came to that."

"Me either. But I warned him not to roll up on me like that. He didn't listen, so that was the result."

I blew out a heavy breath, saddened by everything I'd heard. This wasn't the Legend and Teddy that I'd known over the years. But Teddy wasn't the same Teddy that I met in the beginning either. He was always kind of emotional, but he was usually better at handling himself.

"You know, I'm starting to think that there's a lot more than drinking going on with him."

"Yeah, well, the way he acts makes it impossible for me to have even the slightest amount of sympathy for him."

"I know," I said as I dimmed the lights in the room.

Legend slid out of his shirt, exposing his chest and the gray sweatpants that were pretty damn low on his waist.

Clearing my throat, I looked away.

"You good?" Legend asked in an amused tone.

"Um...yeah. I'm just going to step out and let you finish getting undressed."

"No need. I'm good."

Thinking he'd already wrapped himself in a towel, I turned back to him. But all I saw was dick...big, *black* dick.

"Oh my God!" I called out. "You said you were covered."

"No, I said I was good. You assumed I was covered."

"Well, yeah, that's what people usually say when they are."

"Hmm...not me."

"Legend, please hurry and put your towel on."

"Shit, where is it?"

I glanced around, then realized that I'd forgotten to pull one out for him. "Damn, it's still in the cabinet," I said while gazing across the room. "Okay, so I'm going to ease past you and grab one. Can you like scoot back or sit on the table for me?"

Still smiling, he said, "Sure. I'll scoot back for you."

"Thank you."

I tried my best not to look at him. But it was hard. I mean, his dick wasn't even fully erect, and it was still big as shit. Oh, and beautiful. It was so beautiful.

My mouth watered.

Simone, what's the matter with you? I scolded myself.

Shaking my head, I slid past him without touching his flesh...barely.

As fast as I could, I snatched a towel from the cabinet and tossed it to him.

"You know, for someone that's trying to avoid this interaction, your eyes keep finding their way to my dick."

"What?"

Placing his hand beneath my chin, he lifted my head. "I said, your eyes keep finding their way to my dick."

Unable to keep my thoughts to myself, I dropped my shoulders and whined, "I know. But believe me, I was trying. It's just...I don't think I've ever seen something so...um..."

"So what?" he asked, intrigue in his eyes.

I shook my head. "Nothing. I really shouldn't be here with you like this."

"Mmm...well, I'm not forcing you to be."

"I know."

I tried to instruct my feet to step back, but I couldn't move. My curiosity was eating away at me. With something that looked so good, he had to know what to do with it.

Leaning into my ear, he whispered, "If you want to touch it, just touch it." Slowly, his hand slid into my hair. "But just know, if you do, I can't guarantee that I won't touch you too."

Just hearing those words, I should've walked away. In fact, I should've run away. But I didn't. Instead, I lowered my hand and did exactly what I shouldn't have been doing. I touched it. Not only did I touch it...I stroked it, slowly and intensely, desperate to fill the width of it and to see how far it could stretch.

His moans were like music to my ears and my lower lips started to throb. As if he knew my exact thoughts, he dipped his hand into my scrub pants, not stopping until his fingertips met with my soaked flesh.

I thought I was going to scream just from his touch, but I held it together. It felt so good to feel his fingers floating in and out of me. I moved in a little closer and propped my leg up on the couch behind him, hoping to give him the perfect amount of access to keep hitting all the right spots.

The more he dove between my flesh, the more I stroked his. Both of our moans bounced off the walls. Wanting to make him feel as good as I did, I slipped my hand into my mouth, then returned it to his dick.

He gasped.

The speed of my stroke increased, and I could hear the

smacking sounds of my hand sliding back and forth on his length.

"Fuck!" he called out.

No sooner than those words left his lips, did I feel my insides explode. "Oh my God! Shit!"

He went even harder as he felt my cum rain down on his fingers.

"Damn, you feel good," he whispered.

The depth in his voice made me want to shove him inside of me. But instead, I forced my eyes to open, then stepped back.

Still, his dick looked good.

So good that I almost dropped to my knees and put my mouth around it.

"Um...you should probably go," I said.

Smiling, he reached behind me and grabbed his sweatpants from the massage table.

I tried not to tremble from the feel of his chest brushing against me. But it was a struggle. Especially when he leaned into my ear and whispered, "Something tells me your body hasn't had that kind of experience before." He looked at me to see my response, but I didn't say anything. "Well, just so you know, there's a lot more where that came from, and it only gets better."

I closed my eyes and swallowed hard as he left the room.

As soon as I knew he was out of the spa, I hurried to make sure the door had locked behind him, then slammed my hand over my mouth.

I couldn't stop the tingle that was happening between my thighs. It was like he was still here, stroking and teasing my insides. Lowering my hands, I attempted to calm myself, but it wasn't doing much good.

My cell went off, and immediately, I thought it was Wiz sensing my indiscretion.

But when I glanced down at my phone, I saw Keke's name flashing on the screen.

"What do you want?" I answered.

"Look, I know you don't fool with me, but I think I have some info that you might want to know."

"Does it pertain to me?"

"Not necessarily. It's about Owen."

I rolled my eyes. "Well, it sounds like you should be calling Riah, not me."

"I would, but she has me blocked."

"Hmm...I wonder why."

"Look, never mind all that. This shit is about to go public, and—"

"Look, Keke, I don't care. I've warned my sister about his trifling ass more times than I can count. It doesn't change a thing. I promised her that I would shut my mouth about her marriage, so that's what I'm going to do."

"I hear what you're saying, but I think you need to hear what's about to come out."

"No, thanks. I'll hear it with the rest of the world. Bye, Keke."

14

SIMONE

The drive from the spa to my house was a quiet one.

I had way too much on my mind. The only thing I wanted to do was get home, shower, and close my damn eyes. Wiz was working late, so I didn't have to worry about trying to hide the guilt of another man touching me. At least, not right away. Hopefully, all of that washed away while I was in the shower. I also hoped that the thoughts of Keke's phone call washed away too. Although I'd made a promise to stay out of my sister's marital business, I couldn't help but wonder what was about to come out. For Keke to call me, it had to be something big. The only thing I could think of was that he'd got some random chick pregnant, and she was about to tell the world.

If that was the case, I hoped like hell it would make Riah come to her senses and leave his ass.

Trying to keep my backpack from falling, I adjusted it on my shoulder and unlocked my door.

"Simone, hey," Wiz greeted as he stood up from the couch.

My eyes widened. "What are you doing here? I thought you were working tonight?"

"I was. But I had someone fill in for me. I wanted to talk."

"*Talk*? About what?"

"The hall pass thing."

I frowned. "I think you've made your feelings clear about that. You don't want to do it if I'm going to do it too. The end."

"Yeah, and that's what I want to talk to you about," he said as he walked toward me. "I shouldn't have shut you down like that. It was selfish of me."

Not wanting him to get too close, I hurried out of my shoes and headed toward the kitchen. "It's fine. I'm done with it. Let's just focus on each other."

"I agree, and the first step to us doing that is by me not being selfish."

Confused, I turned to face him. "Wiz, what are you saying?"

It took him a second, but he finally got it out. "I think we should both do it. I think we should both give each other a pass."

"Are you serious?"

"Yeah. I'm hoping it will make our relationship stronger. In fact, I know it will," he said emphatically. "It will free us from any and every question we have about each other."

"But I'm not the one with all the questions. You are."

"Come on, Simone, let's not travel backward here."

Closing my eyes, I shook my head and then returned my gaze to his. "Okay, fine. But we have to set some rules."

"Of course."

We walked over to the dining table and sat across from each other.

I folded my hands together as I placed them down in front of me. "First things first, we have to use protection, and that shit isn't optional."

"Understood, and we can't give each other any information about the person we choose. I don't want to know anything about the nigga you screwed."

"Fine by me. I definitely don't want to know anything about who you choose to screw."

"Good. I'm glad we can agree on that."

"Mmhmm...oh, and it can only be done once. I'm not about to deal with you banging some female repeatedly. I suggest you get everything out of your system the first time around."

"Noted. Anything else?"

"Oh, and it can't happen here."

"Seriously, Simone, you really think I would do some shit like that?"

"Well, you're pretty eager to fuck another chick, so I don't know what you would do at this point."

"I'm not eager. I'm just—"

I lifted my hand. "You don't have to keep saying the same thing. I've heard your side of things. Let's just get it over with so we can get back to our lives."

Standing up, he cleared his throat. "You sure you still want to do this? We don't have to."

"Trust me, if we didn't have to, you wouldn't have brought it back up." He lowered his gaze, then shoved his hands into his pockets, which only proved that there was truth in my statement. "I'm going to take a shower. I've had a long day," I told him.

"Um...okay...I'll be up in a sec."

"Mmhmm," I said as I made my way out of the kitchen.

I took my time going up the stairs, my mind drifting back to the events of the day. Given what I'd done, I couldn't help but wonder if I should still be giving Wiz a hard time. Then I thought about it. The fact that I'd even put myself in the position to do what I'd done was because of his silly ass suggestion in the first place.

When I made it to my bedroom, I started pulling off my clothes.

Just as my mind was finally starting to wind down, I accidentally brushed my hand against my pussy, which was still tingling from earlier.

Damn, I shouldn't still feel like this, I thought.

But that was Legend's effect on me.

Hmm...maybe I should find someone a little less intense. Someone boring.

But why would I do that? I deserve to get everything I can out of the experience. Not only because it will be the only other man I've been with outside of Wiz. But because I want to get some damn satisfaction for being put in this position in the first place. So, if Legend is going to be the guy, I want to be finger fucked until the sun comes up and get some amazing dick in between.

I stepped into the shower and turned on the water. As soon as it was hot as I could stand, I grabbed my washcloth and poured some soap into it. It felt good to let the day wash away from my skin. For a moment, the thought of Wiz being with another woman flashed into my head. I wondered what kind of woman he would choose. Would she be someone like me? Or would she be the complete opposite?

It was weird to think about such a thing. But if this was what it took to get us to a better place in our relationship...whatever.

Damn, I sound just like Riah...dumb as hell.

I shook my head in disbelief. All the shit I gave my sister about her relationship, and mine wasn't any better.

My cell rang.

"I don't know why I brought my phone in here," I said while rolling my eyes.

Trying to ignore it, I continued rubbing soap on my body, then rinsed it away. But within seconds, my phone went off again, which made me feel like it might be an emergency.

I turned off the water, grabbed my towel, and stepped out of the shower.

"This better be important," I said before snatching my cell from the counter. "Nori, what is it?"

"Have you seen the shit that Keke just posted on her blog about Owen?"

Damn, that was fast.

"No, I haven't. But let me guess...he got a bitch pregnant?"

"Honey, I wish."

"You wish?" I said with a chuckle. "What the hell did he do?"

"According to this, he sexually assaulted a woman."

"Wait a minute. Sexually assaulted? You mean like...rape?"

"Yes, and you're not going to like it when I tell you who the woman is."

"Who is it?"

"Nitra."

"Nitra! You mean my assistant, Nitra?"

"Yep."

My mouth dropped, and every bit of air that I had in my lungs quickly disappeared.

What the fuck!

15

SIMONE

I cleared my throat as I walked into my mother's living room and took a seat in the lounge chair next to Nori.

Leaning forward, my mother clasped her hands together and rested them against her chin. "Simone, please tell me that you didn't know about this Owen and Nitra situation."

"I didn't. Well, I kind of didn't."

"What do you mean, *you kind of didn't*?" she replied while frowning.

"It means that I didn't know the details."

"But you knew your assistant was accusing your sister's husband of sexually assaulting her?"

"No." I shook my head. "All I knew was something was coming out, and I only found that out last night."

"From who?"

I rolled my eyes. "Keke."

"Keke?" my mother questioned. "So, she called you?"

"Yeah. She claimed she wanted to give Riah a heads-up. But she couldn't get in touch with her because Riah blocked her.

"Of course. So she called you?"

"Yeah. But I refused to get the details since I told Riah that I would stop having things to say about her husband."

"So, Keke didn't tell you anything?" Nori questioned.

"Nope. I left before she could."

"Damn, this is some crazy shit. Owen's been accused of a lot of things, but sexual assault—"

I scoffed. "With all of the things he's done, I'm surprised this is the first allegation."

Nori's eyes widened. "You don't really think he did it, do you?"

"Is that a trick question?"

"Come on now, Simone, he's a lot of things, but I don't think he's a rapist."

"And I don't think Nitra is a liar. I've known her for a long time and not once has she ever given me a reason not to trust her."

"But why didn't she tell you?"

"Why would she tell me? Riah is my sister, and she was assaulted by her husband. I can't imagine how uncomfortable she felt."

I looked away for a moment, my mind drifting back to my last conversation with her. Everything about her demeanor was off, and now I knew why.

"Okay, well, we have to get this thing under wraps," my mother said. "But most importantly, we have to be there for your sister. She's going to need our support through this. Especially once all the details come out."

Scrolling through her phone, Nori said, "Damn."

"What?"

"The blogs are saying that the assault happened a couple of nights ago at the strip club."

I nodded my head slowly. "Which was the night that Owen didn't come home, and Riah was pissed about it."

"Yep."

"What else does it say?"

"Apparently, it was a private party and Nitra was dancing for someone else, but Owen kept trying to get her to dance for him. It says she refused several times because she's seen how he can get with some of the other girls. But eventually, he convinced her to dance for him because he offered her some extra cash. According to this, things were chill at first. He didn't say much. But then, he started making inappropriate requests for her to do things. She told him no, but—" Nori dropped her shoulders, then her head.

"What? What happened?" I asked.

"It says she felt him shove his fingers inside of her. When she tried to get away from him, he held her in place and refused to let her go anywhere. Instead, he told her to smile and keep moving like she liked it because he had a gun in his pocket."

"Are you serious?" I said as I pressed my hand against my mouth.

"Yep, and because there was so much going on around them, no one noticed that anything was wrong, and it went on for several minutes. Oh, and get this, Nitra isn't the one that put this out to the blogs, it was an anonymous source."

"Really?"

"Yep. I'm assuming that it was someone that she confided in. Then again, it could be her posing as the anonymous source. But why not just go to the police?"

Sucking my teeth, I tilted my head to the side. "Come on, Nori. You see how much shit he's gotten away with already. She probably felt like she didn't stand a chance."

"You got a point," she replied.

My mother stood up. "This is awful. Simone, have you talked to Nitra?"

"No. I tried calling her, but she didn't answer."

"What about Riah?"

Nori shook her head. "She didn't answer the phone either."

"I'll try to call her again," my mother said as she tapped on her cell, placing it on speaker.

It only took a couple of rings for Riah to answer. "Hey, Mama."

"Hey, baby. How are you feeling?"

"Like shit," she blurted. "I can't believe this is happening."

"I know. But it's okay. We're going to get you through this. If you and my grandbaby need a place to stay, you know you can come here."

"Why would we need a place to stay?" she shot back as if she was appalled that our mother even suggested it. "I'm standing by my husband."

Unable to hold back my aggravation, I said, "Seriously, Riah? This man is being accused of rape."

"First off, why the fuck are you even talking to me?" she shouted from the other end of the phone.

"Look, before you even go there, I didn't know anything about this."

"Yeah right. As close as the two of you are, I'm pretty sure Nitra told you that she was going to do this dumb shit."

"First off, she didn't tell me anything. Second, don't try to downplay the situation. The last time I saw Nitra I could tell that something was wrong, but I didn't know what. Now, I know that she was dealing with the aftermath of your bitch ass husband assaulting her."

"Wow, so you're taking her side?"

"Damn right, I'm taking her side. Your husband is a low-down grimy piece of shit that's done more dirt than we can even name. Why wouldn't I believe her?"

"Because she's a fucking liar."

"Alright, alright," my mother said. "Let's not do this. None of us were there, so—"

"I didn't have to be there," Riah said. "I know exactly what happened. Owen told me."

I rolled my eyes. "Oh, and let me guess, he's convinced you that another woman is out for money. Mind you, she hasn't asked for a single dime. Hell, she's not even the one that put it out. Someone else did."

"Bullshit! It wasn't someone else. She just wants it to seem that way so it can look like there was actually a witness. But at the end of the day, Owen and I know exactly what this is," she said. "Your girl has been trying to get at my husband for months. But he wasn't giving her any attention. Apparently, she got fed up when he didn't respond the way she wanted him to the other night and decided to try to embarrass him in the public eye."

"Oh my god! You can't be fucking serious, Riah. There's no way that's what happened."

"Look, I don't have to explain anything to you. Bottom line, your assistant is a liar, and you can't be loyal to her and loyal to me."

"What the hell is that supposed to mean?" I questioned while moving closer to my mother's cell.

"You're *my* blood and when shit hits the fan, you're supposed to have my back. Long story short, you need to fire her ass."

My eyes widened. "What?"

"You heard me. You can't have the woman that's going around spreading lies about my husband working for you. Cut her ass loose."

"Riah, you're tripping."

"No, you're tripping if you think we're going to remain on good terms while you have the enemy working at your spa."

Taking a deep breath, my mother said, "Maybe we should

just see how this thing plays out before making such a drastic decision."

"No, there's nothing to wait on," Riah said. "If my sister has my back, she'll do this. The public needs to know that she's on his side."

"But I'm not on his side."

"Well, if you're not for him, then you're not for me. End of story."

Finally stepping in, Nori said, "Okay, wait a minute. We can't allow this to create a rift between the family."

Riah scoffed. "Sorry, little sis, but it's already done, and you guys have Simone to thank for that."

The line went dead, and my mother looked at us. "This is a mess."

"Tell me about it," Nori whispered.

Scrolling through my cell, I walked toward the door. "I'm leaving."

"Really? You don't care about what just happened?"

"Oh, I care, Nori. But what am I supposed to do about it?"

"Fix it!"

"How?" I replied. "By firing Nitra? I'm not doing that?"

"I'm not saying that."

"Then what are you saying? Because that's what Riah wants me to do."

Nori sighed. "I don't know. But there has to be something. I mean, maybe show a little compassion for what she's going through."

"How can I show compassion for someone who doesn't even show compassion for herself? For years, Owen has shown that he doesn't have any regard for her feelings. He's also shown that he's an entitled asshole that will do anything to get what he wants. I'm sorry, but every bone in my body is telling me that he did that shit, and until I see something that shows me otherwise,

I'm on the side of the person that I trust. If I'm wrong, and there turns out to be evidence to prove that, I will gladly apologize. But until that day comes, I'm not kicking a woman while she's down."

Saying nothing more, I walked out the door and made my way to my car. As soon as I was inside, I pulled up Legend's number and shot him a text.

"Hey, we need to talk. Are you busy?" –Simone

"Nah, I'm at home. I'm about to go downstairs and hit the gym in a little bit. You can still come by though. Unless you want to meet up later." –Legend

"Now is good. I'll be there in a few." –Simone

"Okay. Cool. See you in a bit." –Legend

16

LEGEND

"I just can't believe you two didn't sort this thing out," my grandmother said from the other end of the phone as I stood in front of my gym mirror lifting one weight after the other.

"Look, he crossed me. There's no coming back from that. I'm done."

"I know. I just really hate that. Especially for your fans. They're going to be so disappointed."

"Hold up a sec," I told her as I stopped what I was doing and walked over to the weight bench to turn up the volume on my cell. "Okay, sorry about that. Anyway, I hate our fans are going to be disappointed too. If it was something I thought we could fix, I would try. But Teddy is way too unpredictable at this point, and I have to protect myself."

"I understand," she replied, sadly. "Well, I know you don't get into all that internet gossip, but some of the ladies in the neighborhood came by earlier. They started asking me all of these questions about what was true and what wasn't. They were showing me pictures of the two of you going back and forth at the photo shoot. I had to tell them to mind their own damn business."

I sighed. "I'm sorry about that, Grandma. You know I don't like embarrassing you."

"Oh, sweetheart, you're fine. You didn't embarrass me at all. Those women are nosey as hell. Don't worry about them. How's Eden?"

"The last time we talked, she was keeping her distance from Teddy, which was one of the reasons he went crazy on me."

"Poor thing."

"Yeah. But hopefully, this whole thing blows over soon."

"I'm sorry, Legend, but I don't see that happening. Especially since word got out that you're not doing the festival. People are furious."

"I know." I lowered my gaze, hating that I had to hear those words out loud.

"Oh, how's Kendrick?"

"He's cool. I mean, he's not thrilled about the way things went down, but he understands where I'm coming from. I still think he's holding out hope for me to change my mind once things cool off. But that's not going to happen."

Hearing my gym door open, I turned to see Simone entering the room. Looking beautiful as always, she was wearing a hot pink hooded sweatshirt and some black leggings.

I licked my lips, happy to see her standing in my presence.

"Hey Grandma, let me call you back," I said. "Simone just got here."

"Oh, did she? Let me talk to her."

"I have you on speaker. She can hear you."

Simone smiled. "Hey, Ms. Queenie. How are you?"

"I'm doing good baby. How are you?"

"I'm doing okay."

"Good. How's your sister? I heard the things they're saying about her husband."

My eyes widened, thrown off by my grandmother's

knowledge of the situation. Then again, I shouldn't have been surprised. She may not get involved with every little thing, but her eyes were always on the internet. She talked about her friends being nosey, but she wasn't too far from it either.

Looking just as surprised as I was, Simone shrugged. "Um...she's doing the best she can considering the circumstances."

"Understood," my grandmother replied. "So, do you think he did it?"

Hurrying to put an end to the call, I said, "Bye, Grandmother. Love you."

"What?" She shot back. "I was just trying to get her opinion on the matter."

"Mmhmm...bye."

"Fine. Bye. Love you too," she replied.

I hit the end button on my cell and dropped it into the pocket of my basketball shorts. "Sorry about that. You know how my grandmother is."

"It's fine." Simone sat down on the weight bench and crossed one leg over the other. "She wouldn't be the first person that I've had to explain my opinion to today."

I nodded slowly. "I'm assuming you're talking about having to explain things to Riah?"

"Yep, and it didn't go well at all."

Sitting down next to her, I placed my weight on the floor. "What happened?"

"Shit, what didn't happen?" she spat. "I met up with my mother and Nori this morning to talk about what was going on. The first thing they asked me was if I knew about it."

"Why? Because it was Nitra?"

"Yeah."

"Well, did you know?"

"No. I found out what happened just like everyone else did, and that's what I told her."

"She didn't believe you?"

"That wasn't the issue. She's pissed that I feel like Owen did that shit," she replied. "I don't care how much she loves him and is determined to stick by his side...that man is trash, and if she was smart, she would run as far away from him as she can. But she's not going to. I know my sister. She's going to stand by him and let him make a complete fool out of her like he's done so many times before."

"Damn, I hate that. But you can't force someone to believe something they don't want to believe."

"No, you can't. But I didn't even tell you the worst part."

"What?"

"Riah wants me to fire her."

"Who? Nitra?"

"Yep. She says I'm being disloyal if I allow her to keep working for me because she's a liar."

"Damn, that's fucked up."

"Tell me about it."

"So, what are you going to do?" I asked.

"Not a damn thing. Nitra is my employee, and as far as I'm concerned, she hasn't done anything wrong."

"What about your sister? I'm sure your decision puts the two of you at odds."

"Yeah, but we'll get through this just like we've gotten through anything else. She needs space and time," Simone said. "But never mind all that. I have something more important to talk to you about."

"Oh yeah? What's up?" She didn't say anything right away. Instead, she pressed her hands into her thighs, her demeanor suddenly changing, giving off a vibe that made me feel like she was nervous. "You good?" I asked.

"Um...yeah...I'm fine."

"Wait, is this about what went down between us at the spa? Look—"

"No...well...yes and no," she said. "It's about the hall pass thing."

"Yeah, what about it?"

"Wiz and I have agreed to do it, and....um...I want you to be the person I do it with."

My eyes widened. "Shit, for real?"

"Yes. Well, that's if you're still down to do that sort of thing with me."

"Hell yeah," I spat, but then quickly tried to fix it so I didn't sound so damn thirsty. "I mean, yeah, I'm still cool with it."

"Okay. Cool." She smiled a little, then stood up and turned toward me. "But just so we're clear, there are rules."

"Alright, what are they?"

"For starters, this is a one-time thing."

"Noted."

"Oh, and no one can ever know. Not a single damn person. Do you understand?"

I lifted my hands. "No one will hear shit from me."

"I'm serious, Legend. I don't need everyone in my business."

"Baby girl, I got you. Anything else?"

"Um...no...I think that's it. I'll be in touch to discuss when?" She turned back around and headed toward the door.

I should've let her leave, but I couldn't stop myself from yanking her back toward me and whispering in her ear. "What about right now?"

17

SIMONE

As tempting as Legend's proposition was, there was no way I was going to go through this experience with a man who had probably spent the last hour sweating down to his balls. Not only that, I had way too much on my mind to be screwing him today.

Pressing my hand into his chest, I said, "You really think I want to have sex with you after you've been sweating like crazy?"

"Oh, damn, my bad. I forgot."

"Mmhmm. Besides, my morning started rough as hell, and I'm hungry. So, now probably isn't the best time to be trying to have sex. My attention is in too many other places."

Nodding, he headed to the elevator on the far side of the room, then motioned for me to follow him. "Understood."

"Sorry."

"You have nothing to be sorry about. The last thing I want is for you not to have a good experience. Especially since it's a one-time thing."

"Exactly. I'm glad you understand."

"Sure thing," he replied before escorting me onto the elevator and stepping on behind me. "But I do want to make sure you eat something before you leave. What are you in the mood for? I can have Monty whip us up something."

"Oh, you don't have to do that. I can get myself something on the way home."

He pressed the button to take us to the top floor. "Come on, Simone. Like you said, you've had a rough morning. We can go to my tranquility room, listen to some music, eat, and just stare at the waterfall. It will help you relax."

Letting out a deep sigh, I said, "Damn, that does sound nice."

"I know it does. So, let me help you out just like you always help me out."

"Okay, okay. But I don't want anything crazy."

"Got it. Now, what are you in the mood to eat?"

Placing my finger against my face, I glanced at the elevator ceiling. "I have a taste for a big juicy burger and some steak fries."

"Say no more," he said as he pulled out his phone. "You already know how Monty gets down. His homemade burgers will have you craving his shit every damn day."

"Trust me, I know. I don't think he's ever cooked anything that I didn't enjoy."

I closed my eyes at the thought. Legend's chef was like no other. Even something as simple as a grilled hot dog, he made seem like it was a delicious gourmet dish.

With my arms folded over my chest, I followed Legend off the elevator and into his bedroom. I watched as he held his phone up to his ear, giving Monty instructions for the meal that he wanted prepared. I smiled a little, mesmerized by how well he knew me. Not only did he make sure that my burger buns got toasted, but he also made sure that all the right condiments were put on the side and that an orange soda came along with it. I couldn't remember the last time Wiz ordered for me, or even acted like he gave a damn about what I wanted to eat.

I rolled my eyes at the thought.

Clapping his hands together, Legend walked toward me. "Okay, our food is being prepared, and I made sure that you have plenty of extra everything, including pickles. Is there anything else you can think of?"

I smiled. "No, I think you covered everything. Thank you."

"No problem. Like I said, I want you to be as relaxed as possible for the rest of the day. In the meantime, I'm going to go hop in the shower, then we can head down to the tranquility room. Oh, and the remote is on the nightstand if you want to watch TV while you wait."

"Okay, thanks," I said as I made my way around the bed to grab it. "Oh, and please don't let me fall asleep and end up here all night. You know how that room gets me."

"Don't worry. I'll make sure you're out of here before the sun comes up."

Laughing, I pointed the remote toward the TV. "I'm serious, Legend."

"I'm just kidding. I promise not to let you end up here all night. I know you don't want your man to come looking for you."

I scoffed. "Shit, he's probably out there trying to figure out who he's going to screw. I highly doubt he'll be looking for me."

Grabbing his hygiene bag from his dresser, Legend said, "I still think it's crazy that he would even suggest this. If you were my woman, this wouldn't even be a conversation. I would be too busy fucking the shit out of you every night.

Just hearing him say that made my pussy swell.

I avoided his gaze.

Stay focused on the TV, Simone.

But I could feel Legend's eyes on me...waiting for me to respond.

Taking a deep breath, I said, "Well, that's not the case with me and Wiz."

"And why is that?"

"I don't know. I mean, I guess we just have two different outlooks on sex and what it means in a relationship."

"Oh yeah? And what's that?"

Turning to face him, I placed one hand on my hip. "Aren't you supposed to be getting in the shower?"

"I am. But not until you answer the question."

"Come on, Legend. You know I don't like to talk too much about my relationship."

"Yeah, I know. But given what we're about to do, I feel like I should at least get some kind of details as to how we got here."

Placing the remote down on the bed, I sighed. "Fine. But could you at least get in the shower first? If we start this conversation, you might not be ready when our food is ready, and you know I don't like eating cold food."

He nodded. "Okay, fair point."

"Thank you."

Finally, he stepped into the bathroom and left me alone long enough for me to gather my thoughts on just how much I wanted to tell him. Hell, maybe it was a good idea for us to have this conversation before having sex. Then, he would know exactly what I needed and make sure that I received it.

As soon as he was all cleaned up, he stepped out of the bathroom.

I watched as he tossed his sweaty clothes into the dirty clothes basket that was in his closet, noticing that he'd traded his navy blue basketball shorts for a pair of red ones, along with a dark t-shirt and some black socks.

I nibbled on my bottom lip, trying to understand why something so simple turned me on. But between that, and the crisp soapy aroma that was coming from his skin, it was taking everything in me not to climb all over him.

"Our food should be ready," he said. "You ready to head downstairs?"

Clearing my throat, I said, "Yeah."

"Cool. After you," he said while motioning toward his bedroom door.

I smiled.

After stopping by the kitchen to grab our food, we took the stairs to the basement floor.

When we made it to the tranquility room, the sound of cascading water greeted my ears, transporting me to a peaceful state of mind. I loved everything about it. Especially the breathtaking waterfall that was right outside of the open patio door while also still being inside Legend's home.

Around the waterfall were lush green plants of all shapes and sizes. The air was filled with the fresh scent of damp earth and the gentle whispering of leaves. The soothing sound of flowing water was music to my ears and gave me so much peace as I watched Legend prepare our blankets on the floor near the patio.

As soon as he finished, I sat down comfortably across from him and started to dig in.

For the first few moments, we sat in silence, enjoying the meal that Monty had prepared for us.

"This is so damn good," I said as I wiped the ketchup from the side of my mouth. "I would kill to know what Monty seasons these fries with."

"Trust me, he'll never tell. Everyone who's ever had them has tried to get the recipe. He's not having it."

"I bet." I chuckled. "So, just how many women have you given the romantic picnic lunch treatment to?"

He smirked. "Say what?"

"You heard me. How many women have you given this treatment to while allowing them to taste Monty's seasoned fries?"

"Does it matter?"

Shaking my head, I laughed. "That many, huh?"

"Hey, most of the women I've had in my circle love to eat."

"Hmm...I bet."

"But, I can tell you one thing no other woman has ever done but you."

"Oh yeah? What's that?"

"Come down to this room."

"Really?"

"Yes, *really*. This room is my place of peace, which means only someone that I feel is special enough and gives off good vibes can step in here." He placed his hand on my cheek. "You've always given nothing but that, so your energy is forever welcome into this space."

For a moment, I just stared at him, and once again I could feel the throbbing between my thighs. But this time, it was something I couldn't shake. Not only was my pussy pulsating, but I could feel the seat of my panties becoming drenched in my juices.

Although we'd eaten quite a bit, we still hadn't engaged in the conversation he'd asked me about earlier, which was somewhat good and bad. I needed him to know what I'd been missing, so he could give me everything I needed. I didn't want whatever moment we shared to be wasted. But something told me that no matter what I said or when I said it, he was going to make sure that I was satisfied.

With that in mind, I moved the plates that separated us and crawled over to him. "Don't make this a waste of my time," I whispered.

"Baby girl, that's one thing I'll never do. Trust me." He shoved his hands into my hair and yanked me forward. The moment our lips collided, a fire ignited within me, and I knew there was no turning back.

18

LEGEND

Wasting Simone's time was the furthest thing from my mind, and after seeing her take off all her clothes, I was determined to prove it to her.

Standing in front of me, she slid her fingers between her lower lips and then placed them into her mouth.

Damn...okay.

That shit was definitely a turn on...and freaky as hell.

But today wasn't the day for her to show me how freaky *she* was. It was my job to show *her*.

I snatched her toward me, then pressed my mouth against her neck. Taking my time, I trailed kisses from the center of her chest down to her belly button. I could feel her body trembling against me. Especially once I made it to her pussy.

Looking up at her, I said, "Tell me what you want me to do to you."

She lowered her gaze, a smile spreading across her face. I could tell she was pleasantly surprised by my question.

Tucking her bottom lip between her teeth, she placed her hand against my mouth. "I want you to fuck me with your tongue," she whispered. "I want you to fuck me hard."

"Say no more."

That was all I needed to hear. There wasn't a part of her body that I planned to leave untouched. When this was all over, the chances of her wanting to be touched by anyone else would be zero. She was going to have to force herself to climb back into bed with her man again, which was something I didn't even want to think about. It was all about right now...and *right now*, she was with me.

That fool had no idea the mistake he'd made. But I got the feeling that he would know soon enough.

Making myself comfortable, I took a seat while still between her thighs, then laid back. "Sit on my face, baby girl."

She smirked then lowered her body slowly.

The moment her pussy touched my lips, I plunged my tongue inside of her and allowed my fingers to press against her sensitive flesh. Her moans filled the air, giving me just what I needed to keep going.

The taste of her reminded me of all my favorite fruits. So sweet that I knew I would forever be addicted.

I could see her eyes rolling to the back of her head as she feverishly rotated her hips. Fucking my face was all that mattered to her, and I was greatly appreciative of the honor.

"Fuck, Legend, fuck."

Her aggressive whispers made my dick swell to the point that it ached, making me question how much longer I could go without diving inside of her. Trying to calm myself, I surrounded my dick with my hand and stroked it slowly. As if she could feel the shift, she looked over her shoulder, then repositioned herself so that she could get on all fours. Before I knew it, her ass was in my face and her mouth was taking in my manhood.

I squeezed my eyes shut, trying not to let out the growl that was rumbling from my chest. But something told me that was exactly what she wanted.

For several minutes, the two of us took on the challenge to see who could make the other cum first. With the way she was slurping on my shit while caressing my balls, I was convinced that she was about to be the reigning champion. But a part of me just couldn't allow that to happen. Easing my head back, I took a moment to stare at her pussy. It was beautiful and soaking wet.

Using two fingers, I slid inside of her, then covered the rest of her with my tongue. Her head sprung back as she squealed. Without question, I knew I had her, and when her thighs started to shake, my fingers went into overdrive.

"Oh...my...God," she panted.

Within seconds, everything inside of her flooded onto my fingers, then into my mouth. I wasn't walking away without savoring the honey that she held hostage between her legs.

"Mmhmm...give me all of that shit," I whispered.

I could feel her body becoming unhinged and when she had nothing left to give, she collapsed onto the floor. I slid my tongue along the crease in her back, enjoying the sight of her pleased expression as her eyes remained closed.

"Fuck, Legend! What are you trying to do to me?"

"Give you everything you need," I told her, then kissed the top of her head. "You thirsty?"

"Um...yeah. Can you pass me my drink, please?"

Nodding, I grabbed the tumbler cup that was filled with orange soda and handed it to her. "Don't drink too fast. I wouldn't want you to choke," I teased.

She laughed. "Trust me, after what I just had in my mouth, I think I can handle a straw."

Taking a seat on the edge of the couch, I chuckled. "You were definitely sucking the shit out of me. You almost had me too."

"Mmhmm...I can tell, which is why your ass decided to pull out all the stops and fuck me with your fingers *and* your mouth."

I shrugged. "I couldn't let you win. I'm supposed to be the one making *you* feel good."

Standing up, she strolled my way, then climbed onto the couch to straddle me. "Oh, no worries, you're definitely doing that."

I nodded. "Good to know. I'm glad to hear that you don't have any complaints."

"Oh, but I do have just one," she said her lips inches away from mine.

"Really? Tell me what it is so I can rectify it."

"Although I love everything you can do with your mouth and your fingers, you've yet to show me what you can do with your dick," she said as she reached beside me to grab the condom that I'd placed there before we started.

Nodding, I grabbed it from her hand and slid it on as she watched me with a finger between her teeth. It was crazy to see how she was determined not to miss a thing.

I placed my hands on her hips and eased her down, inch by inch.

Smiling, she stared into the ceiling until she fully covered me, then she lowered her gaze to mine and said, "I think your dick likes me."

"Oh, baby, it fucking loves you."

Laughing, she tossed her head back, then rotated her hips with precision. I pressed my face into the center of her chest, reveling in how good it felt between her thighs. I had on a condom, but she was so wet that it felt like nothing was there.

"Mmm...yes...fuck me!" she whined.

My tongue made its way to her nipple, which was begging for me to surround it. The more she whined and bounced up and down on my shit, the more I took her in. I was intoxicated by her, and I couldn't imagine why the man she was with would ever give me an opportunity like this.

Opening her eyes, she slowed up the pace and glanced out at the water. "I wish we were under that waterfall," she whispered.

Tightening my arm around her, I rose from the couch. "Keep your legs around me."

She smiled, knowing exactly what I was about to do.

This moment was all about her. Whatever she asked for, it was my duty to provide it.

I took my time, walking us through the water while also making sure our tongues were intertwined. Kissing was Simone's specialty. As it should be, her lips were made for it.

The second we found ourselves close to our destination, she let out a giggle and looked at me. "You're really going to fuck me under there?"

"Is that what you want?"

She glanced over her shoulder, then back at me. "Yes."

Not saying another word, I stepped forward and took in her laughter as the water showered our heads, and then I positioned her against the rock wall that was behind the waterfall.

She sucked on my bottom lip, then pressed her hand against the back of my head, her mouth widening to take in my tongue. I shoved myself deeper inside of her, unable to resist the feeling that was now coming over me.

This shit is different.

A growl came from my mouth, which was met with a moan that Simone couldn't hold in.

Consumed with passion, our bodies collided continuously.

"I'm about to cum," Simone called out.

It didn't take long for me to do the same, and when I did, I squeezed her hips so fucking tight that my fingerprints remained behind.

For several seconds, we didn't say a word. Instead, we just held on to each other while trying to catch our breaths and reveled in the high that neither of us wanted to come down from.

I could feel her lips on my neck, which made my insides tingle in a way they'd never done before. It caught me so off guard that I felt like I should reposition myself, but at the same time, I didn't want to move. I didn't want *her* to move. I loved the feel of her near me. I loved how comfortable she seemed.

Slowly, she eased her legs from around me and placed her feet beneath the water. Removing her head from my neck, she stepped back to look at me. I could tell she wanted to say something, but I knew she wouldn't.

I kissed her cheek. "I hope I gave you everything you wanted."

Still, she didn't say anything. Instead, she kissed me.

Before I knew it, we were breaking one of the rules that she'd put in place.

Clearly, one time wasn't going to be enough.

19

SIMONE

I leaned my back against my shower wall. The water was falling in front of me, and all I could think about was the waterfall that Legend had screwed me under earlier.

A smile spread across my face.

The things he did to me...

Is that what I've been missing?

I shook my head, trying to toss back the thought, but immediately I was reminded of how many times I allowed him to do it. Granted, I shouldn't have gone against my own rule. But I needed to experience Legend more than once. I needed to know that what he'd done the first time wasn't just a dream. Thankfully, it wasn't, and each time just got better and better. By the third time, I had to force myself out of his presence. What should've been a couple of hours turned into damn near all night.

Luckily, Wiz hadn't made it home yet. I was hoping that he was out having his pass, which meant I could climb into bed and get lost in my previous reality. It was much better than the one I had to return to.

I tilted my head to the side.

The fact that I was thinking like this was really sad. I should've felt some sort of guilt for wanting to be anywhere but in the same space as Wiz. But I didn't. Oddly, there was a twinge of relief with the thought that I might not see him until morning. The longer I was able to sit with my thoughts, the better.

Hearing a knock, my head shot toward the bathroom door.

"Hey, babe," Wiz said from the other side, "are you going to be in there much longer?"

Damn it.

"Um...no. I'm about to get out now. Is everything okay?"

"Yeah, everything's fine. I was just hoping we could talk."

Again? What now?

"Okay. Just a sec," I said as I turned off the water and stepped out of the shower. I wasn't feeling his tone. Trying to hurry, I grabbed my robe, slipped it on, and peeked out the door. "What's up?"

He sat at the edge of the bed and motioned for me to come sit down next to him.

Now, he was freaking me out for real.

"Wiz, what is this about?" I whined. "You're scaring me."

"I'm sorry. I don't mean to scare you."

"Okay, then tell me what's going on."

He took a deep breath, then cleared his throat. "You know I love you, right?"

"Um...yeah."

"And I've loved you since we were kids?"

Irritated by the way he was dragging things along, I groaned and then sat down next to him. "Wiz, please quit beating around the bush. What are you trying to say?"

He took a long pause, then lowered his gaze. "I don't think we should do this hall pass thing. I just think we should take a break from each other."

Looking at him like he was crazy, I said, "What?"

"I just feel like all of this is a lot. The idea of being with someone else while we're together doesn't sit right with me."

"But taking a break from me does?"

"I mean, not necessarily. But at least I wouldn't have to sit with the guilt of being involved with another woman while *with* my woman."

"But Wiz, we talked about this. We made rules. We agreed that everything was fine."

"I know. But the more I thought about it, the more I realized how ridiculous it was. Being with someone else while together isn't okay, and I don't want that for either of us."

"So, you're saying that you want to be able to fuck as many people as you want freely?"

"No, that's not what I'm saying at all."

"You sure? Because that's what it sounds like." Shaking my head, I said, "You know what? Never mind. If breaking up is what you want, then fine."

"I didn't say we were breaking up. I just said that I think we should take a break. You know? Give us some time apart. I really think that's all we need."

"Wiz, cut the bullshit. I'm sick of the back and forth with you. You have no idea what you want," I told him. "But the one thing I'm starting to realize is that you clearly don't want to be with me."

"Don't say that."

"Why not? It's the truth. You went from laughing about a hall pass with your boys to trying to convince me that you were just talking shit. Then you started to feel some type of way about both of us doing it, only to tell me that you're okay with it. Now, you don't want us to do it at all, but we should take a break from each other." I stood up. "Like, make up your fucking mind. Either you want this, or you don't, and all signs are pointing to *you don't.* So, with that being said, I'm going to go on about my business."

I tried to move away from him, but he grabbed my hand. "Okay, maybe you're right. Maybe I don't know what I want. But the only way I feel like I'm going to figure that out is if we take some time apart. I know it might sound ridiculous to you, but—"

"Like I said before, if that's what you want, then fine. But while you do that shit, what do you expect me to do in the meantime?"

"Wait for me," he replied.

I jerked my head back. "Are you serious?"

"Just give me some time to sort things out."

"And how long is that supposed to take?"

He stepped away from me. "Honestly, I don't know. But I promise you, it's going to make us both better."

I scoffed, then rolled my eyes. "Yeah okay."

"I'm serious, Simone. I know some time apart will do us some good."

"Mmhmm...so what's the plan for us as far as living arrangements?"

"I talked to my boy, Sean. He's cool with me staying with him for a while."

My eyes widened in disbelief. "Wow, you really have been thinking about this, huh?"

"Please don't take this the wrong way, Simone."

"I really don't know how else to take it." I turned away from him and started pacing the floor. "All of this is so out of the blue, and the fact that you waited until after the damn pass—"

"After the pass?" he questioned, confusion in his voice. "I told you that I didn't think we should do that. I haven't slept with anyone."

I stopped, my mind catching up with the words I'd said out loud. Clearing my throat, I spun around. "I mean—"

"Wait a minute." He looked me over, his eyes assessing every inch of me. "Where have you been tonight?"

"What do you mean?"

"You heard the question, Simone. You're showering pretty late. Where have you been?" He glanced down at his watch. "It's after midnight."

Realizing there was no way I was getting out of telling the truth, I threw up my hands. "Fine, I was out doing what we agreed to."

"Doing what we agreed to?" he replied in alarm. "You were out fucking someone else?"

"The way you're saying it makes it sound—"

"What? Like the truth?"

"No, it makes it sound bad."

"That's because it is bad," he shouted, then let out a chuckle before turning away from me. "I can't believe you. You really went and screwed someone else. What happened to all that shit about not being able to even *think* about another man touching you, huh? What happened to all that?"

"Nothing happened to it."

"Oh, but clearly something did. The fact that we only had this conversation yesterday, and you already spread your legs for someone else says a lot. Shit, you came at me crazy about the situation, but you were the first to do it. I guess I wasn't the only one that had been thinking about it."

"Oh, please, Wiz. Don't you dare try to turn the tables on me. The thought hadn't even crossed my mind until you said something."

"I don't believe you."

"I don't give a damn about what you believe. It's the truth."

"Who is he?"

"What?"

"Who is the nigga that you fucked?"

I shook my head. "I'm not telling you."

Gripping my wrist, he yanked me toward him. "Yes, the hell you are."

"No, I'm not." I snatched my arm from his grasp and then looked at him like he was crazy. "Have you lost your fucking mind? Don't you ever put your hands on me like that again."

"And don't you ever let your pussy touch another nigga again."

I glared at him.

This was a side of Wiz that I'd never seen before. The inflamed look in his eyes was deadly, and the rage in his voice scared me a bit.

"Okay, I think you need to take a moment and cool down," I told him. "How about you go ahead and go to Sean's."

"I'm not going any fucking where. I want to know what you did, and with who."

"I already told you I'm not telling you that."

"Did you suck his dick?" he shouted. "Did he eat your pussy like you've been begging me to do?"

Done with the conversation, I waved him off and walked toward the door. "I'm going downstairs. When you're done acting like a weirdo, let me know."

"Oh, so I'm acting like a weirdo now?"

"Yes, you are. Just minutes ago, you said that you felt like we needed to break up, and now you're tripping because I slept with someone else, which was something that we agreed to and something that would've probably happened once we were broken up anyway."

His eyebrow shot up. "Clearly, you didn't listen to what the fuck I said earlier. I requested that we take a break, not break up."

"Oh my God, Wiz. It's the same damn thing."

"No, it isn't. But after finding this out, you're right, breaking up is the correct term."

"Wait...what?"

"I'm not repeating myself. I'm sure you heard me."

I shrugged. "Yeah, I heard you, but I want to make sure I'm fully comprehending. So, are you saying that you're done with me for good?"

"Yep, that's exactly what the fuck I'm saying."

"Wow, *really*? You're calling it quits because of something that was your idea?"

He looked at me and shook his head slowly. "The fact that you went and screwed someone else without giving it a second thought tells me that I was right for the way I've been feeling all this time. Our relationship isn't at all what I thought it was. What you did was fucked up, and I don't know if I can ever forgive you for that."

Eyeing him in disbelief, my mouth dropped.

Is he serious right now?

He can't be serious.

"I'll be back to get my shit tomorrow." He stormed out of the bedroom and rushed down the stairs.

A few seconds later, I heard the front door slam.

With my mouth still open, I glanced around the room, unsure of how I should feel.

Pulling me from my thoughts, a loud beep came from my cell.

"Since what we had was a one-time thing, I hope you don't mind me saying that it was some shit that I'll never forget. I hope you enjoyed the experience. Goodnight Simone." – Legend

Looking up from my phone, I hurried over to my closet, threw on some clothes, and strolled out of my bedroom. "One-time thing my ass."

20

SIMONE

Rolling over, Legend wrapped his arms around me from behind and pulled me in closer to him. I could feel my bare ass resting comfortably against his dick. "So, you want to tell me how you ended up in my bed again last night?" he asked.

"Not really."

He kissed the back of my neck. "I don't believe that. In fact, I got the feeling you wanted to tell me last night, but you decided to let something else speak for you instead." He cupped my lower lips, which sent a tingle down my spine.

I almost opened my legs to let him in. But I knew if I did, I wouldn't get shit done today. Besides, this couldn't keep happening. Even though Wiz and I were no longer together, continuing a fling with Legend was a bad idea.

Forcing myself to think clearly, I turned around to face him. "Wiz and I broke up last night."

"Really?"

"Yes, and I'm still kind of all over the place about it."

"I see. I knew something was up. The way you were fucking definitely said you were trying to blow off some steam."

Laughing, I said, "Oh my God, was I too rough."

"Nah, not at all. I like it any way you give it. I could just tell you had some other shit on your mind."

"Yeah, I did."

"So, what happened?"

Sitting up, I lifted the sheet to cover my breasts, then rested my head against the headboard. "A lot. At first, he told me that he didn't think we should go through with the pass because he felt like we should just take a break. Then—"

"Wait...did you say, *take a break*?"

"Yes. That's what he told me."

Legend frowned. "What the hell is going on in this man's head?"

"I wish I could tell you. But long story short, he went from saying that, which caught me off guard, to deciding that he was done with me for good after I slipped up and told him that I'd already taken the pass."

Lifting his fist to his mouth, Legend's eyes widened. "Oh, shit!"

"*Oh, shit* is right. That fool went crazy. He completely flipped things around on me, made me feel like I'd done him some huge injustice, and then made it seem like my actions were the final straw for our relationship."

"Damn, did he say that?"

"Not in those exact words."

"Wow, that's messed up."

"Yeah, so now I'm questioning everything."

Legend sat up and scooted closer to me. "Don't question yourself. You didn't do anything wrong. He's the one that put this shit in motion. If he didn't want it to happen, he never should've put the idea out there."

"That's basically what I told him. But he insisted that I was the one that had been thinking about it long before him. Then he asked me who I did it with, if I sucked your dick and if you ate my pussy like I'd been begging him to do...it was insane."

Legend gave me a confused gaze. "Hold up...you had to beg this fool to put his mouth on you?"

I lifted my shoulders, then said, "Yeah, and it still didn't happen."

"You've got to be kidding me."

"I wish I was."

"So, let me get this right. You've been with his ass for ten years, and he never even dipped his tongue in it?"

"Nope."

Laughing, Legend shook his head vigorously. "Nah, I refuse to believe that shit."

"Well, believe it. It's one hundred percent the truth."

"Are you sure he's into women?" he asked, then quickly waved me off. "You know what? I'm not even going to come for that man's manhood like that. All I can say is, I don't know one man that doesn't like eating pussy, and I damn sure don't know one that wouldn't fall to their knees to eat yours."

Blushing, I pressed my hands against my face. "Okay, enough about that."

"Nah, there's never enough about that. In fact..." Legend slid under the covers, then made his way on top of me.

"What are you doing?"

Instead of answering me, he spread my legs and slid his tongue inside of me. My eyes rolled to the back of my head, enjoying the sensation that came with him darting in and out of my flesh.

"Legend, I told you—"

"Mmhmm..." he mumbled in between the smacking sounds that came from my wetness.

Damn it, Simone, you have to get a grip. At this rate, this man is going to fuck you into a coma.

Lowering my hands, I gripped his face and pulled him from beneath the covers. "Legend, please, we can't keep doing this."

"Why not? You're a free woman now, which means I can eat this shit as much as I want."

My pussy jumped in response.

"Believe me, as tempting as that sounds, it's a terrible idea." I slid from under him and scooted out of the bed.

I searched around the room for my clothes. Then, I remembered that he ripped them off the moment he realized why I was at his front door.

Snatching his white tank and his basketball shorts from the floor, I hurried to slip them on.

"Damn, you look good as hell in my shit," he said before standing up to meet me where I stood. "But we'll get back to that. Now, what's so terrible about us continuing what we started?"

"Everything, Legend. Not only am I not in the right headspace due to a breakup, but you're my client and my friend. It was different when we agreed to do this once. It meant that once it was over, we would go back to our regular lives. I would go back to my relationship, and you would go back to screwing whoever you screw in your free time."

He laughed. "Whoever I screw in my free time?"

"Yeah. You're famous, which means you can get whatever woman you want on a regular. Oh, and with the way you use your dick, I'm sure your phone is ringing like crazy from someone trying to get as much of it as they can."

"Don't make this about other women. This shit is about you...about us."

"Legend, I'm in no position to keep going with you. When any part of you is inside of me, I don't think. It's literally like everything around me doesn't matter. All I care about is you and what you're doing to me."

"Okay, that's even more reason to keep going. It will help take your mind off the bullshit. Especially with your ex."

"No! I can't just fuck my problems away. I have to face them head-on. Move through them."

Dropping his head, Legend blew out a heavy breath. "Alright, fine. I don't agree with it, but I'm going to respect your decision."

I walked closer to him and placed my hands on his cheek. "Thank you."

"Mmhmm."

I could tell that he wasn't feeling my decision. But I was grateful that he was choosing to accept it. Clearing my throat, I said, "I should probably get going."

"Yeah. I'll walk you out."

"Legend, please tell me that this won't change things between us."

Pulling me into a hug, he said, "Nah, we're good. No matter what, I want you to be happy, and I do understand that you're dealing with a lot. Especially after being in a relationship for so many years."

"Too many years," I spat. "Feels like time wasted."

"Don't think of it that way. Think of it as a lesson learned."

"Definitely."

"But, since you're not letting me solve all your problems with my dick anymore, how about you let me help you out in another way."

I looked him over in suspicion. "What do you have in mind?"

"Well, you know I only have a few more shows to do. How about you come on the road with me?"

"Oh, wow...I don't know."

"Come on, Simone. It will help you get all this crazy stuff off your mind. Plus, you still owe me for not making it to my last show."

I sucked my teeth. "Um...I gave you a free session, remember?"

"Oh, damn. You did, huh?"

"Mmhmm...sure did."

"Okay, fine. Just come because I want you to, and no this isn't me still trying to screw you. Even though I would love to, I'm concerned about your well-being first. I won't be good on the road unless I know you're good. Besides, I think you'll enjoy it."

"Oh, really?"

"Mmhmm," he said, then held up his hand. "Take some time to think about it. I have a few more days before I get back on the road. If you're still not feeling it after giving it some thought, then I'll leave it alone."

Sighing, I said, "Okay, I'll think about it."

My cell rang.

Looking at my screen, I sucked my teeth. "It's Wiz."

"I wonder what the hell he wants."

"That makes two of us," I answered my phone, then placed it on speaker. "What?"

"Where the hell are you? The spa isn't even open yet, so I know you're not at work."

"None of your business. Why are you calling me so early in the morning?"

"Because I came to the house to get my things, and you're not here."

I frowned. "Okay, well, I didn't know you needed me there to get your stuff."

"I don't. I was just trying to figure out why you weren't here, and why the bed looks like it hasn't been slept in."

"Wiz, in case you forgot, you broke up with me last night, which means where I sleep is none of your concern anymore."

"Cut the bullshit, Simone. Where the fuck are you? Are you with that nigga you cheated on me with?"

"Cheated? Is that what we're calling it now?"

"I'm calling it what it is."

"No, you're just saying dumb shit."

"And you're out being a hoe."

My eyes widened. *Did this fool just call me a hoe?*

Before I could fully process my thoughts, the phone was snatched from my hand and Legend pressed the end button. "Don't waste another breath on his bitch ass," he spat, fury resting in his eyes. "Out of respect for the situation and you probably not wanting him to know you're with me, I grabbed your phone instead of putting him in his place. But I won't do that shit again. Next time, I'm going to say what I need to say, then find out where he is."

Turned on by his response, I tucked my bottom lip between my teeth, then nodded. "Okay."

He shook his head and smiled. "Why are you looking all giddy."

"No reason."

"Yeah, whatever."

Forcing myself to push back the horny signals between my thighs, I returned to the discussion of Wiz's shitty phone call. "I can't believe him. He's never acted like that before."

"He's in his feelings," Legend replied. "You're about to see his true colors come out, and it's not going to be pretty."

Taking a seat on the bed, I said, "I see. Maybe I should take you up on that offer to get away after all."

"Most definitely, and in the meantime, avoid contact with him as much as possible. If need be, you can stay here another night. That way you can give him enough time to get all his things out of your place."

"Oh, no, I can't do that. I'm sure you have business to handle, and isn't my mother coming by here to meet with you later today? I can't be seen here."

"It's fine. I've got more than enough space. She won't even know you're here."

"Yes, she will. My car is in the driveway."

"It's cool. I'll have Mya move it into the garage."

"Legend—"

"It's settled. You'll stay here one more night to steer clear of Wiz's bullshit and to relax. I can call Eden and have her pick out some stuff for you to wear, so you can be comfortable."

"Legend, I don't need a stylist for clothes to lounge around in. Besides, I can just throw on something of yours and grab some things from the store. The outlet mall is close by. I'll just go there."

"Okay, fine. How about we go together?"

I laughed. "*You*...go to the outlet mall? Are you even allowed to do that? You know, without people trying to harass you and take pictures while you shop?"

"I mean, I don't do it often, but yeah I can. All I have to do is put on some sweats, a hat and some shades. No one will even know it's me."

"Yeah, okay."

"I'm serious. I've done it many times. You know what? Let's just get dressed. I'll prove it to you."

Intrigued by the idea, I said, "Okay, let's do it."

21

LEGEND

"This is so good," Simone squealed as she tossed a pretzel bite into her mouth and strolled beside me down the bricked walkway of the outlet mall. "It's been so long since I had these. When I was little, we would come here and get them all the time."

"Yeah, Brookie's is the best pretzel shop in the city. Thankfully, it's still early. Later in the afternoon, this place gets crazy." I tugged on her hat to make sure it stayed as low as mine, then toyed with her puffball that was sticking out the back. "You look cute as hell."

"Thanks," she said with a giggle. "What is it about the simple look that always seems to get a man's attention? I could be out here dressed to perfection. Hair laid, face beat and all the right jewelry to match the outfit...a man might not say two words to me. But let me come out with a bare face, hair barely combed, and nothing but some damn lip gloss. Every man I cross paths with is staring me down like I'm the finest thing walking."

I shrugged. "Shit, that's easy. We love a woman in her natural state. To us, if you look fine as hell with none of that extra shit on, we know what we're going to get when we wake up to you.

Don't get me wrong, it's nice to see a woman dressed up and all that, but we don't know if that's the real woman. Between the makeup, the weave, and all the body enhancements, it's hard to tell the real from the fake, and most of us just want the real. It's as simple as that."

"Hmmm...okay. I hear you."

I pulled apart my soft pretzel and shoved a piece into my mouth while trying not to be overwhelmed by how pretty she was. But it was hard. Although they were big as hell on her, she managed to make my navy blue sweats look like they were made just for her.

Dabbing the corners of her mouth with a napkin, she said, "Why do you keep stealing looks at me?"

"My bad. I just think you're beautiful, that's all."

"Is that right?"

"Yeah. I've always thought you were beautiful. But I tried to stay quiet since you had a man."

"Oh, so now that I don't, you feel free enough to say it, huh?"

"I ain't even going to lie to you...yeah, I do. And I'll tell you that for as long as you allow me to."

Smiling, she lowered her head. "You're making me blush."

"Good. That's what I'm trying to do." She glanced behind us, then looked back at me, prompting me to place my hand on the small of her back. "Don't worry, no one knows that Cade is with us. That's the whole point of him walking so far back."

"I know. It's just funny that he's with us but not really with us."

"Yeah, I know. But trust me, if some shit goes down, you'll know he's with us."

She laughed. "I bet."

Her cell rang.

Simone lifted her phone to look at the screen, then let out a loud groan.

"What's wrong?"

"It's Wiz again. He won't stop calling me."

"And he probably won't stop anytime soon. The fact that he ended things with you, and you haven't tried to reach out to him is probably killing him."

"Reach out to him? Why would I do that? He made it pretty damn clear that he was done with me. I'm just trying to give him the space that he asked for."

"I know that's how you see it, but I can guarantee you that he doesn't see it that way. Especially after knowing that you were with someone else."

She stopped and looked at me with a lifted brow. "How do you think he sees it?"

"If I had to guess, he's tripping hard about the fact that you're not begging for him to take you back, which lets him know that your interest is elsewhere. As far as he's concerned, you're probably off fucking the man that you slept with."

Shaking her head, she continued walking. "Why doesn't that surprise me? He dumps me, then gets mad because I'm not sitting at home crying about it."

I shrugged. "I know. It sounds messed up, but that's how it is sometimes."

"Yeah, well, I need him to realize that calling me like a maniac only makes me want to stay as far away from him as possible. Especially since he's only calling to see where I am, and who I'm with."

"Unfortunately, that thought isn't crossing his mind right now." Not thinking, I lifted my hat to scratch my head.

"Legend?" I heard someone call out.

My head darted to the right of me.

It was Keke.

She rushed our way but was stopped by Cade stepping in front of us. "Keep it moving ma'am."

Keke stepped back, but that didn't stop her from bombarding me with questions. "So, are you really not doing the Rhythm City Festival? Are things *that* bad between you and Teddy?"

I ignored her, not willing to give her the slightest bit of input.

Just the sight of Keke made my skin crawl, which was unfortunate because she was an attractive woman. Small in stature, cute little round face and an edgy pixie cut that made it clear that she wasn't your typical journalist.

Grabbing Simone's hand, I turned back in the direction we'd just come from. "I guess our fun time is over."

"Definitely," she replied.

"Simone? Is that you?" Keke questioned from behind us. "Wait a minute, I didn't know you and Legend were a thing. What happened to Wiz?"

"None of your business, and we're not a thing," Simone spat over her shoulder. "We're just friends. You already know that."

She snickered. "Oh, well, he's not holding your hand like you're *just* friends."

"That's because you're out here harassing the shit out of us. Can't you find someone else to drive crazy today?"

"I'm not trying to harass anyone. I'm just trying to get Legend's side of things," she said. "But since you're here, how do you feel about what's going on with your assistant? Does she still work for you?"

"You know damn well I'm not answering that."

"Don't be like that. We're family."

Pissed, Simone spun around. "Girl, get the fuck on. You and I haven't been family for years. I don't see you sitting around the table at family dinners."

"That's because y'all act like y'all too good to be around me."

"No, it's because you're too damn messy," Simone said.

"You'll do anything to get a story. You've made that clear on several occasions."

"I'm just doing my job, Simone."

"Okay, well do that shit elsewhere and leave me the hell alone."

"But—"

"You heard what the hell she said." I gripped Simone's hand tighter, then helped her into my Range Rover.

As soon as we were both inside, the driver sped out of the parking lot.

I pressed my head back into the seat, then looked over at Simone. "You good?"

"Yeah, I'm cool."

"You sure? I know you weren't trying to be seen. Especially by your cousin."

"No, I wasn't. But oh well." She shrugged. "Her ass is always lurking somewhere."

"Hell yeah."

"I just don't understand her though. I mean, I get that she has to do her job. But there has to be a line drawn when it comes to family. That should be off limits."

"It should, but Keke doesn't give a damn about that. If it's juicy, she's reporting it. She doesn't care who it is or who it hurts."

"I know, and I hate that." Scooting closer to me, Simone rested her head on my shoulder. "Thanks for coming with me to grab some clothes. It really took my mind off things. Well...for a little while."

"You're welcome. I wish I could've made your escape last a little longer."

"It's all good. I'm sure the rest of the day will be cool. When we get back to your place, I'll probably hang out in the theater room and find a good movie to fall asleep to."

I nodded. "Sounds like a good plan."

"Oh, do you have some red wine?"

"Of course. Do you want me to have Monty bring you some to the theater or—"

"I'll go to the wine room and grab it myself. It will give me a chance to just stand around and admire how many options you have."

Laughing, I shook my head. "Of course."

"Look, some of us aren't blessed to have a crazy amount of random rooms in our home with unlimited shit to choose from."

"Well, at this point, what's mine is yours, so..."

"Oh, so we're on *that* level now?"

I shrugged. "Might as well be."

"Damn, I should've gotten dumped sooner. I didn't know that being single came with all these perks."

Planting a kiss on the top of her head, I said, "Baby girl, you have no idea."

22

SIMONE

Despite not sleeping at home, I was well rested.

Just as I'd planned, I spent the remainder of yesterday in Legend's theater room scarfing down snacks and watching movies. I even turned off my phone so I couldn't be interrupted by Wiz's constant calls.

It was the perfect day. So perfect, that I fell asleep in Legend's comfy movie chair. I probably would've stayed there for the rest of the night if he hadn't carried me to one of his guest bedrooms.

He was the perfect gentleman, which made it almost impossible to keep my word and not try to screw him while I was half asleep.

I sighed at the thought...*Damn, I really wanted to.*

But I had to be stronger than my emotions. It was way too soon for me to be getting caught up with another man. Especially Legend. I couldn't tell if I was in a trance from his extremely talented tongue, along with his massively well-trained dick, or if I was finally dealing with genuine emotions that had been suppressed since we were kids.

Either way, now wasn't the time to be trying to figure that shit out.

I needed to focus on me.

Pulling into the parking lot of my spa, my eyes widened. Although I'd been warned by one of my employees about the alarming amount of press outside of my building, I didn't expect it to be this bad. They were everywhere, and the only thing keeping them from storming inside was the armed guard that Legend had hired to stand outside the door.

I stepped out of the car, somewhat hoping to go unnoticed. But as soon as my sneakers hit the pavement, all eyes were on me, and everyone came rushing toward me while asking a million questions.

"Simone, do you think your brother-in-law assaulted your assistant?"

"Whose side are you on?"

"Alright, back up," the guard instructed while reaching for me. "Give the lady some room."

I couldn't have been more grateful for his presence. Seeing so many reporters and bloggers outside of my establishment was insane. It definitely put me on edge, which meant Nitra was probably feeling ten times worse.

The moment I stepped inside, I walked to the back to see if she was at her desk.

She was there, slumped over with her head on her arms.

"Are you okay?" I asked.

"I'm so sorry," she cried as she lifted her head. "No one was ever supposed to know. I'm so embarrassed."

"You have nothing to be sorry or embarrassed about. This isn't your fault."

"But it is. I confided in someone about what happened and now your business is paying the price for it." She wiped a tear from her face. "The majority of our clients are celebrities and wealthy people. We've already had several people call and cancel because of all that shit outside."

Damn.

"She's right," one of my employees, Asana, said as she walked toward us. "We've had several cancellations. It wasn't like this yesterday though. I'm guessing last night's interview really put the focus on us."

"Interview? What interview?" I asked.

"You haven't seen it?" Asana said before pulling it up on her phone and showing it to me.

I sat on the edge of Nitra's desk while listening to Owen's every word. He went on and on about how he was innocent and how Nitra was just mad about him not accepting her advances. Then he said that Nitra probably wasn't making enough money at the spa, which he made sure to name, and that she was just after money like every other woman who had accused him of ridiculous things.

"That asshole," I said before slamming Asana's cell back in her hand. "He named my business on purpose."

"Why would he do that?" Asana asked.

"Because him and my sister are pissed that I'm still allowing Nitra to work here."

Nitra stood up. "Well, maybe you shouldn't."

"Maybe I shouldn't what?"

"Allow me to still work here. Look at what it's doing to your business. This shit isn't okay," she said before reaching down in the drawer and pulling out her purse. "I should leave."

"Don't you move," I demanded. "I'm not about to let anyone run you off. Especially when I've yet to see proof that he didn't do it."

"That's the thing...there is no proof. It's just my word against his, which is why I never wanted to say anything in the first place. No one gives a damn about what a stripper has to say."

I dropped my head, hurt that she felt that way. But sadly, she was right, which only hurt me even more. "You know, it pisses me off that his shitty reputation doesn't speak for itself."

Sighing, Asana said, "That's the price we pay as women. Our bodies are labeled as temples, but we're the only ones that are required to treat it as such. Most men feel like they can do whatever they want to us, and we should be okay with it. Hell, society has made it clear that it's no big deal. Especially when it comes to celebrities." She shook her head and chuckled. "I can count on both hands how many times I've been out at one of these celebrity parties and been groped by men. Then, when I said something to them about it, they told me that I was asking for it because of what I was wearing or just because I was there."

"See, that's some bullshit," I blurted.

Hearing some commotion in the front, I hurried to see what was going on.

Much to my surprise, it was my sister.

"Riah, what the hell are you doing here?" I called out.

"Where is she?"

"Who?"

"Don't play with me, Simone. Where is your lying ass assistant?" she shouted. "Did you fire her like I told you to?"

Aggravated, I slammed my hands against my hips. "Riah, get the hell out of here."

"I'm not going anywhere. I want to see for myself if you really don't give a damn." She looked over my shoulder. When her eyes narrowed and her nostrils flared, I knew she'd seen Nitra. "Bitch don't hide now! Bring your lying ass out here."

"I'm not lying," Nitra called out. "Your husband assaulted me."

"No, the fuck he didn't. You're just like every other hoe out here trying to come up. Well, I'm here to tell you, we're going to handle you just like we've handled all the rest. But your stupid ass won't get a single dime. I'll see to it."

Appalled, I looked my sister up and down. "Why are you fighting this man's battles?"

"Because I'm his wife. I'm not just going to sit back and be quiet. It's my job to support him."

"Not when his ass is wrong."

She shoved me. "Quit saying that."

"Riah, don't put your hands on me."

"Well, don't say shit to make me."

Trying to maintain my composure, I closed my eyes for a second, then walked to the door and opened it. "You need to leave."

"Or what?"

"Quit playing with me Riah. The last thing I want to do is put my hands on you. But if you make the wrong move, you know I will."

Knowing I wasn't lying she stared at me, her nostrils flaring. "You're wrong as hell for choosing that girl over me," she snarled.

"Look, I've been very clear about where I stand on the situation. You don't have to like it, but you need to respect it."

"I'm not respecting a damn thing. I thought there was a chance of us fixing this, but now I see that's not going to happen." She moved closer to me. "When your little assistant gets exposed for the liar that she is, don't come back to me apologizing. I'm done fucking with you."

We held each other's gaze for a few seconds. Until, finally, I lifted my head a little higher. "I'm sorry to hear that, sis."

Pissed, Riah stormed out of the building, waving off the media frenzy as she headed to her car.

A part of me felt terrible that it had come to this. But this was the result of her only wanting to see things from her distorted perspective.

Turning back toward Nitra, I said, "Sorry. My sister shouldn't have come at you like that."

"It's fine."

"No, it's not fine," I told her before glancing around the room in concern. "Honestly, I don't think it's safe for you here. At least not while everything is so fresh."

"I agree," Asana chimed in.

Shoving my hands into my pants pockets, I said, "I'm not firing you, but I think you should take a leave of absence with pay. Just until this thing blows over."

Nitra shook her head. "I can't ask you to keep paying me while I'm not here."

"You're not asking me. I'm telling you what I'm going to do. You and EJ still have to eat. Now, grab your things, I'll have the guard walk you to your car and make sure you get home safely."

"Are you sure?"

"I'm positive." I followed her to her desk to get the rest of her things, then escorted her to the door and gave the guard instructions to get her home.

Overwhelmed by everything that was going on, I hurried back to my desk and pulled out my phone to send Legend a text.

"Yes, I will go on tour with you. I need to get away ASAP." –Simone

"Say no more. I'll have Mya send you the details in a few." –Legend

"Thanks." –Simone

"Sure thing. I promise you'll have a good time." –Legend

"Great. I need it." –Simone

"I know you do." –Legend

23

LEGEND

Kendrick stood on the other side of me as I dribbled the ball behind the free-throw line. We were in my backyard talking shit and playing basketball to blow off some steam.

"You ready to see me win?" I teased.

"Man, just shoot the ball," he shot back. "Oh, and while you're at it, feel free to tell me that you've changed your mind about the festival. You know Ms. Regina hasn't canceled our set yet."

"That's unfortunate," I replied before tossing the ball in the air and watching it drop into the hoop. "I'm not changing my mind."

He shrugged. "I figured it was a long shot. Just thought I'd check."

"Yeah, well, make that your last time. I'm not even thinking about that festival anymore. My mind is on finishing up this tour. Speaking of which," I said as I pulled my cell from my pocket, "I need to double check and make sure Mya sent Simone the flight information. We fly out on Tuesday."

"Wait, Simone's going with you?"

"Yeah. I figured getting away for a little bit would be good for her. She's going through a lot right now."

"Oh, really?"

"Yes, *really*?"

"You sure that's all it is?" he questioned with a lifted brow. "I saw that video of the two of you at the outlets a couple of days ago."

I jerked my head back. "Where?"

"It's all over the internet. Someone recorded you guys trying to get away from Keke."

"Shit. I didn't know anyone else saw us."

"Well, they did, and now the whole world has seen you guys too."

Trying to make light of it, I shrugged. "It's really not that big of a deal. It was just two friends hanging out."

"Mmhmm. Well, the way you two were holding hands didn't give *just friend* vibes. It was more like, *I'm with my girl, so y'all need to mind your business*."

I waved him off. "Stop reading into shit. I only grabbed her hand after Keke showed up. I was trying to get us out of there."

"I hear what you're saying, but that's not what the people are saying. In fact, the people have questions. Specifically, Wiz."

"*Wiz*? When did you see his ass?"

"Actually, he called me."

I frowned. "He called you?"

"Yeah. Apparently, him and Simone broke up, which I'm assuming you already know." He eyed me for a moment, but I didn't respond. "Anyway, he claims she cheated, and since the two of you are all over the internet holding hands, he's trying to find out if you're the nigga she cheated on him with."

"First off, that fool is lying. Simone didn't cheat on him."

Kendrick grabbed the ball from the ground and tucked it underneath his arm. "Sounds like you know what happened."

Remembering that Simone didn't want what went down between us to be discussed, I said, "Look, I don't know what the hell he's talking about. I just know Simone's not that kind of woman."

"Well, that's not what it sounds like. He's convinced that she slept with someone else, and if he broke up with her, then something happened. I don't see any man ending things with a woman like Simone over some bullshit."

Before I could say anything further, Kendrick's cell beeped, and he shoved his hand into his pocket to grab it.

"What the hell?" he shouted as he stared at the screen.

"What?"

"Man, you won't believe this." He held his phone in the air so I could see it. "Teddy is requesting a paternity test from Eden."

Squeezing my eyes shut, I shook my head. "See, that's exactly why I'm not messing with that fool. He's taking shit way too far. He knows damn well that's his kid."

"Oh, and get this...Keke questioned him about whether or not you could be the father."

My eyes widened. "Hell naw! I know you're fucking lying."

"Nope. Look right here." He pointed to the last sentence of her blog post.

There was no mistake...she definitely said that shit, and he did absolutely nothing to dispute the possibility.

"I can't believe this." I pulled my phone back out.

"What are you doing?"

"Calling Eden," I replied. "I know she's probably fuming."

As soon as she picked up the line, all I heard was, "Can you believe this shit? This idiot is asking me for a paternity test. *Me*...of all people. He has a lot of fucking nerve."

"Yeah, I know."

"He's such an asshole."

"Look, just give him what he wants so he can shut the hell up."

She scoffed. "*Give him what he wants*? I'm not doing a damn thing."

Surprised that she didn't agree, I said, "But don't you want to dead this shit?"

"Yeah, I do. But I'm not giving in to his little temper tantrum. He didn't come to me and ask me to take a test. I found out like everyone else. He's doing this for attention. He knows the truth, which means I'm not wasting my time playing his little game."

"I hear what you're saying, but—"

"End of discussion," she spat and changed the subject. "I'm going to send you the outfits I put together for the rest of your show. Make sure you keep an eye on your phone. I need your feedback ASAP."

"Um...okay," I replied a little thrown off. But given how heated she was, I knew it was in my best interest to just go along with what she was saying. "Oh, I need you to do me a favor and pull a few looks for Simone."

"Really? She's coming to one of your shows?"

"Actually, she's going on tour with us."

"Ohhhhh...wow...that's new."

"Yeah, I know. But she needs a break, so I suggested she come and enjoy the tour."

"Hmm...okay."

"Chill, Eden. I can hear the wheels turning in your head."

"What? I haven't said a thing," she replied. "But I do have to ask...how does her man feel about this trip?"

"They broke up," I blurted without giving it a second thought.

"Damn, for real?"

"Yep. Anyway, I'll keep a lookout for the photos. Talk to you later."

She giggled. "Don't be trying to rush me off the phone."

"Bye, Eden." I ended the call, then returned my attention to Kendrick who was now eyeing me in suspicion.

"You fucked that girl, *didn't you*?"

"Who? Eden?" I frowned. "Man, nah. You know I wouldn't—"

"Hell no! I'm talking about Simone."

I shook my head, then waved him off. "How did we get back on this shit?"

Grinning, he placed his fist against his mouth and raced toward me. "Damn, you really did." He slammed his hand against my shoulder. "How was that shit? Was it as good as I imagined?"

Furious that he'd even thought about it, I said, "Keep talking and I'm going to fuck you up."

"My bad," he said before lifting his hands. "Let me get off your territory."

"Didn't we talk about this? I ain't no damn dog and neither is she."

"Right. Sorry."

"Let's go inside. I need to take a shower."

Still smiling, Kendrick said, "Okay. But you do know that I know you fucked her, right?" I Ignored his words and continued walking. But Kendrick being Kendrick, he just kept talking. "Man, the way your ass is avoiding the question is telling on you. Not to mention, you're too damn hostile."

I spun around and clenched my fists while looking him in the eyes.

Recognizing that enough was enough, he finally retreated. "Okay, I'm done with it. But I suggest you come up with a better way to answer the question. Because if you bump into Wiz, that nigga is going to ask you, and that guilty ass response you're giving ain't going to cut it."

24

SIMONE

I sat across from Legend, admiring every inch of his private jet as we floated above the clouds. The inside was flawlessly designed with soft, plush leather seats and rich, dark wood. The seating area was spacious and equipped with all the latest technology, including high-speed internet, which made it easy for me to check in and view the spa cameras whenever I wanted.

"How long have you had this thing?" I asked. "It looks brand new."

"It's been a little over a year. I always said that I would get one whenever I was able to afford it."

I nodded while still looking around. "Well, you did good."

"Thanks. Oh, if you get tired or just want some privacy, there's a bedroom in the back. It has a king size bed, silk linens, and plenty of fluffy pillows. You'll fall asleep in no time."

"Okay. Good to know."

Smiling, he hopped up from his seat. "Oh, and before I forget, I've got something for you."

"Really?"

"Yep." He reached behind my seat and then handed me a large gift bag.

"What's this?"

"Just open it."

I lowered my gaze and pulled the decorative tissue from the bag. Butterflies fluttered in the center of my stomach as I pulled out the plush white robe with my name embroidered on the front and a pair of thick furry socks. "Oh, wow, this is so sweet. I love this."

"Yeah, I wanted you to be comfortable. Also," he walked into the lavishly decorated dining and lounge area, which was near the front, "I thought you might like a little afternoon snack, so I had Monty whip you up a little something this morning."

I couldn't stop myself from smiling as he placed the medium-sized plastic container in my hands. "Oh my God, Legend. I knew I smelled something familiar when I got on here." Giddy, I grabbed a piece from one of the glazed donuts and shoved it into my mouth. My eyes slid closed as the perfect combination of sweetness and buttery flavor melted against my tongue. "This is so good. Thank you."

"No problem." He returned to his seat.

After finishing up my donut, I glided my feet into my fuzzy socks, grateful for his thoughtfulness. Although his actions may have seemed like small gestures to him, it felt so big to me. Knowing that he was paying attention to the tiniest of things just to make me smile, made me feel warm and fuzzy inside.

Once I had them comfortably on my feet, I reached into my purse and grabbed my cell.

I had a new voicemail.

"God, I wish Wiz would stop calling me," I whispered. "The messages he's leaving on my voicemail are insane."

"What is he saying?"

I shook my head. "Nothing worth repeating."

"Simone?"

Dropping my shoulders, I said, "Ever since our little run-in with Keke hit the internet, he's been leaving messages asking me if you're the one I cheated on him with."

"Oh...yeah...Kendrick told me that he was going around asking questions."

"He's what?" I said as I gazed at him with wide-eyed shock. "He asked Kendrick?"

"Yep."

"That asshole," I blurted. "What the fuck is his problem?"

"I already told you."

"Yeah, I know. But how do I make him stop? It's getting ridiculous. The phone calls, the text messages, asking people about who I'm screwing...this shit is not okay."

"No, it's not. Do you want me to have a chat with him?"

Shaking my head vigorously, I said, "No."

He laughed. "What? I just asked if you wanted me to talk to him, not kill him."

"No, but I know you. If he says the wrong thing, that conversation is going to turn into a brawl. That's not what I want or need right now."

"Come on now, Simone, give me a little more credit. I can keep it together long enough to let him know to stop harassing you. We're both grown men."

"Oh, so you think he's going to be okay with the guy that he thinks I screwed telling him to stop calling his ex?"

Shrugging his shoulders, Legend stood up, then placed his hand on the arm of my seat while leaning in close to me. "Quite frankly, I don't give a damn what he's okay with. I just want him to stop fucking with you," he whispered, then moved in even closer, forcing our lips to almost touch. "Oh, and stop acting like what that man is thinking isn't true. Bottom line, I did fuck the shit out of you, and he has every right to be worried that he's lost you. I damn sure would be."

I swallowed hard while trying not to grab his face and

tongue him down. "I...I didn't say that you didn't," I whispered. "But he's accusing me of cheating, which is something I didn't do."

"No, you didn't, which is why you should let me talk to him."

Shaking my head, I said, "You can't. You've got enough on your plate with the Teddy situation. I'll handle Wiz."

"You sure?"

"Yes. I'll just keep ignoring him. Eventually, he'll get the picture and leave me the hell alone."

He took a step back, then returned to his seat. "Did you get the locks changed at your house yet?"

"No, but it's at the top of my list when we get back in town."

"Simone, that's three weeks from now."

"Relax, Legend, it's fine. He can't do or say anything to me if I'm not there."

"I know, but—"

"Look, I promise I'll get it taken care of as soon as I get back."

"Oh, I know you will. Because I'm going to call the person to get it done for you."

I laughed. "Seriously?"

"Yep. You're not about to have me losing my damn mind about a nigga walking in on you whenever he feels like it."

"Damn, you almost sound like you're my man."

He shrugged. "I'm just doing what I would do if I was."

I shook my head. I didn't need him to see how hard I was blushing. "You're funny."

"I don't see how. I'm dead ass serious."

"And that's why you're so funny."

"Hmm...okay. I'm glad you think so."

There was a moment of silence as we sat and stared at each other. It should've been awkward, but it wasn't. It felt right. It felt perfect.

"So, what's up?" Legend said, purposely breaking our silence. "You down for a massage?"

"Um...sure. Are you feeling tense?"

Laughing, he shook his head. "I'm talking about for you?"

"Wait...you want to give *me* a massage?"

"Yeah. I figured it was the least I could do while we're on this flight. I'm sure it will help take your mind off all the headaches back home."

"I don't know," I replied with a hesitant expression. "I've never had a man give me a massage before."

Legend frowned. "Damn, did that nigga do anything for you?"

"I thought you were supposed to be helping me not think about him?"

"My bad. You're right," he said. "You definitely have to let me give you a massage now though. You deserve that kind of experience."

"Yeah, but that experience might lead to something else, and we agreed—"

"I know, I know. Look, I promise I'm not trying to get you half-naked so I can get between your legs. I honestly just want to make sure you're comfortable."

Appreciating his efforts, I said, "How about a foot massage? That way I can see just how good you are with your hands, and I won't be tempted to let you feel on other things."

Amused, he nodded. "Okay, that's cool."

"Cool."

Rubbing his hands together, he moved over to the seat next to me and pulled my feet into his lap. "Is that comfortable for you?"

"Yeah, it is."

I watched him as his fingers went to work, making sure to sink deep into my flesh. My body started to tingle, and before I knew it, so did something else. I closed my eyes, trying to hide my pleasure.

"You can stop fronting," he said. "I know this shit feels good to you, and I know you thought you were getting off easy by getting a foot massage. But me doing this is equivalent to me rubbing on your pussy. I can make you orgasm just from touching your toes."

"Why are you doing this to me?" I whined.

"I told you. I'm trying to make sure you relax. I plan to do that whether we fuck or not."

At this point, fucking him was exactly what I wanted to do. I could feel the seat of my panties getting wetter and wetter. Yanking my feet from his lap, I said, "How about we watch a movie?"

He eyed me with a smirk. "Whatever you want baby girl."

"I want you to stop touching me."

"You sure about that?"

I paused for a moment, then took a deep breath. "No. But I can't handle your hands on me anymore."

Before I could say anything else, he stood in front of me. "Fine. I'll keep my hands to myself."

"Thank you."

"But my mouth...*that's* a different story." He dropped to his knees and yanked me to the edge of my seat. Before I knew it, my leggings were down to my ankles and his tongue was sliding through the side of my panties.

If stopping him was an option, I damn sure didn't feel the need. Instead, I just closed my eyes and let him do what he wanted to do. Without a doubt, he was relaxing the shit out of me, and with the way I was feeling right now, I was probably going to let him do it over and over again.

25

LEGEND

I stood in front of my hotel window, admiring the stunning view. It was a beautiful blend of urban and natural sites, making it the perfect place to relax and take in the energy of the city. I only had a couple of hours before I had to be at the arena for my show. But my mind was so far from that. Instead, I was focused on what I'd done to Simone earlier.

I was trying my best to respect her wishes, but every time I saw her, my fucking mouth watered. Since I couldn't be inside of her, I figured there was no harm in tasting her. I couldn't shake the urge to hear her moans. It was a melody that I wanted to endure every day.

I lowered my gaze, somewhat aggravated that what should've just been about sex had turned into me wanting so much more.

"Fuck," I blurted through clenched teeth.

"You good?" Eden questioned as she stepped into my room pushing a clothing rack.

"Um...yeah...I'm fine."

"Stop lying. What's on your mind?"

"Nothing."

Sucking her teeth, she placed one hand on her hip and eyed

me with a lifted brow. "I'm not going to tell you again to stop lying."

"Fine. I'm falling hard for Simone."

"Oh, really?"

"Yes, *really*," I said. "I thought I could play the game and just fall in line with whatever she wanted to do, but shit isn't playing out in my favor."

"Okay, so did you tell her how you feel?"

"Not exactly. I mean I've joked about certain things, but I haven't just come right out and said that I'm feeling her."

Nodding, she smiled then pulled a black jacket from the rack and tossed it on the bed. "Sounds like you have quite the dilemma."

"Tell me about it. If I would've known she was going to have my ass hooked like this, I would've never slept with her."

"You had sex with Simone?"

My heart sank, realizing that I'd said too much. "No, what I was trying to say—"

"Nope, don't you dare try to fix it now. You meant exactly what you said." She smiled and moved closer to me. "You have to tell me what happened? How did you two end up sleeping together?"

"I can't tell you. I shouldn't even be talking about this."

"Well, it's too late. You've opened your big mouth and now I want to know all the sexy details."

I shook my head. "If I tell you, Simone will kill my ass."

"Look, I promise not to tell a single soul. This stays right here, between you and me."

Taking a deep breath, I said, "You swear?"

"Girl scout promise."

I jerked my head back. "You were a girl scout?"

"No, but it sounded like the right thing to say."

"Well, try again. I'm not buying that one."

She stuck out her hand and shoved her pinky in my face. "Fine, I pinky swear."

"That's more like it."

Rolling her eyes, she locked her pinky with mine. "Now, tell me what went down."

I returned to the window and shoved my hands into my pockets. "It started with her lame ass boyfriend wanting a pass."

"What kind of pass?"

"A pass to have sex with someone else."

"Are you serious?"

"Yep," I replied. "At first, she was talking to me about it, but making it seem like it was about a friend of hers. I could tell by the way she was talking that it was about her. So, I told her that if her friend went through with it, she should tell her that I was down to do it with her."

"Wait...so you were trying to talk her into letting you fuck her friend?"

Turning around, I looked at Eden like she was crazy. "Did you not hear the part where I said that I knew the friend was her?"

"Oh, right. Sorry, I forgot," she said before waving me off. "Okay, keep going."

"Anyway, eventually, she told me the truth and she chose to take her pass with me."

"Hold up, don't tell me they broke up because she had sex with you?"

"Yes and no."

She shook her head. "I'm not following."

"Apparently, the day we got together, her man decided that he didn't want to go through with the pass, but she let it slip that she already had."

Eden slammed her hand against her mouth. "Oh, shit! I know his ass flipped out."

"He sure did. Ol' boy was so pissed that he accused her of cheating and broke up with her."

"What? You're lying."

"Nope."

"Wow, that's just like a man. He was all good until he found out that she didn't waste no time getting some dick."

"That's exactly what happened."

"Okay, but never mind that idiot. How did you end up falling for her? Did she put it on you that damn good?"

I squeezed the back of my neck. "I hate to admit it, but yeah she did. I haven't been able to stop thinking about it since."

"I see," Eden replied. "So are you sure this isn't just about sex? That shit can definitely cloud your judgment."

"Trust me, I started off asking myself the same thing. But I've been feeling Simone since we were kids. I just knew better than to act on it. Between my career and her being in a relationship—"

"And the random women you have a habit of screwing on the regular," Eden added.

"You can chill on all that. I'm single, so I can do as I please," I said. "I've been in relationships before, and cheating was never an issue."

"Yeah, but that was ages ago. You're in a different tax bracket now. Women are going to be throwing themselves at you left and right."

"That's the least of my worries."

Seeming somewhat convinced, Eden nodded her head slowly. "Okay, I hear what you're saying. So, what are you going to do about it?"

"That's the thing. I have no idea. I want to respect her time and space, but whenever I'm with her, I can't stop myself from thinking about what it would be like if we were more."

"Then you should tell her that. Make it clear that what you feel for her is about more than sex."

"But how?"

"I don't know. That's for you to figure out. Oh, and make sure you let her know that you're in no rush. Well, that's if you can."

"Shit, I've waited this long. I'm sure I can wait a little longer if it means seeing where things can go between us."

"Knock, knock," Simone said as she peeked in from the other side of the room door. "Cade let me in. I hope that's okay."

"Yeah, it's cool," I replied.

Leaning into my ear, Eden whispered, "I would suggest you wait until after the show before saying anything." She returned her attention to Simone. "You look good as hell girl. That dress fits you like a glove."

"You think so?" Simone questioned as she stood gracefully, her curves heightened by the form-fitting red dress that hugged her figure. Her smooth skin glowed in the lights, complemented by her dark, cascading curls that framed her face perfectly.

"Of course, you do," Eden replied. "I hate to brag, but I'm damn good at my job."

"You sure are," I mumbled.

"What was that?" Eden teased.

"Um...nothing," I blurted before walking toward Simone and admiring the delicate spaghetti straps that adorned her bare shoulders. "Did you get the flowers I sent to your room?"

"I did," she replied. "They were beautiful. Thank you."

"You're welcome."

"Um...can I talk to you for a sec?" she asked.

"Of course." I looked over at Eden, giving her the cue to leave. Catching my hint, she nodded and then strolled out of the room. I looked back at Simone. "What's up? Everything okay with your room?"

"Oh, yeah, everything's perfect. I couldn't have asked for a better view."

"Okay, cool. What's wrong?"

Taking her time, she moved in closer to me. "Legend, what happened on the jet got me thinking."

Shit, maybe I shouldn't have done that, I quickly thought.

"Oh yeah? About what?"

"Us," she said, then cleared her throat. "Clearly, the two of us are struggling to keep our hands off each other. I'm not sure if it's just because the sex was so good or if there's more between us. But either way, I can't shake this feeling of wanting to find out." She eyed me as I opened my mouth to speak, then placed her finger over my lips. "Let me finish." I nodded, then allowed her to continue. "Before I say anything else, I need to know if you have feelings for me or if I'm just imagining it."

"It's definitely not a figment of your imagination."

She giggled, then tilted her head to the side. "Are you sure this thing between us isn't just about you wanting to fuck me whenever you want to?"

"I can promise you that it's not just about that. Simone I've had my eye on you since the day I met you at your mom's office."

"Wait...what?"

"Yeah. But I knew I wasn't ready, and you were always with ol' boy."

"And you think you're ready now?"

"Shit, that's what I'm feeling."

Once again, she laughed as she lowered her gaze. "You're funny."

"What? I'm just being honest."

"Yeah, well, I don't know what I feel right now. I mean, I know that I have feelings for you. But like I said, I'm still not sure if it goes beyond sex."

I shrugged. "It's all good. How about we take the time to find out?"

"You sure about that? It could take months. Especially since I'm still dealing with a breakup."

"Baby girl, I've waited this long. I can wait a little longer."

Staring at me, she smiled, then circled her arms around my neck. I thought she was going to say something else, but she didn't. Instead, she lowered my head so that my forehead rested on hers and continued looking into my eyes.

Not wanting to miss the opportunity I closed my eyes and pressed my lips against hers. She didn't resist, which gave me the green light to lower my hands to her waist.

I wasn't sure where this moment would take us, but I was damn sure ready to explore.

26

SIMONE

Four weeks later

"Well, well, well. Look who came to see me," my mother said as she stepped into her office and hugged me. "I feel like I haven't seen you since you got back in town from Legend's tour, and that was a week ago."

"Yeah, I know. I've been so busy. It's tough not having an assistant."

Taking a seat behind her desk, my mother sighed. "Have you talked to Nitra at all?"

"Nope. I haven't been able to get her on the phone since I got back. I'm not sure if she's avoiding me or if I should be worried." I leaned back in my chair.

"Why would she be avoiding you? I thought things were good with you two?"

"They were," I replied. "But she's probably avoiding me after I tried to convince her to press charges against Owen right before I left."

"You did?"

I sighed. "Yeah, and I really shouldn't have hassled her about it. She's going through enough as it is. But I just wanted it to be clear that she wasn't alone, and that I was one hundred percent on her side."

"Well, that's probably not easy for her to grasp since you're somewhat related to the man she's saying did this to her."

"I'm not related to that sicko. Please don't ever say that again."

My mother shrugged. "Sorry. You know what I'm trying to say though."

"Yeah, I know. Anyway, I'm going to keep trying. Hopefully, she picks up my call at some point."

"Knock, knock," Legend said as he stepped into the office. "How are you lovely ladies today?"

Although he was talking to both of us, he was looking directly at me. I tried not to smile too hard, but I couldn't help it.

"We're good," my mother replied. "What you up to?"

"Nothing much. On my way to the studio. I've been feeling inspired since I got back in town."

Once again a smile spread across my face. "Oh yeah?"

"Mmhmm...my next project may be the best thing I've ever done."

My mother nodded. "Good. That's exactly what I want to hear."

Giving me one last glance, he said, "Well, I'll let you ladies finish talking. I just wanted to stop through and say hello."

"Alright," my mother replied. "Go make a hit."

"Sure thing," he said before returning his attention to me. "See you later." The way he said it, I knew he was confirming instead of just making small talk.

I nodded in agreement and tucked my bottom lip between my teeth while watching him leave the office.

The time I spent with Legend on tour was better than I could have expected. Although I'd allowed him to put his mouth on me while we were on his jet, I only let it happen once. For the remainder of his tour, we kept things on a level that was just about spending time with each other. There wasn't a second that didn't feel pure with him, and our best moments were the moments we spent in silence. It was in those minutes that I could tell that we truly enjoyed being next to each other. Whether it was me resting my head on his shoulder while lounging around in his dressing room before a show, or him sitting in bed next to me while trying to figure out the word of the day before his grandmother. It was so genuine and sweet, which was something I'd never experienced before.

Pulling me from my thoughts, my mother said, "Hmm...that was interesting."

"Huh? What...what was interesting?"

"That exchange the two of you just had that you think I didn't notice."

I looked away from her. "I have no idea what you're talking about."

"Oh, you most certainly do, and now you're going to tell me what happened on this tour."

"Nothing happened."

"Simone don't even try it. You're my child. I know when something is up with you. I know when you're different, and sweetheart, you're definitely different. Not to mention, when I flew in to see his show in Chicago, you were so giddy that I barely recognized you. But I didn't have time to address it then, and I didn't want to ruin whatever happiness you were feeling in that moment."

Pressing my hands against my face while attempting to hide my smile, I said, "Is it that obvious?"

"It most certainly is. Now, are you ready to tell me what's going on?"

"Okay, fine." I took a deep breath and leaned further back in my chair. "What I'm about to tell you stays between us."

"Alright."

"I'm serious Mama. That means you can't tell Nori or Riah."

"I won't."

I gave her a long glare, then I crossed one leg over the other. "Okay, so, Legend and I spent a lot of time together while he was on tour. We did the simplest of things, and it was amazing in every possible way."

"That's great, baby. I'm happy to hear that."

I lowered my gaze. "But as good as it feels, it also feels scary."

"Scary? Why?"

"Because I'm still fresh off a breakup. I shouldn't be so quick to jump into things. But it's like I can't help it. Legend makes me feel things that I've never felt before, and it's things that I don't ever want to be away from."

"Well, just enjoy that. Is he pressuring you for more?"

"No, he's not. He's agreed to go as slow as I want to go."

"Good."

"But that's the thing...although I know and feel like I should take it slow, I also feel like Legend is the one. I mean, it's not like he's some random man that I don't know. I've known him for years, and I've always been comfortable with him."

"Okay, well here's a bigger question. How do you feel about Wiz? Are you still in love with him?"

I paused for a moment, then looked down into my lap. "This is going to sound crazy, but I don't think I've ever been in love with Wiz. I think I've *loved* him. But that's it."

"Oh, wow."

"Yeah, I know," I replied. "But, in my defense, he's the only man I've ever been with. We've done everything together. But the more I look back over the last few years, the more I realize that we weren't even friends. There was no genuine laughter between us. It was just moments of us trying to force ourselves to truly enjoy each other."

"Really? I didn't know it was *that* bad between you two."

"I know. We've done a good job of making things look good in front of others, but when it's just the two of us, there's nothing there."

"Well, do you want my opinion?"

"Yes, of course," I replied.

"Sounds to me that you guys grew up and grew apart. You two were very young when you got involved with each other. Your life was different, your views were different. What worked for the two of you back then, doesn't work for you now," my mother said. "I know people are always in love with the idea of high school sweethearts staying together and getting married. But the reality is, that doesn't always work out. People evolve and begin to see things differently as they get older. Sometimes they even begin to love differently. That's not your fault or his, that's just the way it is, and sometimes we just have to accept that. We have to accept that eventually, we have to find someone that can meet us where we are now. Not the person who we were before. I think both of you felt that way, but neither of you knew how to express it."

I closed my eyes as my mother's words seeped deeper into my mind. I couldn't deny anything she was saying. In fact, in a way, I felt like it was what Wiz was trying to express to me when the hall pass conversation came about. It didn't make a lot of sense to me then, but it made a hell of a lot of sense to me now. More so now that I'd come across a man who met me where I was today.

Standing, I said, "What you just said makes so much sense, and as much as I hate to admit it, Wiz pretty much said the same thing, but I wasn't ready to hear it."

"And that's understandable. That's a hard pill to swallow after being with someone for so long."

"Yeah, it is," I replied. "I've been avoiding him, but maybe I should make plans to talk to him."

"I agree. It's important that you close that chapter of your life before entering a new one. If you don't, it's only going to make things more challenging for you."

Nodding, I said, "Noted."

"Okay. Good," she said. "Oh, and you're still coming to the Entertainment Excellence event on Saturday, right?"

"Of course. I wouldn't miss it."

"Okay, good. I want you and your sisters to ride there with me. I'll text you later and let you know what time to meet up at the house."

I groaned. "Are you sure that's a good idea? You know Riah and I still aren't on speaking terms. Putting us together will probably do more harm than good."

"I don't want to hear that. The two of you need to work this thing out."

"I know, but I don't think the night that you and several other major players in the entertainment industry are being honored would be the best time to do that. It might ruin everything."

"Well, it sounds like you two need to figure out how to be on your best behavior. I'm going to tell you just like I told her...I want all my children with me. End of discussion."

Dropping my shoulders, I said, "Alright," then turned toward the door. "I better get going. I have some shopping that I need to do. I'm supposed to be going to some party with Nori tomorrow night, and I have no idea what I'm wearing."

"Okay, baby." She planted a kiss on my cheek. "You have a good day."

"You too. Love you."

"Love you too."

I strolled out of the office, trying to shove back the aggravation that came along with the thought of having to see my sister in a couple of days. We hadn't been in the same room since she'd acted a fool at my spa. Although things seemed to have calmed down in the blogs, I wasn't sure if things were calm between us. But for the sake of my mother, I was willing to come together and play it cool. Hopefully, Riah had sense enough to do the same.

27

LEGEND

"Bro, that shit sounds fire," Kendrick said as I stepped out of the booth and sat down in the chair next to him. "I want to call it baby-making music. But it's like some real deal love shit."

"You think so?"

"Hell yeah. You're going to be dodging pussy for days after you drop this album." Giving me a smirk, Kendrick rested his hand on my shoulder. "Just make sure you toss a few this way."

I laughed. "You can have them all."

"Oh yeah?"

"Yeah."

"Damn, she really has your ass whipped, huh?"

"What?"

He sucked his teeth. "Fool, you heard me. I know pussy whipped when I see it, and that's exactly what you are. Simone must be putting it on you tough."

"Man, chill, we're not even having sex."

"Mmhmm...tell that shit to someone that doesn't know you."

"I'm for real. We've just been hanging out, and it's been nice. Like, on another level kind of nice."

"Wait, like on some relationship type of shit?"

"Not necessarily. She's still taking things slow after her breakup and I'm respecting that."

"But you want it to be more, huh?"

I took a deep breath. "I shouldn't be having this conversation with you."

"Yeah, well, you've already started. Besides, I'm not going to say shit. I know how touchy this situation is. Wiz is losing his damn mind right now."

"I see. I told Simone she needed to change the locks on her crib, which she finally did last week."

"Damn, I know he's tripping hard, but I don't think he would be dumb enough to try anything. Some niggas just don't take breakups well. Especially after finding out their ex is kicking it with someone else."

I shrugged. "Either way, I don't want Simone to take any chances. Better to be safe than sorry."

"True. But enough about that," Kendrick replied before looking at the studio engineer. "Let's get into this music. Play that shit back."

Within seconds he did just that.

The soft sound of an electric guitar filled the room as the drummer set the steady beat, creating a smooth, sultry rhythm. The keyboardist added a soulful melody, while the bassist laid down a steady groove that set the foundation for the song. Finally, I entered, my voice drenched with emotion as I croon about love.

I closed my eyes and nodded my head slowly, enjoying the feelings that my music was bringing to the surface. Memories of my time with Simone flooded my thoughts, reminding me of every moment between us that I'd made sure to capture.

As my thoughts consumed me, I continued to drift into another place, allowing the song to carry me until it couldn't anymore.

"That was amazing," Simone said as she stepped further into the studio. "Is that going on your new album?"

"Hell yeah," Kendrick jumped in.

"Um...more than likely," I replied. "I'm just playing with some things right now."

"Well, you should add that to the list. It sounds really good."

"Thank you," I said while looking her over like it was my first time seeing her today. She was wearing a cream sweater dress with brown leggings and boots that stopped just at her thigh. "You look nice. Where are you headed?"

"I was on my way to the outlets, but I wanted to stop by and see what you were working on before I left. You seemed excited when you stopped by my mom's office."

Standing, Kendrick placed his hand on the engineer's shoulder. "Aye man, let's give these two some privacy before they snatch each other's clothes off in front of us."

"Bro, chill," I shot back.

"What? I'm just saying. I know that look."

"Whatever, just get out."

"I'm going," he said as he followed the engineer out the door.

Dropping my shoulders, I looked at Simone. "My bad. He's been on my ass ever since Wiz questioned him. I haven't told him anything though. Well, not about us having sex."

Waving me off, she said, "At this point, it doesn't even matter. Wiz has said enough, so the rumors are making their rounds. All I can do now is try to diffuse the situation with him as much as possible."

"How do you plan on doing that?"

"Even though I don't want to, I guess I need to try and have a conversation with him. Maybe if we talk, he'll stop acting crazy and we can finally close the door on this thing." She walked over to me and then climbed into the chair to straddle me. "Then, you and I can actually take things to the next level."

Surprised to hear what she was saying, I cleared my throat. "And by next level, what exactly are we talking about?"

"Being together."

"Are you sure? I know it hasn't been that long since we first talked about things."

"No, it hasn't. But I was talking to my mom about us, and she helped me put some things into perspective."

"What did she say?"

"Honestly, I would prefer to wait to have that conversation if you don't mind. I need to get things handled with Wiz first."

Nodding, I said, "I don't mind at all. Whenever we decide to take the next step, I want you to be in a good place with things."

"Good," she replied in a relieved tone. "Now, I just got to figure out when I'm going to talk to him. He's usually busy on the weekends, and I have quite a bit going on myself right now. Maybe I'll just wait until Monday."

Pulling her closer to me, I said, "So, I got to wait four whole days before possibly having you all to myself for good? That's a long ass time."

Her head fell back as she let out a bout of laughter. "It's not that long."

"Yes, it is. But I guess I'll keep being patient."

"And I truly appreciate you for it."

"Oh yeah? Prove it."

"What do you want me to do?"

I placed my hand against my chin as I leaned further back in my chair. "Shit, I know I can't touch you like I want to, but nothing's stopping you from touching yourself and letting me watch."

"Oh, wow, you want me to get freaky right here in the studio?"

"I mean, yeah, if you're down."

She giggled, then stood up. "Say no more."

A smirk spread across my face as I watched her unzip her

boots, then slide her leggings down to her ankles and kick them to the side. I could feel my dick pressing against my sweats as she walked toward me, then leaned over to kiss me.

As our tongues intertwined, I could hear her hands sliding back and forth against the wetness that was now covering her pussy.

Suddenly, she forced herself away from me and backed away until the heels of her feet met the couch. I watched in awe as she lowered herself onto the edge and spread her legs so I could see the sparkle between her thighs.

My hand slid into my sweats, not stopping until I was surrounding my dick.

There was no way I could just watch, and she knew it.

Tucking her bottom lip between her teeth, she smiled at me with her eyes. "Why are you hiding it from me? I can't be the only one with everything out."

"I got you," I said, then pulled my dick out and stroked it slowly.

"Mmm...thank you." She kept her eyes on me, then slid two fingers inside of her pussy. It didn't matter that someone could walk in at any moment and see us. In fact, I think that was exactly what turned her on.

With every second that passed, our strokes got more intense. I could feel my veins bulging from my thick flesh. My growls bounced off the walls of the room, which couldn't be heard from a single person on the other side.

I watched as her head fell back and her fingers moved faster inside of her.

"Fuck, fuck, fuck! I'm about to cum," she called out.

"Shit, me too."

Unable to resist, I rushed across the room and dropped my head between her legs, allowing my mouth to meet her fingers.

She gasped for air and pressed her hands against the back of my head, forcing my tongue to capture all her juices as they flooded from between her walls. The taste of her did something to me, leaving me no choice but to lean my head back and catch the explosion that raged from within me.

She watched in admiration as the tip of her finger rested between her teeth.

Once she saw that I'd let go of enough, she sat on top of me and rested her face against mine. "Soon enough, all of that will be inside of me."

I smirked. "Baby girl, you keep talking, and it's going to be a lot sooner than you think."

As soon as I said those words, the door flew open, and Kendrick walked in. "Oh, shit, my bad." He placed his hand over his eyes. "I was just coming back in to see if y'all saw the shit that Keke posted."

Simone groaned, "What now?" then turned toward the couch to grab her phone.

Although she still had her sweater dress on, it wasn't covering anything when she bent over to reach inside her purse.

I stood up and adjusted my sweats, then got Simone's attention so I could toss her clothes her way.

Still staring at her phone, she hurried to slip them back on.

"Um...can I uncover my eyes now?" Kendrick asked.

"Yeah, man, you're cool," I told him.

I moved over to Simone and stared at her cell as she made it to Keke's website. "Oh, wow," I said, surprised to see the headline.

Kendrick stepped further into the studio. "Looks like Eden agreed to take that paternity test after all. Hopefully, it will put an end to all this bullshit and things can get back on track."

"I hope so too," I said.

Clearing his throat, Kendrick looked between the two of us, but he didn't say anything. Instead, he just nodded and smiled.

Finally, after a few more odd ass seconds passed, he said, "I guess I'll let you two finish up."

"Oh, trust me, we finished," Simone blurted before looking back at me smiling. "Call me later."

"Will do." I licked my lips while trying to keep my composure as she walked out of the room.

Damn, she's sexy.

"Whipped," Kendrick uttered.

"Shut the hell up."

"What? I'm just speaking the truth, and after what I saw, I can't even blame you."

"*What you saw*?" I frowned. "Bro, please don't tell me you were watching us?"

"Nah, man, I'm talking about the way she was sitting on your dick when I walked in. I know that ass had to be bouncing like crazy."

"Whatever. Let's just get back to this music. I'm feeling inspired all over again."

Laughing, he sat down in the chair next to me. "I bet you do."

28

SIMONE

Standing on the massive table in front of me, Nori reached down to grab my hands. "Girl, are you going to sit there all night and act like you're allergic to dancing?"

"If it means not being seen by my ex, yes," I shouted over the music. "Why in the hell didn't you tell me that Wiz was going to be the DJ at this club?"

"Because I knew if I did, you probably wouldn't have come."

"You're damn right I wouldn't have come."

"We still haven't talked. The last thing I need is to have a run-in with him tonight."

Letting out a heavy sigh, Nori hopped down from the table and then sat down next to me. "Sis, the man is working. He doesn't have time to come and say anything to you. I really think you're worrying yourself over nothing."

"That's easy for you to say. You're not the one he's harassing day after day."

"Okay, you make a valid point," she replied. "How about this? I'll keep an eye out and make sure he doesn't come anywhere near you."

"Girl, bye. You'll probably be so drunk in the next twenty

minutes that you won't even be able to see what's in front of you."

"Look, if it means you'll get up off your ass and have a good time, I won't have another drink for the rest of the night."

"I can't ask you to do that. You didn't come here to babysit me."

"Don't think of it as babysitting. Think of it as me looking out for you the same way you would look out for me."

Dropping my shoulders, I smiled, then leaned in to hug her. "Thanks, little sis."

"Anytime."

I grabbed her drink from the table and then took a quick sip. "Okay, now whose birthday are we here celebrating?"

"Twan," she quickly answered.

"The rapper, Twan?"

"Yep." Her eyes lit up with excitement. "Mama said he's looking for new management, so when I got an invite to his party, I figured it would be the perfect opportunity to see what's up. Not to mention, he's super fine."

I looked toward the front of the club as he stood on stage tossing back a bottle of champagne, his tattooed chest making it hard to look away.

Twan *was* fine as hell, and if he wasn't the same age as Nori, I might have been even more intrigued. But younger men weren't my thing.

Tapping me on the shoulder, Nori said, "Oh, look, your boy just walked in."

At first, I had no idea who she was talking about. But once I turned toward the main entrance and saw Cade motioning for people to get out of the way, I became fully aware.

The second my eyes landed on Legend, a smile spread across my face and butterflies fluttered in my stomach. "I didn't know he was coming tonight."

"Hmm...this should be interesting," Nori said with a smirk.

"What should be interesting?"

"Well, I'm pretty sure I saw Teddy walk in about twenty minutes ago, and if I'm not mistaken things got pretty ugly the last time they were in the same room together."

Immediately, I glanced around the club. "Oh God, that's not good at all."

"It sure isn't. But, hopefully, they'll keep their distance and be on their best behavior tonight."

"Yeah, I hope so. Because I'm pretty sure Keke is somewhere lurking around here, and she won't hesitate to blast whatever goes down on her stupid ass blog."

"You already know."

Placing her drink back down on the table, I said, "I'm going to the restroom. I'll be back."

"Okay. Well, I'll be here making sure that Wiz doesn't leave the stage."

I laughed. "Thank you."

"Sure thing."

Smiling, I made my way down the stairs that led to the bottom floor. I listened as Wiz shouted the next song and reminded everyone whose birthday it was.

I nibbled on my bottom lip, contemplating if I should make my way to the VIP area to talk to Legend. I wanted to, but the last thing I needed was for Wiz to see us together and somehow cause a scene.

You know what? I'm just going to take my ass to the restroom and go back where I was.

I strolled past the bar and squeezed my way through the crowd of people who were standing around talking. Halfway to my destination, I felt a hand touch my arm. Nervous about who it might be, I turned around slowly.

Much to my surprise, it was Owen.

I snatched my arm from his grasp. "Please don't ever touch me again."

"Damn, it's like that little sis?"

"I'm not your fucking sis."

Giving me a sleazy grin, he said, "Come on now, Simone. Don't be like that. We need to do a better job of getting along. You know, for your sister's sake."

"Nigga, fuck you. Hell will freeze over before I try to get along with you. Especially after what you did to Nitra."

He rolled his eyes. "Please don't tell me you still believe that bullshit?"

"You damn right I do," I shouted. "You may have my sister fooled, but I don't believe a single word that comes out of your mouth. You've been doing dirt since the day Riah met you, and its only gotten worse. You think because you're some big-time football player, you can get away with doing whatever. But eventually, you're going to leave a trail so thick that you can't talk your way out of your bullshit. I can't wait until that day comes."

He scoffed. "Wishful thinking sweetheart."

"Fuck you, Owen."

Smiling, he leaned closer to me and whispered, "You can keep acting like I'm the only one doing dirt, but word around town is Wiz dumped your ass because you're out here spreading your legs for someone else." He took a step back, then looked me over. "Sounds like you need to be worried less about what I'm doing and focus on getting your own house in order."

Taking a hard swallow, I looked away from him and forced back the urge to bitch slap him. I refused to give him the satisfaction of knowing that he'd gotten under my skin. Instead, I remained still until I could feel his presence lessen around me.

When he was no longer near, I took a deep breath and placed my hands on my hips.

"You good?" I heard Legend say while behind me.

"Yeah, I'm fine."

"You sure? I saw you over here talking to Owen. Did he say something crazy to you?"

"Trust me, it's nothing worth repeating." I waved away the thought, then looked at Legend. "Why didn't you tell me you were coming tonight? I told you I would be here."

"I didn't want you to be tripping. I was planning on keeping my distance, but then I saw you looking upset."

"And you couldn't resist coming over here, huh?"

He wrapped his arm around my waist and yanked me forward. "No, I couldn't."

Knowing that someone was probably watching, I should've pushed him away. But the way my body melted against his, I didn't want him to let me go."

"Damn, you two look mighty comfortable."

Recognizing Teddy's voice, I turned around. "Hey, Teddy. How are you?"

"I'm cool," he replied as he leaned in to hug me. The sharp and bitter aroma of alcohol oozed from his pores. "Long time no see."

"Yeah, it has been a minute. Are you having a good time tonight?"

"Mmhmm," he mumbled before forcing his bloodshot eyes to look at Legend. "You know we need to talk about what went down at the photo shoot."

"Nah, I'm good on that," Legend replied in a nonchalant tone.

"Oh, are you?"

"Mmhmm."

"So, you're just going to keep playing me like that?"

"I'm not playing you like anything. You've done some fucked up shit lately. You and I have nothing to talk about."

Teddy stumbled, then lowered his hands in front of him to try to keep himself steady. "Look, man, I know I've—"

"Hey," Kendrick stepped in as he placed his hand on Teddy's back, trying to hold him up, "perhaps right now isn't the best time to be having a conversation."

"I agree," I chimed in.

"I'm good," Teddy insisted.

"Nah, you're not good," Kendrick told him. "You can barely stand up."

Grabbing Legend's hand, I said, "Come on, let's step outside for a sec. I need some air." I peeked over my shoulder to make sure Cade was nearby.

Like always, he was right there and ready to move.

Nodding, Legend followed my lead, and Kendrick moved Teddy in the opposite direction.

We were almost outside when I heard Wiz shout, "Damn, so you're really going to flaunt the nigga you fucked in my face?"

My eyes widened as I spun around. "Wiz, please don't do this here."

"Why not? You brought it here."

Trying to diffuse the situation, I walked over to him. "Look, I know you want to have a conversation, and we can do that. Just not here. Name the time and the place."

"Fuck that, Simone. You've been ignoring me for weeks because you're out here being a hoe."

Before I knew it, Legend was in Wiz's face. "Make that the last time you call her anything other than her fucking name."

"Damn," Wiz shot back, then nodded his head slowly. "Oh...yeah...y'all definitely fucking. If I wasn't convinced before, I'm damn sure convinced now."

Legend scoffed. "I don't give a damn about you being convinced. Whether I'm beating the pussy up or just playing with it, that still doesn't give you permission to call her out of her name."

"Is that right? So, what the fuck do you call her?"

Before he could respond, Cade stepped between them, and I grabbed Legend's hand. "Let's go. He's not worth it."

"Baby girl, I told you if I ever heard him call you out your name again, I was going to see him."

"I know, but—"

"Baby girl, huh?" Wiz interrupted. "So, that's what you call her?"

Laughing, Legend stepped forward and confidently slid his hand down his beard. "Damn right. But that's nothing. You should hear some of the shit she calls me when I'm nose deep in her pussy nigga."

With rage in his eyes, Wiz lunged toward Legend, but Cade caught him and knocked him on his ass. "Not today, my friend."

"Legend, please, can we just leave?" I called out.

Not saying a word, he nodded and motioned for me to walk ahead of him.

As fast as I could, I made my way to the exit and stormed out the door.

What a fucking shit show.

29

SIMONE

"How are you feeling?" I asked Legend as we walked into my house. "You were pretty quiet on the way here."

"My bad, I just needed to cool down."

"Yeah, I know. Tonight was a lot." I placed my hand on his cheek. "I really do appreciate you coming to my defense."

"Always."

"But I also have to say that I don't want you jeopardizing your career trying to protect me."

"Baby girl, my career is fine." He lowered his lips to mine, then squeezed my ass. "As long as I get to do this at the end of the night, it's all worth it."

Laughing, I wrapped my arms around his neck. "You really go hard for me, huh?"

"Harder than you could ever know." He purposely bumped me.

"I wasn't talking about that, sir."

"I know. I just wanted to be clear."

"Oh, you're definitely clear."

"Good," he said before slapping my ass. "It's late as hell. Go get yourself some rest. I'll call you later."

Disappointed, I frowned. "You're leaving?"

"Well, yeah. I figured you would probably want to be alone."

"That's the last thing I want," I replied.

"Oh, well excuse me. Did you want to grab some clothes and head back to my place?"

"Um...no. How about you stay here?"

Looking me over with a lifted brow, he said, "Really? You want me to stay here?"

"Yes, I do," I said with a laugh. "Is that a problem?"

"Not with me," he replied. "I'm just surprised. You haven't asked me to stay the night here since we started doing whatever it is we're doing, so—"

"I know. That was because Wiz still had keys to my place. But now that that's no longer an issue, I don't care about any of that."

"Say no more," he said as he pulled off his jacket.

I grabbed it from his hand and then hung it up in my living room closet. "Make yourself at home. I'm going to get out of these clothes and hop in the shower."

"Hmm...how about I help you?"

I pressed my hand into his chest. "You most certainly cannot. We're still trying to figure things out. Sex isn't on the table."

"Who said anything about having sex? I was just trying to help you get undressed."

"That's what you say now. But the second I take off my clothes, you're going to find some way to stick your fingers where they don't belong, and I don't think I'll be able to stop myself this time."

Lifting his hands, he said, "Alright, fine. I'll hang out down here while you shower."

"Great. Like I said, make yourself at home." I walked toward the stairs, then stopped. Suddenly, the feeling of doing the opposite of what I had in mind came over me. "You know what? The weather isn't too bad tonight, we should get in the hot tub."

He shrugged. "Sounds good to me. I don't have any trunks though."

"You're wearing boxers, right?"

"Yeah, but I can't guarantee they're going to stay on once I get in the water."

I cleared my throat. "It's fine. I'll keep my distance if they don't."

"Alright. But don't say I didn't warn you."

"Whatever. I'll be fine." Smiling, I turned away from him and scurried up the stairs. Although the night had turned out to be a lot crazier than I expected, I was glad that things were finally settling down on a good note. I was probably pushing the limit by letting Legend stay the night. But after that run-in with Wiz, I was feeling on edge, and I didn't want to be alone.

Pleased that he wasn't going anywhere, I took my time changing into my swimsuit.

When I made it back downstairs and stepped into my backyard, I heard smooth and soulful music coming from the nearby speakers. The soft lights that were strung up in the trees swayed along with the rhythm, adding to the relaxing and sultry atmosphere.

"Comfortable?" I questioned as I walked toward Legend who was already in the hot tub.

I removed my robe and tossed it on one of the lounge chairs.

"Very," he replied, his eyes stuck on me. "That's a sexy ass swimsuit."

"Thank you. I just got it," I said while twirling around to give him a full look.

Although I didn't wear it often, orange was my color, and my little two-piece proved it.

Legend slipped his hands beneath the water to reposition himself. "Yeah, you stay on the other side of the hot tub. I'm not going to make it if you don't."

I laughed, then stepped into the water. "We have to work on practicing restraint. We're supposed to be focusing on what things look like for us outside of sex."

"I know, and I feel like we've done a damn good job so far. What I feel for you goes way beyond what's between your legs. I don't think we need to keep going through the same test to prove that."

"Okay," I swayed my hands back and forth as I made myself comfortable across from him. "So, for fun, let's say our testing period is over and we take things to the next level—"

"You're talking about being in a relationship, right?"

"I'm talking about what we want beyond a relationship," I said. "The mistake I made with Wiz was thinking we wanted the same things, and when I realized that wasn't the case, I thought I could change that. I don't want to make that mistake again."

"Understood."

"So, even though you've heard me mention these things before, I need to make sure my needs are very clear. I want marriage, I want kids...and most importantly, I want a happy life with a man who knows that I'm the one. There shouldn't be a question in his mind about that."

Smiling, Legend stood up and glided through the water until he was directly in front of me. "What you're asking for is easy."

"Legend, I'm serious. I don't want to be in some bullshit ass relationship again."

"You won't be."

"You sure about that?"

"Simone, I can guarantee you that. I'm nothing like Wiz. I know what I want, and it's all the things you want."

"Including me?"

"Damn sure including you." He moved between my legs, and immediately I noticed his boxers were floating on the other side of the hot tub.

Smiling, I tucked my bottom lip between my teeth and wrapped my legs around his waist. With the tip of his dick, he slid my swimsuit bottoms to the side and pushed himself between my folds.

After the night we'd had, this was everything I needed.

It was crazy to think that this feeling was once something I was only able to crave. With Wiz, sex was a chore rather than a connection of souls that were meant to be making love. But with Legend, it felt like our souls were always intertwined. His determination to make sure that *our* bodies were pleased was the only thing that mattered in every moment. It was something I never wanted to escape, and I got the feeling he would never let me.

Floating with the rhythm of the water as our bodies continuously collided, I relaxed my lower muscles even more, making sure to give him all the access that he desired.

30

LEGEND

Leaning against the kitchen island, I took a bite out of the grilled cheese sandwich that Simone had made us for breakfast. I could feel the rise of her cheeks as she smiled while keeping her face pressed into my back.

"It's delicious, isn't it?" she said.

I couldn't lie, she had the art of fixing a grilled cheese sandwich down. Not only was it flavored with just the right amount of butter, but it was nice and crisp without being burnt.

"It is."

She kissed my cheek. "I told you I could make a mean grilled cheese. Just wait until I make you my world-famous peanut butter and jelly. You might drop down on one knee right then and there."

"Oh, really? It's that good?"

"Sure is."

"Hmm...okay, I guess I'll have to see."

"I guess you will."

Still smiling, she moved to the other side of the island and took a bite of her sandwich. For a moment, I just remained quiet, watching her every move. Her level of comfort put my mind at ease. But I couldn't help but want to talk more about what we'd discussed last night. I needed to know if she was really open to taking things to the next level between us.

I lifted my glass of orange juice and then took a short sip. "So, about last night..." I started, but she quickly intervened.

"Last night was so crazy. I still can't believe Wiz acted the way he did," she said. "Sometimes it's really hard to believe that he's the same person I was in a relationship with."

"Yeah, I know. It's like that sometimes."

"Oh, and did you see the blogs this morning? They have a picture of you and Wiz face to face with each other like at a damn boxing match."

Frowning, I said, "I'm not surprised at all. Keke knows how to get a good photo."

"Tell me about it. Oh, and there are also some clips of you and Teddy going back and forth. But you can't hear what's being said."

I shook my head. "I'm not even going to stress myself about that shit. It is what it is."

"I hear you," she replied. "On another note, I hope things go smoothly at this event tonight. I don't want me and my sister to ruin it for my mother. Especially knowing how excited she is about it."

"As long as you guys remember that this night is about Ms. Regina, I'm sure everything will be fine. Besides, I'll be right there. I won't let you do anything crazy."

Pretending as though she was praying, she slammed her hands together and lifted her eyes to the ceiling. "Thank God."

"Now, about last night—"

Simone's cell rang, forcing me to squeeze my eyes in aggravation.

"Oh, it's Nitra," she said before answering the call and

putting it on speaker. "Nitra, hey. Where are you? I've been trying to get in touch with you."

"Yeah, I know. Sorry, I'm so late getting back to you."

"It's fine. Are you okay?"

"I'm fine. Well, as fine as I can be," she said. "I'm no longer in Ballman Hills though."

Frowning, Simone walked over to the dining room table and took a seat. "What do you mean? Where are you?"

"Honestly, I'd rather not say. Just know that me and EJ are safe, and we'll be gone for a while."

"Why?"

"It's a long story that I don't want to get into."

"Nitra, please don't shut me out. Tell me what's going on."

A frustrated sigh came from the other end of the phone. Then there was a short moment of silence before Nitra finally said, "Someone broke into my house and completely trashed it."

"What?"

"Yes. They broke picture frames, dishes, my glass table, and so much other stuff."

Simone pressed her hand against her mouth. "Oh my God. I'm so sorry. Were you guys there?"

"Thankfully, no. But it scared the shit out of me to come home to that, and for my baby to see it...I was mortified."

"Do you know who did it?"

Once again, Nitra fell silent, which told Simone everything she needed to know. "It was Owen wasn't it?"

"I don't have any proof, but yeah, I think it was his way of warning me to keep my mouth shut."

Dropping her shoulders, Simone said, "Nitra, you shouldn't let him get away with this. I know this isn't what you want to hear, and I promised myself I would leave you alone about it, but I still think you should press charges."

"With what evidence, Simone? I told you, it's just my word against his."

"I know, but—"

"Look, what he did to me was terrible. But I'm not risking my life or my baby's life over it. It's not worth it. I'd rather just leave town and move on with my life."

I lowered my gaze and shook my head. Hearing what Nitra was going through made my stomach turn. No one should be treated the way she's been treated. But that was the shitty society we lived in, and given Owen's track record, he was going to do it plenty more times and get away with it.

Leaning back in her chair, Simone said, "I hate this happened to you."

"Yeah, me too. But I'll be fine. I'm a strong girl."

"Yeah, you are," Simone replied. "I wish you would've called me sooner though. I would've been there for you after the break-in."

"Simone, you shouldn't be in the middle of all this. You and your sister are at odds right now because of me."

"No, we're at odds because of her dirty dick ass husband that she continues to defend. That's not your fault."

"Yeah, well, I feel like it's my fault," Nitra said. "Anyway, I have to go."

"Okay, well, at least call and let me know how you're doing."

"I will."

"You promise?"

"I promise."

Letting out a deep sigh, Simone said, "Take care of yourself, Nitra. I love you girl."

"I love you too."

The line went dead, and I could see the disappointment in Simone's face.

I made my way over to her and placed my hand on her shoulder. "Are you okay?"

"No, I'm not. This never should've happened to her. She doesn't deserve this."

"I know. It's terrible. But that fool will get exactly what he deserves. People like him go through life thinking they got away with things. But in the end, their souls didn't."

"Yeah, well, him and his soul better not ever come near me again."

"Simone, please don't do anything crazy. You know I won't hesitate to put my hands on someone for getting out of line with you."

She shrugged. "All I'm going to say is, if we cross paths anytime soon, you better be ready to go to war. Because I'm letting his ass have it."

Taking a deep breath, I lowered my head and pressed my lips against her cheek. "Whatever you say, baby girl. I'm on whatever you on."

31

SIMONE

"That pantsuit is fire," Nori said as she held up my hand to watch me twirl around in our mother's living room.

"Thanks, sis. I thought you might like it."

"Mmhmm...I might have to come and raid your closet. I need to see what else you got."

"Don't even try it," I said before snatching my hand from hers and laughing. "You don't have room to add anything else in your closet. You have more stuff than you'll ever wear."

"It's called having options."

"No, it's called being obsessed." I looked over at Mama as she sat on the couch and slid her feet into one of her heels. "Wouldn't you agree?"

"I mean, you do have a lot of clothes, Nori."

"Wow, Mama, you're really siding with her?"

"No, I'm just saying, you could afford to give a lot of that stuff away. You hate wearing things more than once, so what's the point of keeping it?"

Sucking her teeth, she rolled her eyes. "I like memories. Each outfit is tied to something that was important to me."

I laughed. "Oh my God, you're being dramatic as hell right now."

"No, I'm not. I'm just being honest."

"Yeah, okay." I glanced down at my phone to check on the time. "Mama, what time did you tell Riah to be here?"

"The same time I told you and Nori to be here."

"Which was thirty minutes ago," I blurted.

My mother stood up. "Yeah, I know. I don't know why she's so late. Let me try to get her on the phone."

I watched as my mother walked off, then turned my attention to Nori. "Being on time has never been one of her qualities."

"Please don't start," Nori griped. "You agreed that you were going to focus on making tonight pleasant. No bickering."

Lifting my hands, I said, "Okay, fine. I'm done."

"Good."

"But while we're chatting, what the hell happened to you making sure that you kept an eye on Wiz last night?"

"Um…yeah…about that—"

"Mmhmm…you failed. End of story."

"Okay, but in my defense, I was dancing in my own little world. I didn't even see him get off the stage."

"Yeah, that's obvious," I said. "It was almost a damn blood bath on the dance floor."

"Oh, I saw. What did Wiz and Legend say to each other?"

"Nothing worth repeating."

Returning to the living room, Mama said, "Okay, she should be walking through the door any minute now."

"Finally," I replied.

No sooner than I said those words, Riah walked inside.

I lowered my gaze to stare at my cell, and she hugged everyone in the room but me.

Play nice, I told myself. *Don't be the reason your mother's evening is ruined.*

I took a deep breath, then grabbed my purse from the coffee table. "The car's outside, right?"

"Um...yeah," Mama replied. "Let's get a few pictures, then we can head out."

"Sounds like a plan," I said before meeting her near the fireplace.

"Oh, wait a minute," Riah said. "Let me go grab Owen. He's waiting outside."

I frowned. "What the hell is he doing here?"

"What do you mean? He's my husband. Why wouldn't he be here?"

"Because he wasn't invited." I turned to Mama. "You didn't invite him to ride with us, did you?"

"No, I didn't."

Riah sucked her teeth. "She didn't have to invite him. Like I said, he's my husband. He can go wherever I go." She leaned out the doorway and waved him inside.

I took in a breath, then closed my eyes. "Riah, if his punk ass comes in here, I'm going to go the fuck off."

"You're not going to do a damn thing."

"After the shit he did to Nitra, yes the hell I am."

"Oh my God. Let that shit go. It was all a lie."

"No, it wasn't, and your husband knows it too. That's why he had her house broken into."

Riah jerked her head back and looked at me in disgust. "Is that what she told you?"

"It doesn't matter what she told me. Bottom line, your husband is trash and you sticking by his side only makes you—"

"That's enough!" Mama stepped in. "I'm not going to stand here and let the two of you call each other names."

Riah huffed, then folded her arms over her chest. "Well, tell that to Simone. She's the one spewing nonsense."

"Nothing I'm saying is nonsense. You just don't want to

believe the truth. The same truth that's been put in your face multiple times, but this time it's ten times worse. Owen is a sick freak who likes to take advantage of women."

"Wow, you're still going around spreading bullshit, huh?" Owen said as he stepped into the house, a smirk resting on his face.

Immediately, my insides started to boil.

"I'm not going," I told Mama.

"What?"

"If he's riding with us, I'm not riding. I will take my own damn car."

Riah sucked her teeth. "Well, if he's not riding then neither am I.

"Oh my God," Nori groaned. "This is ridiculous. Everyone needs to get their shit together. This night is about Mama. There's no reason we should be standing here going back and forth about whose riding with who."

"We wouldn't be if Simone wasn't being so damn childish," Riah spat.

Nori scowled. "Oh please, this isn't all on Simone. You knew damn well she wouldn't be cool with Owen riding with us. You did this shit on purpose."

"No, I didn't."

"Yes, you did, and I'm not here for it. All of this is uncalled for."

"Nori's right," Mama agreed. "This shouldn't even be an issue. Since it's my night, it's my decision. I think it would be best if Owen just met us at the event."

Riah opened her mouth to speak but was interrupted by Mama's ringing cell.

Holding up her finger, Mama stepped away to answer it.

"Well, I guess that's settled," Nori said. "Your husband's not riding with us."

Riah frowned. "I don't agree with this."

"It's okay, baby." Owen kissed her cheek. "I'll see you there."

Mama returned to the living room. She radiated a sense of deep sadness and simmering anger, as if she had been wronged and was struggling to contain her emotions.

"You good?" I asked.

"No, I'm not good." She passed me her cell.

"What's this?"

"Just press play," she said while keeping her eyes on Owen.

I lowered my gaze and did as she asked.

Nori walked over and watched with me.

At first, I didn't know what I was looking at. But then I noticed a familiar face on the screen. In fact, I noticed two. It was a video of Nitra as she danced in front of Owen.

"Is this what I think it is?" I questioned.

My mother didn't say a word. But the fearful look on Owen's face spoke loud and clear.

"What's going on?" Riah asked. "What are you guys looking at?"

She tried to walk toward me, but Owen quickly yanked her back. "Baby—"

"Don't you dare," I shouted, then shoved the phone into Riah's face. "Here's the evidence you've been waiting for."

She moved in closer to get a better look, then turned up the volume. But all that could be heard was the clinking of glasses, people laughing, and the occasional whoops and cheers from the crowd as they tossed money at strippers who were dancing in the distance. But even though there was no way to tell what was being said between Owen and Nitra, the video made it very clear what was being done to her.

Owen reached for Riah again. "Let me explain. It's not what it looks like."

Turning around, she shoved him in the chest. "It looks like you were assaulting a bitch with your damn fingers!"

"Riah, baby, you can't trust everything you see. Especially on somebody's grainy ass phone."

She shoved the cell in his face. "This doesn't look grainy at all. In fact, it's crystal clear. That's you, and that's her...and the shit you're doing doesn't look like it's something she's enjoying."

He took a hard swallow and stared at the phone.

"Mmhmm...that ass is caught," I said.

"Fuck you, bitch," he blurted.

Before I could process what he'd said, Riah slammed her fist into his jaw, causing him to stumble back.

The room fell silent.

Me and Nori looked at each other.

"What the fuck is wrong with you?" Owen shouted, his hand pressed against his face.

"Don't you ever call my sister a bitch again. I don't give a damn how you feel. When it comes to my blood, you keep that shit to yourself. Matter of fact," she stepped away and walked toward the kitchen.

We all looked around, unsure of what she was about to do. But the second we heard one of Mama's knives slide out of the wooden block that was sitting on the kitchen counter, we knew what was up.

Oh shit!

Mama raced toward Riah and tried to grab the knife from her hand, but Riah snatched it away.

"No, Mama. This son of a bitch has embarrassed the hell out of me time and time again. It's time he pays for that shit."

My eyes widened, and I hurried to grab her waist, forcing her to fall back on the couch. "You're right, he does deserve to pay," I told her. "But *you* don't. If you kill his ass, you'll be the one to go down."

"Yeah, sis," Nori chimed in while standing behind the couch. "He's not worth it."

"I want his ass to die," she screamed. "Right now!"

We wrestled with her...until finally she weakened, and Mama maneuvered the knife from her grasp.

Riah's sobs filled the room, making it impossible not to feel the hurt that she was consumed with.

I turned around to see if Owen showed an ounce of remorse for what he'd done. But he was gone.

32

SIMONE

On any other day, I would've been a lot more social at a major event. But instead, I was hiding in the corner of the room sipping on punch that I wished had been spiked with alcohol. I was trying to do too many things...avoid Wiz as he strolled around the room chatting like he hadn't acted a complete fool the night before and take my mind off the hurt that my sister was feeling after learning the truth.

But the last part was hard since Riah wasn't answering any of my calls. Right now, I had no idea where she was or what she was doing.

Taking a deep breath, I glanced around the room and admired the space we were in. This year's ceremony was being held at The Crystal Palace, which was a spacious black-owned venue that was known for hosting some of the most over-the-top celebrity events and weddings in Ballman Hills.

"Hey," Legend said, pulling me from my thoughts. "How are you feeling?"

"I could definitely be better," I replied. "I can tell people are trying not to stare while also staring. It's annoying as hell. Especially since this night is supposed to be about my mother."

"Yeah, I know. It's pretty messed up. How's Riah?"

"Terrible. When we saw the video, we were literally in the middle of arguing about her wanting Owen to ride here with us."

"Damn. So, he was there when you guys watched it?"

"Yes, and he tried to trick us into believing that it wasn't what it looked like."

"*It wasn't what it looked like?*" Legend shot back. "That video was clear as day. Nothing about what went down looked consensual."

"That's exactly what we told him. But long story short, he ended up calling me a bitch, and Riah punched the shit out of him."

"Oh, damn!"

"Mmhmm...it gets even worse though," I said. "Riah went to the kitchen and grabbed a knife. We had to climb on top of her so she wouldn't chop his ass up."

Legend's eyes widened. "Are you serious?"

"Yes! I can't make this shit up."

"Wow, that's a lot. I'm surprised y'all still showed up."

"Trust me, if it wasn't for my mom, I definitely wouldn't be here."

"Yeah, I get it."

"Anyway, how are things going with you this evening? You look nice," I said as he stood confidently in his well-tailored dark suit. If it weren't for the fact that we were only fifteen minutes into the event, I would've yanked his ass to the nearest bathroom. But I couldn't risk it. Knowing us, we would end up missing everything.

Smiling, he said, "Thanks. You know I had to get clean for Ms. Regina's big night." He looked me over and licked his lips. "I see you felt the same way. You look good as hell tonight in that pantsuit."

"Thank you. I wish I felt good."

He leaned over and whispered in my ear. "Don't worry. I'll be sure to make you feel good later."

"Is that right?"

"Mmhmm...just tell me what you want me to do."

I placed my hand under my chin and then peered into the ceiling. "I'm sure I can think of a few things."

"Just let me know. I got you."

I opened my mouth to respond but realized that everyone was making their way to their seats. "Looks like I'll have to wait to tell you what I'm thinking. Things are about to get started. Where's your seat?"

"Right up there," he said pointing to one of the tables that was near the stage on the other side of the room.

"Damn, we're nowhere near each other."

"Yeah, I know."

I sighed, hating that we were going to be so far apart. But I knew I would see him after, so I forced myself to be happy with that.

Placing my hand on Legend's chest, I kissed his lips. "I'll see you later."

His eyes widened. "Oh, so I'm getting kisses in public now?"

"Mmhmm."

"Okay," he said while nodding with appreciation. "I'm with it."

I smiled. "I figured you would be."

Before I turned to walk away, I could feel his hand brush against my ass, making me smile even harder.

When I made it over to the table, Nori was already comfortably seated. Leaning, she whispered into my ear. "Well, if you two were trying to be discreet about your little love affair, you failed tonight."

I rolled my eyes. "Stop being nosey."

"It's not being nosey when shit is made obvious."

"Whatever. Just focus on the stage. They're about to start."

Keke plopped down in the chair behind me and said, "Oh, wow, I wasn't expecting to be seated this close to you guys."

I eyed her with disgust. "Then why the hell are you?"

"Your guess is as good as mine."

"Whatever," I shot back. "I know you. If you're right here, it's because you wanted to be. What bullshit do you have up your sleeve tonight?"

"I don't know what you're talking about."

"Yeah, okay."

"But...um...since I'm here, how are you guys feeling about that footage of Owen? Pretty damn incriminating, huh?"

"It's exactly what his ass deserves. I hope like hell Nitra takes this as her cue to press charges against his ass." Turning around, I said, "How long have you had that footage anyway? I always knew you wouldn't have released that anonymous accusation on your blog unless you had some sort of evidence, but I wasn't willing to put myself through the headache of dealing with you to find out."

"Damn, that's cold," she replied. "Anyway, I haven't had it for that long. When I shared the accusation, I only had a piece of the evidence. It took some work to get the rest."

"I wonder if Nitra knows." I reached into my purse and pulled out my phone to pull up my texts.

It took me a minute to figure out what to send her. I couldn't imagine what it felt like to know that there was footage going around of the assault that so many had accused her of lying about.

After pondering over my thoughts for a few more seconds, I finally sent the text.

"Hey, have you seen the blogs about Owen?" –Simone

A few seconds passed, then a message came through.

"I have." –Nitra

"How are you feeling?" –Simone

"Honestly, I don't know how to feel. On one hand, I'm glad the truth is out there. But on the other, I'm mortified at what that truth looks like and everyone seeing it." –Nitra

"I threw up just from seeing the little bit that I saw." –Nitra

I closed my eyes, attempting to shove back the tears that were creeping to the surface.

"I'm so sorry. I know that had to be awful to see." –Simone

"It was. But I'm just glad that someone came forth with evidence. It was probably the only way anyone was going to believe me." –Nitra

"Yeah. Well, I just wanted to check on you. I'm currently at the Entertainment Excellence event for my mother." –Simone

"Okay. Thanks for checking on me. Oh and tell Ms. Regina I said congratulations." –Nitra

"I will." –Simone

"And before you ask, yes I'm going to make sure his ass goes to jail. I've already talked to my lawyer." –Nitra

Happy to see those words, I closed my eyes and smiled inwardly.

"I'm glad. Let me know if there's anything I can do. I got you." –Simone

"Will do. Thank you." –Nitra

"No problem." –Simone

Relieved, I closed out our texts and dropped my cell back into my purse.

"So, how is she?" Keke asked. "Is she going to the police?"

I sucked my teeth and turned my attention to the stage. "None of your damn business."

"Come on, Simone. This is a big deal. People should know how the victim feels now that she's been vindicated."

"Well, they'll have to ask her."

"Simone—"

"Shhh...someone is speaking." No longer interested in entertaining Keke with conversation, I gave my full attention to the host as she gave an introduction of who she was.

Shortly after, the woman smiled, then said, "Well, I won't bore you guys with too many details about myself. Let's get started. To start things off, here's a brief video of all our honorees tonight. Lower the lights please."

I glanced over at my mother as she sat at the honoree table that was in the center of the room. I couldn't have been prouder. This was a moment that my mother had dreamed of. When she started her management company, her goal was to help African American music artists get the representation they deserved in a tough business. Now, it was so much more. Not only did she work hard to represent those in music, but she worked hard to represent those in other parts of the entertainment industry as well. What was once a company of just *her* taking on clients became a company where she hired other talented managers to do the same, and she deserved every bit of the acknowledgment the city was giving her.

Still smiling, I returned my eyes to the screen, which had finally lit up, but what was showing had absolutely nothing to do with my mother. Instead, it was a clip of my backyard.

At first, I was confused.

What the hell is going on?

Then, when I saw the video switch to Legend standing in front of me and his boxers floating in the water behind him, I immediately knew.

Oh my God. This is from last night.

My eyes widened and I shot up from my chair. "Turn it off," I shouted. "Turn it off now!"

Suddenly, my vision became blurred. I could only hear the

commotion in the distance and gasps as the sounds of me moaning blasted through the speakers.

I stumbled away from the table, trying to get as far away from people as I could. But the journey to the exit seemed endless. I couldn't get there fast enough.

Why was this happening?

A million questions raced through my mind as I continued to rush toward the exit doors.

I could hear the bloggers questioning Legend as he tried to make his way to me.

"Is that you in the video?"

"Are the two of you together?"

"Who did this?"

I stopped to see what his response would be. But before he could say a word, Nori snatched me out of the room. "Let's go, sis."

33

LEGEND

Sitting at the edge of my bed, I stared at the third text that I'd sent to Simone since last night. She still hadn't replied, and I didn't understand why. Granted, I knew she was embarrassed by the video of us having sex being shown at the Entertainment Excellence event, and even more devastated that it was now all over the internet. But avoiding me wasn't the answer. I needed to know that she was okay.

Giving up on getting a response, I scrolled through my call logs so I could call Ms. Regina. But before I could make the call, my grandmother's name popped up on my phone.

"Hey, Grandmother," I answered. "Everything good?"

"I don't know. I feel like I should be asking *you* that question since I hear that your penis is being blasted all over the internet."

I dropped my head, then squeezed my eyes shut. "So, you heard, huh?"

"Mmhmm...I sure did. Now why are you going around making sex tapes? Is this some publicity thing? Are you under new management? Because this definitely doesn't seem like Ms. Regina's style."

"No, Grandma, it's not a publicity thing. I had nothing to do with that video."

"Hmm...you sure?"

"I'm positive."

"So how did it get out?"

"I have no idea."

"Did Simone record it?"

"I don't know. I haven't had a chance to talk to her."

"You haven't?" My grandmother replied. "Why not?"

"She's not answering my calls."

"Damn it, Legend, please tell me you didn't secretly record this woman and—"

"No, I would never."

"It's okay. You can tell me the truth. I won't judge you. Well, maybe a little bit. Because you have to be more careful about stuff like this. I know how men are. Y'all like to record your little sexcapades for your collection. Then, someone hacks your phone and—"

"Grandmother, I'm telling you I didn't do this."

There was a momentary pause...*damn, if my grandmother thought this way, did Simone?*

Shit.

"Okay, I believe you," my grandmother said. "I just had to check and be sure. I know damn well I raised you better than that."

"Yeah, you did. I would never disrespect a woman like that. I just can't believe you doubted me."

"I'm sorry. I just know all kinds of things go on in that crazy world you're in."

"Yeah, but that's not one of them. Not for me," I said. "But if you thought that way, then there's a huge chance that Simone does too, which may be why she's avoiding me."

"That's a strong possibility. Rosemary and Mildred seem to

think that it might have been you. They stopped by earlier today."

"What did you tell them?"

"I told them that my grandson wouldn't do that. Then I came right home and called you, hoping and praying that I was right."

I took a deep breath, then stood up.

This wasn't good at all. If a few old ladies were sitting around gossiping and questioning if I had anything to do with it, that meant that so were others.

"I need to go. I have some calls to make."

"Alright. Get this thing cleared up. I don't want you being dragged through the mud for all this nonsense."

"Neither do I," I replied. "I'll call you later. Love you."

"Love you too."

The line went dead, and I tossed my cell on the bed. "Fuck! If it isn't one damn thing it's another."

There was a knock at my bedroom door, then my assistant peeked in. "Hey, you have a visitor."

"Who?"

"Kendrick."

I sighed. "Send him in."

She nodded, then disappeared out of the doorway.

When Kendrick stepped into the room, he was all smiles. "Damn, bro, I didn't see the entire video, but you are definitely a lucky man."

Looking at him like he was crazy, I said, "Say something else like that and I'm going to make you get the fuck out."

"My bad. I was just paying you a compliment."

"Trust me, it isn't necessary. I don't need anyone telling me shit about my woman."

"Oh, so she's your woman now?"

I paused, then shook my head. "Never mind all that. Why are you here?"

"I was just coming through to check on things. How's Simone?"

"Hell, I don't know. She's not answering my calls."

"She's pissed at you, huh?"

I shrugged. "I don't know. Didn't I just tell your ass that she's not answering my calls? At first, I thought it was because she was embarrassed. But after talking to my grandmother, I'm wondering if it's because she thinks I had something to do with the video?"

"Well, did you?"

"Hell no! I don't do that recording shit."

Kendrick jerked his head back. "Really? Never?"

"Never!"

"Damn, you're missing out. It's pretty amazing to look back at. Not only that, you get to see just how well you performed."

I frowned. "I don't need to see how well I performed. I know my skills."

"I mean, yeah, but—"

"You know what? I'm done talking about this shit with you." I turned away from him, and then something crossed my mind, prompting me to look back in his direction. "Do the women you record know that you're recording them?"

"Oh, most definitely. I always get the woman's permission and make sure she's down with it. I'm not trying to get caught up in no mess."

Although I still didn't like what he was saying, at least I knew that he wasn't being a complete idiot. "Hmm...okay."

"I'm serious. Now, I do know a few niggas that don't give a damn if the chick is down for it or not. They record anyway and have whole parties showing the shit. You wouldn't believe how many women I've crossed paths with and recognized them from one of the videos."

I looked him over with disgust. "Are you serious?"

"Hell yeah. It's crazy."

"So, you're telling me you've seen these videos for yourself?"

Smiling, he shrugged. "I mean...it's no different from watching porn, right?"

"It's definitely different. The people in porn videos have agreed to have themselves recorded and are making money off the shit."

"Not always."

"Man, whatever."

He shrugged. "I'm just saying."

"Do me a favor and don't say shit else. Matter of fact, just leave. You being here is just making my day worse."

"Damn, for real."

"Yeah." I stood in place, waiting for him to turn around and walk out. When he didn't, I took a step forward. "Do you need me to escort your ass out?"

He lifted his hands. "Nah, I'm good. Looks like you need some time to cool off."

"Kendrick, please get the fuck out before I break your neck."

"Alright, alright. I'm going."

I didn't say anything else. I just watched as he strolled out of the room.

Still, my brain was reeling from the things he'd just told me, and the fact that he didn't see anything wrong with it. But I shouldn't have been surprised. Kendrick was known for playing close to the line that shouldn't be crossed when it came to disrespecting women. More and more, I was questioning if our friendship was worth holding on to. But it wasn't an easy decision to make. I'd already cut Teddy off for his bullshit behavior. I wasn't ready to lose another one of my childhood friends.

Feeling overwhelmed, I walked into the bathroom and turned on the shower. I needed to relax. Maybe after a hot shower and a few hours in the tranquility room, I would have a better mindset and know what to do next.

34

SIMONE

"Fresh pancakes coming right up," my mother said as she walked over to my dining room table carrying a plate with a stack of pancakes that almost touched her chin.

Nori rubbed her hands together. "Mmm...I can't wait to dig in. I'm starving. Did you bring the butter too?"

"No, but you can get your lazy behind up and grab some."

Nori frowned, then pushed her chair back from the table and strolled over to the refrigerator.

As grateful as I was for my family staying with me after last night's craziness, a part of me wanted to be alone. I needed time to think and understand how something like this even happened. Especially since my mother's security team didn't find any hidden cameras around my home. The only thing that made sense was that someone planted the camera and came back for it later.

Just the thought made me cringe. Granted, I knew I'd always talked about doing wild things when it came to sex, but not like this. This was completely out of my control, and it wasn't my choice.

"You want regular syrup or strawberry?" my mother asked.

"Regular," I replied as I pulled on the drawstring to tighten my hooded jacket.

"Simone, you're inside. You don't have to hide yourself."

"Yeah, I'm inside, but I can hear the people outside waiting for me to come out so they can take pictures and ask me a million embarrassing questions," I said. "Just my luck, someone is at one of the windows trying to see through the damn blinds."

"Well, if they are, I'll be more than happy to remind them of why they should have stayed their ass on the curb." She nodded toward her purse, reminding me of the gun she always kept nearby.

"See, and that's what I don't want," I said.

Returning to the table, Nori sat down in the chair across from me. "What did I miss? What don't you want?"

"For Mama to go crazy and start shooting some random paparazzi person for trying to peek through the window."

"Oh, yeah." my sister shook her head. "We definitely don't want that. I'm not trying to make any prison visits."

My mother jerked her head back and then sat down next to me. "Prison visits? No ma'am. It would be considered self-defense. This is private property."

Waving my hand, I said, "Can we stop talking about shooting people? I'm already on edge from last night."

My mother nodded. "Sorry."

"Yeah, sorry, sis."

"It's okay," I replied.

"So...um...have you talked to Legend?" Nori asked.

"No. He's called, but I haven't answered."

My mother looked me over in confusion. "Why not?"

"Honestly, I don't know."

"You don't know?" Nori frowned. "Wait...you're not blaming him for all this, are you?"

"No, of course not. Well, I don't think I am."

"Hmm...I don't know, Simone. It sounds like you are, and if that's the case, I don't think it's fair."

"Look, I know that. But right now, it's kind of hard for me to focus on someone else while my titties and God only knows what else is the hot topic of the internet."

"Don't worry about that," my mother said. "I've been on the phone since last night working on getting the video pulled from the blogs."

Nori scoffed while cutting into her pancakes. "You can have it taken down from the blogs all you want, but it's still going to be all over the internet. Once stuff like that hits the web, it's there for life. Even when you think it's not."

"Knock, knock," Riah said as she stepped inside my house. "Did you guys know the front door was unlocked?"

My eyes widened as I looked between my mother and Nori. "Who left it unlocked?"

"Oops," Nori said. "My bad."

"Really? You want one of those crazy ass people to come into my home?"

"No, of course not. I went out to grab something from my car and I guess I just forgot when I came back in."

Feeling my insides fuming, I stood up, but Riah held up her hands to stop me. "It's fine. I made sure it was locked. No one else is coming in."

"You sure?"

"I'm positive," she replied before making her way into the kitchen and pulling out a chair. "I'm pretty sure I already know the answer to this, but how are you doing?"

"Terrible," I replied a little hesitant to say anymore since I should've been asking her the same question.

Sensing what I was thinking, Riah said, "I'm fine. Now, let's not make this about me today. Keep talking."

Too defeated to go back and forth, I accepted her statement

and continued with what I was saying. "I was just telling Mama and Nori how I have no clue how many of my body parts are all over the internet since I haven't seen the full video."

"Well, it's just your titties and ass, which looked amazing. You two definitely gave the world a show."

"You watched the whole thing?"

"Not necessarily. But I will say that a lot happened in the beginning. Kudos to you two for getting the right angles."

"No, there's no kudos to us. I had nothing to do with this video."

"Oh..." she paused for a moment, then tilted her head to the side. "So, this wasn't some fun and games thing the two of you recorded that ended up getting leaked by mistake?"

"No, it wasn't. I had no idea that a video existed."

Confused, Riah said, "Well, if you guys didn't make the video, who did?"

Before anyone could respond, my mother's cell rang.

"Excuse me," she said and stepped away from the table.

Leaning back in her chair, Riah folded her arms over her chest. "So, I do have to ask...what exactly was the status of you and Legend's relationship when this went down? Because from the looks of things, it looked like you two were making love instead of just fucking. I mean, there were a few moments of fucking, but—"

"Riah, I thought you said you didn't watch the whole thing?" I interrupted.

"I didn't. But it was pretty long. I'm sure I stopped before making it to the end though."

Nori frowned. "You know that's messed up, right? How do you watch a sex tape of your sister?"

"Look, when I come to Simone's defense, I need to know what I'm defending. I can't do that unless I know the facts."

"Whatever," I said while rolling my eyes. "To answer your

question, things between Legend and I were pretty intense by that point. We'd just had a conversation about taking things to the next level, which was beyond sex."

"Oh, really?"

"Yes." Suddenly hit with something that hadn't even crossed my mind until this very moment, I said, "What if this was one of Teddy's antics?"

"What do you mean?" Riah questioned.

"What if he had someone record us and purposely made sure that it was shown at the event because he knew that it would hurt me, which would then hurt Legend?"

Nori frowned. "You really think Teddy would do something like that?"

"Why wouldn't he? You saw what he did to his baby mama while trying to stick it to Legend."

"Yeah, but this is a bit extreme."

"It is," I said. "But when has that ever stopped Teddy before?"

Riah shrugged. "She has a point."

Returning to the kitchen, my mother let out a deep sigh, and then said, "I just got off the phone with one of my assistants. She said that Owen was arrested this morning."

My eyes shot over to Riah.

She remained still, closed her eyes for a moment, then opened them again. "Good."

"Are you okay?" my mother asked.

"I'm fine."

She was saying the words, but I knew they weren't real. What woman would be fine after learning that her husband was a rapist?

"Well, just know that we're here for you," Nori said, "and you don't have to play strong for us. We know it hurts."

"I'm fine. Really?"

"No, you're not." I blurted. "How could you be? This is someone that you loved and that you stood by repeatedly. He went out and did whatever he wanted to do with no regard for his family. You have the right to be angry. You have the right to be sad."

"Yeah, well, right now I'm just numb," she spat. "I don't feel anything at all. Will that change at some point? Probably so. But for now, I feel empty, and I would really like to stop talking about it."

I could hear the hurt in her voice, which pained me deep in my soul. Not wanting to cause any further damage, I nodded and said, "Understood. Just know that I'm here to talk if you need me."

"Thank you," she replied. "Oh, but before we shut the conversation down, I do want to apologize for the way I treated you." She lowered her gaze. "You were right for feeling the way that you felt when it came to him. Hell, deep down, I had my doubts too, but I didn't want to believe it. Not after everything he promised me, and the life we'd planned together. It just wasn't fair."

"No, it wasn't fair," I said as I grabbed both of her hands. "It wasn't fair to you, and you deserve so much better." I stood up and pulled her into my arms. "At the end of the day, you did what you felt was right. You stuck by your man until the evidence proved that you couldn't. Now, you just have to learn from your mistakes and move on."

"Well, I've definitely learned from this disastrous mess. I'm done trusting men."

Leaning forward, Nori said, "So, wait...does that mean you're going to start messing with women?"

Riah's eyes widened. "Hell no! Don't get me wrong, I love to look at women, and I even might play around a little bit for fun. But a relationship? Nah, that's never going to happen," she said.

"I'm just saying that I'm taking a break and focusing on myself for a while. With everything that's going on now, I have a long road ahead of me, and I've got to prepare myself for that."

Nori stood up and moved toward us. "Well, just remember that you don't have to go through this thing alone."

"That's right," I said. "We're family, which means we will forever have each other's back."

Smiling, we wrapped our arms around each other.

"Um...I hate to break this sisterly moment up," Mama said as she held up her cell and looked at me. "Someone wants to talk to you."

Eyeing her in confusion, I said, "Me?"

"Yep."

"Who is it?"

"Legend."

35

LEGEND

I paced back and forth in my living room.

I wasn't too thrilled when Ms. Regina told me that Simone needed a minute and would call me back. I just wanted to jump through the phone and shake her. I needed Simone to listen to me and understand that I would never do anything to hurt her. But instead, I held back, swallowed my pride, and told Ms. Regina that I would be waiting for her call.

Twenty minutes had passed since I was given that excuse. I was tempted to call back, but I knew that wouldn't get me anywhere. The last thing I wanted to do was apply too much pressure. I didn't want to lose Simone, which meant I had to give her the time that she was requesting.

"Hey, Teddy's at the gate," Mya said as she stood in the middle of the living room floor.

"Who?" I replied, convinced that I'd heard her wrong.

"Teddy."

I let out a light chuckle. "You can tell him to turn back around. He's not welcome here."

She nodded, then returned her cell to her ear to relay the message.

Teddy was the last person I wanted to deal with right now.

"Legend," Mya spoke again while placing her cell against her chest. "He says that he knows you don't want to see him, but it's important, and he would really like to come inside and talk."

"*Talk?*" I shot my assistant a stern glare. "Why are you telling me this? I already gave you my answer."

"I know, sir, but he seems pretty adamant and—"

Dropping my shoulders, I shook my head. "You know what? Just let him in. Let's get this shit over with."

"Okay." She turned away from me and did as I asked.

I slid my hand down my face. *Whatever you do, don't let this fool get under your skin,* I told myself. *You have enough on your plate as it is.*

I closed my eyes, then breathed in and out slowly.

It wasn't long before Teddy walked inside and stood in front of my door just a few feet away from me. "Hey. Thanks for allowing me to come in. I know you're not feeling me right now."

"You're right, I'm not. Why are you here?" I shoved my hands into my pants pockets and looked him over sternly.

"So...um...I'm sure you heard the news about the paternity test results, huh?"

"Actually, I haven't. I've been dealing with my own shit these days."

Nodding he said, "Oh...yeah...right, the sex tape. How are things with that? How's Simone?"

"I'm good. But that's none of your concern. What's up? What does the paternity results have to do with me?"

He cleared his throat, then shrugged. "Nothing, really. Just thought you would be happy to know that I'm the father."

Looking at him like he was crazy, I shook my head. "But we all knew that though. Even you knew that. You just wanted to do stupid shit to get under Eden's skin." I clapped my hands together. "Bravo...you definitely did that shit."

"Look, I just wanted to make sure that everything was on the up and up. I wasn't feeling the way she'd been moving lately."

Waving him off, I said, "But why would you bring me into that shit? Not once have I ever been disloyal to you. There was no reason for you to imply some bullshit that you knew wasn't true all because you were in your feelings or drunk as hell."

"I wasn't drunk. I'd only had a few drinks when—"

"Bro, with you, that's all it takes. You're an alcoholic, Teddy. That's what alcoholics do."

Moving toward me as his nose flared. "I'm not a fucking alcoholic."

"Yes, you are, and until you get some help, I'm done fooling with you. You're not about to keep putting me in bad situations."

"Damn, for real? It's like that?"

"Yep. It's like that."

"But what about the festival? What about our fans?"

"I already told you where I stand when it comes to the festival. I love our fans, but—"

"What if I agree to get help? Would you do it?"

I tilted my head to the side trying to see if he was serious. The show was right around the corner, which meant he could easily agree to it today and say that he changed his mind once the festival was over. But a part of me didn't want to believe that he would do that, and an even bigger part of me wanted to believe that this would be the push that he needed to get some help.

Feeling optimistic, I said, "I would."

"Really?"

"Yeah. I mean, I'm pissed at you. But that doesn't change the fact that I want you to be okay."

A flicker of hope twinkled in his eyes. "Would you consider continuing the group too?"

I shook my head. "I can't do that. I know you don't believe it, but I really think it's time for us to move on. There's so much more out here for us."

"You mean for you," he blurted.

"Teddy—"

"Nah, man, it's cool. I'll figure my shit out. But first, I'm going to get myself together. You know how I feel about my fans. I can't let us go out without giving them what they deserve."

I lifted my shoulders. "Hey, I feel you on that."

"So, are we good?"

I shrugged. "Look, as long as you do what you're supposed to do we'll be good."

"Shit, at this point, I really don't have a choice. Eden's threatening to file for full custody and talking about leaving the damn state if I don't get it together."

"Oh, damn."

"Yeah, I think she's fed up with my ass for real this time."

"As she should be. You've put that woman through hell."

"Yeah, I know."

My cell rang.

It was Simone.

"Oh, shit," I said as I looked up at Teddy. "I've got to take this. Mya will see you out."

I didn't stick around to hear his response. Instead, I made my way up the stairs and hurried to answer the call. "Simone, hey."

"Hey. You wanted to talk?"

"Yeah, I did. I was kind of hoping you would let me come over so we could have this conversation face-to-face."

She sighed. "Well, given what's going on outside of my front door, I don't think that's going to happen today."

"Wow, it's that bad, huh?"

"Yes, and unlike you, I don't have a house out in the middle of nowhere with a security gate and guards to keep people out."

"Well, you know I don't mind sending someone over there to make sure you're safe. Just say the word."

"No, it's fine," she replied.

There was a moment of silence, which gave me some time to contemplate what I was about to say next.

Taking a deep breath, I said, "So, I want to say this, and I hope like hell you believe me."

"What?"

"I had nothing to do with recording or leaking that video of us. I would never disrespect you like that."

"Legend, I know that. What would even make you think that I would've blamed you for this?"

I shrugged. "My grandmother asked me if I did it, and that was because her friends asked her, which then made me wonder if you thought the same."

"Well, no, I didn't. But something else did cross my mind."

"Okay...what?"

"Teddy," she replied. "Do you think he could've done this?"

Surprised, I shook my head. "That hadn't even crossed my mind."

"Yeah, I know. But seeing as he's been so determined to get back at you, it somewhat makes sense."

"I don't know, Simone. I just saw him, and he didn't give me that vibe."

"Okay, fine," she said in frustration. "Well, if he didn't, who the hell did?"

"I don't know. What about Keke?"

"I've thought about that. But what would be her motive?"

"Hell, what was anybody's motive?"

Simone let out a loud groan. "I don't know, Legend. All I know is no one gave a damn about me until they saw me with you."

Confused, I said, "So...wait...you *are* blaming me?"

She let out a deep sigh, then fell silent.

I waited patiently, wanting to hear that I was wrong.

But when she finally spoke again, all she said was, "I...I should go."

"Simone don't shut me out. If you and I are going to take things to the next level—"

"Maybe taking things to the next level isn't such a good idea," she interrupted.

"What? You don't mean that."

"But I do. At least for now. There's too much going on."

"I get that. But I don't think we should put things on hold between us. If you need some time, I'll give you that. Just don't—"

"I can't talk about this anymore. I have to go. Bye, Legend."

36

SIMONE

I sat at my desk, staring at the bouquet of red roses. They were beautiful, and they smelled just as fresh as the others. It had been five days since I told Legend that we should take a break from each other, and every day he made sure to send roses to my office with a card letting me know how much he valued me, loved me, and that no matter how long it took, he would wait for me.

"Knock, knock," Nori said as she stepped into my office all dolled up.

"Hey." I stood up and walked around to hug her. "You look extra pretty. What have you been up to?"

"Nothing much. I just came from my meetup with the matchmakers. They were taking pictures, so I had to make sure I was cute."

"Oh okay. Well, like always, I hope everything works out."

"Girl, me too. I'm ready to find my husband and have a bunch of little Nori's running around."

Lifting my shoulders, I said, "I still think you should consider just going on a regular date with a regular guy?"

"Is Legend just a regular guy?"

This time I rolled my eyes. "First of all, that's not even a fair question. I didn't go looking for Legend. We kind of just fell into each other's lap."

"Mmhmm...y'all did a lot more than that, honey."

"Seriously, Nori?"

She laughed. "What? Too soon?"

"Yeah, way too soon."

"Okay, my bad. But speaking of Legend, have you changed your mind about things yet?"

"No, I haven't. I still think we need to be apart for a while. Hell, maybe forever."

She lifted her hand. "Okay, I've tried to give you space to deal with this whole situation. But your silly ass way of thinking has got me confused as hell. How long are you going to punish him for this?"

"I'm not trying to punish him."

"Well, that's exactly what you're doing," she replied. "And I think it's all bullshit, so tell me what's really going on."

"Nothing's going on."

"Yes, it is, and you need to tell me what it is right now. What's got you treating him like this?"

Unable to hold back what was consuming my thoughts, I blurted, "What if this whole situation is just a sign?"

"A sign? For what?"

"That Legend and I shouldn't be together. I mean, at first, I was just really overwhelmed by the sex tape situation. But now that I've had some time to think about things, I've come back to the conclusion that I had all along...it's too soon for me to be getting involved with someone else right now."

"You can't be serious."

"Yes, I'm very serious. My energy shouldn't be focused on someone new. I should be focused on myself, so I don't make the same mistake that I made before," I said. "For years, I thought I was with someone who loved me unconditionally, and I thought we were on the same page. But we weren't."

"First of all, you're trying to compare a relationship that started as teenagers to a relationship that's building as adults. No matter how you try to slice it, they're nothing alike. Your teenage mind is nowhere near what it is today, and the same goes for Wiz. The two of you were together when everything was all butterflies and rainbows." She placed her hand on my shoulder. "Despite what people want to think, puppy love is really a thing, and I think that's exactly what the two of you had. But what you have with Legend is so far from that. It's a bond that stemmed from a friendship and that has been nurtured over the years. I don't think there's any doubt about what either of you wants. Now, you just have to trust it, and shut up about all of that other shit."

I jerked my head back and looked her over. "Damn little sis, tell me how you really feel, huh?"

"I sure will, and your ass better listen too."

I glanced at my cell to look at the time. "Shoot, I need to get going. I'm supposed to be meeting up with Keke for lunch."

"Meeting up with Keke? Why?"

"I just want to make sure I've ruled out every possible person that may have had something to do with this sex tape thing. I don't think it was her, but she might be able to find out who did," I said. "We're meeting at one of the restaurants in Mama's office building. You want to come?"

"I would, but I've got a meeting to get to."

I grabbed my purse from my desk and followed her out of my office. "Well, I'll catch up with you later. Love you."

"Love you too. Oh, and call me later and let me know how things go."

"Will do." I watched her as she walked out of the spa, then

turned my attention to Asana. "I'm heading out for a meeting. If you need me, call me on my cell."

"Sure thing," she replied. "Oh, and it's still a few paparazzi out there, but not as many as before."

"Okay. Cool." I stepped out the door and motioned for the guard to walk me to my car.

The few people who were standing outside bombarded me with the same questions that everyone had been trying to get the answers to since the video leaked. But I just shoved my shades over my eyes, hopped in my car, and sped out of the parking lot.

It didn't take long for me to make it to Ballman Towers, and like always, the paparazzi were outside waiting to catch a glimpse of whatever celebrity was walking in and out of the building. I hurried inside, drowning out their words like I'd done to the others.

I hopped on the elevator and rode it to the thirty-fifth floor. Sizzle and Smoke Bar and Grill was one of my favorite restaurants in Ballman Towers. Not only did they have the best nachos, but their frozen margaritas never disappointed. They were huge and they always got the job done.

"Good afternoon, Ms. Baltimore," a young woman greeted while shooting me a sweet smile and grabbing a menu from behind the podium. "How many will be dining with us today?"

"Actually, I'm meeting someone here. I'm not sure if she's arrived or not." I glanced around for a few seconds before finally seeing Keke tucked away in a booth just a few feet away. "There she is right there."

"Alright," the host replied. "Right this way."

Smiling, I nodded, then followed her to the booth and sat down. "Thank you."

"No problem. Your server should be with you shortly," she said before tapping the table and walking away.

Leaning back, Keke sat her phone down on the table. "Well, I must say that I was surprised when you asked me to meet you for lunch. What's this about?"

"First off, this is completely off the record, so you better not be recording me on that thing."

"I'm not."

"You sure about that?" I picked up her cell and tapped on the screen to see if there was any sign of anything being recorded.

She chuckled. "Damn, is my word not good enough?"

"Given everything I've been going through...no it isn't."

She nodded. "You know what? Fair enough. I'm pretty sure that sex tape has you on edge. Never expected to see that."

"Yeah, and since we're on the subject, I'm just going to cut to the chase. Did you put a camera in my backyard?"

She closed her eyes and then opened them again. "What?"

"Look—"

"No, you look," she shot back. "I've been seen as the villain for years, and I've let it ride. But this, this is where I draw the line. I would never do some shit like that to you, and I damn sure wouldn't put it out for the world to see. I have more class than that."

I stared at her for a moment, making sure her words were true. Dropping my shoulders, I sighed. "Okay...I didn't think that you did."

"Then why ask me?"

"Because I needed to be sure," I said. "But what I really wanted to ask you was if you'd heard anything from some of the other bloggers? I know you guys run in the same circles, and I know a lot of you talk. Has anyone mentioned anything?"

"Anything like what?"

"About putting a camera in my backyard or sneaking around my house...*anything*?"

She shook her head. "No, I haven't."

"Okay, well, seeing as you know how to get information. Maybe you could try to find out for me."

She shrugged. "I mean, I can do a little digging. But what makes you so sure that it was someone from the media? This looks like this was done maliciously. No blogger has a reason to do anything like that to you or Legend."

"Yeah, but—"

"You know, there was a lot of talk about how pissed off Riah was about you keeping that girl working for you. Have you ever considered that maybe she had something to do with this? Maybe she wanted to embarrass you the same way she felt like you were embarrassing her."

"Embarrassing her?"

"Yeah, by not having her back and taking your assistant's side over hers."

I jerked my head back with disgust. "What? No. There's no way my sister would do something like this?"

"Are you sure about that?"

"I'm positive, and I would appreciate it if you would stop trying to point the finger at her. I know my flesh and blood."

Keke shrugged. "Okay. I was just trying to help."

"Yeah, well, that's not it, so you can stop trying now."

"Will do."

Finally making it to our table, the male server pulled a pen from his apron. "Are you ladies ready to order?"

"Actually, I'm about to head out," I said as I stood up.

"Damn, you're leaving already?" Keke questioned. "I thought we were having lunch."

"*You* can have lunch. I have something I need to do." I turned away and strolled out of the restaurant.

Thankfully, my mother's office was just a couple of floors down. She was just the person I needed to talk to.

The more I thought about what Keke said, the more I

thought about how pissed Riah was with me for taking Nitra's side. Not to mention, her reaction to the sex tape was pretty weird. She was acting like it wasn't a big deal. Maybe there was a bigger reason for that...one that hadn't crossed my mind at all.

Damn, did Riah do this shit to me?

37

LEGEND

"How are you feeling?" Ms. Regina asked as she stood in front of the mini bar that sat in the corner of her office pouring herself a drink. "I know it's been pretty tough these days. Have you talked to Simone?"

"Nah, not since the day I asked you to put her on the phone."

"Oh, wow, that's been a few days."

"Yeah, I know. But when I did talk to her, she made it clear that she needed some space, and she didn't know how long she was going to need it," I said.

"I see, and how do you feel about that."

I leaned back in my chair as I watched her take a seat behind her desk. "I'm not thrilled about it. But I also know that I have to respect her wishes. I just hope she doesn't get so caught up in her mind that she ends up changing her mind about us."

"I hope she doesn't either. I like you two together. I think you make her truly happy."

"Thanks."

"I will say this...I know my daughter very well." Ms. Regina took a sip from her glass and then shook her head. "When she gets overwhelmed, she shuts down and it's hard to get through to her. Between all of the craziness with Wiz and having to deal with the world chiming in on her having sex with you...I know she wants to climb into a hole and stay away from everyone."

"I can understand why she might feel that way. But I'm the last person she needs to run away from. I've got her back just like she's always had mine," I said. "In fact, I'm a little surprised by her response to things since she's always been so quick to help me when I've been at my worst."

"Oh, it's easy for her to be there for others. But when it comes to herself, she struggles. But hopefully, she'll let you back in and you can help her through all of this."

I nodded. "I hope so too. Oh, did she tell you that I mentioned Keke as potentially having something to do with things?"

"Yeah, she did. Speaking of Keke, she's meeting with her for lunch today." Ms. Regina glanced down at her watch. "They should be at Sizzle and Smoke right now."

"Oh, really?"

"Yep. I'm interested to hear how that conversation goes. I'm hoping I don't get a phone call from security asking me to come up there and pull Simone off of her."

"Damn." I scooted forward. "Do you think we should go up there?"

Ms. Regina shrugged. "If I don't hear from her soon, maybe. But for now, let's talk about the festival. How have rehearsals been?"

"Surprisingly, rehearsals have been pretty smooth."

"Good. So, has Teddy been on his best behavior?"

"He has. In fact, at our last rehearsal, he showed me the rehab facility he's planning to go to after the festival."

She smiled. "Okay, good. I'm happy to hear that."

"Yeah, me too. I hope he follows through. I want to see him get better."

"Trust me, we all do."

Feeling my cell vibrating, I pulled it from my pants pocket. "Oh, this is my grandmother. You mind if I step out for a sec?"

"No problem. I've got a few calls to make anyway."

"Cool." I hurried out of the office and answered the call. "Hey, Grandmother. You good?"

"Well, yes and no."

"What's wrong?"

"The knob on my damn bathroom door fell off again. I've called the people to come by and fix it, but it's taking too long. Do you think you have time to do it for me?"

"Um...yeah."

As soon as I said those words, I saw Simone walk off the elevator. She was focused on her phone, so she didn't see me.

Like always, she was effortlessly beautiful, which made me eager to think of the right thing to say to her. But I couldn't. Instead, I just continued to stare, then cleared my throat once she was close enough to hear me.

Noticing that I was on the phone, she gave me a brief smile and waved.

Grateful for the little bit of interaction, I greeted her with the same gesture, then opened the door for her to go into her mother's office.

"Thank you," she said.

"You're welcome." My eyes lingered on her for several seconds, then I forced my attention back to my phone call.

"Legend, did you hear what I just said?" my grandmother questioned.

"Oh, um...no. I'm sorry. Repeat it for me?"

"I said that I think the lock on my front door needs to be changed too. Some of the ladies said they saw some young folks lingering around here. They think they might be trying to break into places."

"What?"

"Mmhmm."

"Well, have there been any break-ins?"

"No, but I want to be sure no one gets in here."

"Grandmother, the locks you have on your door are good. I also check your security cameras regularly and make sure nothing fishy is going on over there."

"Yeah, I know. But it would just make me feel better if I had fresh locks. These things are old."

"Well, you wouldn't have to worry about any of that if you would move in with me. I have tons of space and—"

"Nope," she interjected. "Not doing it. Just get me new locks Legend. You never know, someone who lived here before may still have their key. Oh, and while we're talking about you checking up on me...no one else has access to these fancy video cameras that you have around here, do they? You know I like to walk around naked."

I frowned. "Grandmother...please."

"What? I'm asking a legitimate question."

I paused, my mind quickly jumping to Simone and all the cameras she had around her house.

"Um...let me call you back," I said. "I need to take care of something."

"Okay. Just don't forget about these locks. I want them done today."

Nodding, I said, "I'll get it taken care of."

"Thank you."

The line went dead, and I rushed into Ms. Regina's office and looked at Simone. "Sorry to interrupt, but I have a question."

She looked me over with a lifted brow. "Okay. What's up?"

"You have security cameras inside and outside of your home, right?"

"Yeah."

"And you can look at your camera footage through an app, right?"

Eyeing me in confusion, she lifted her shoulders. "Yeah, Legend, what are you getting at? You think someone hacked into my security cameras or something?"

"Well, that depends...does Wiz still have access to the app as well."

Realizing what I was getting at, her eyes widened, and she slammed her hand against her mouth. "Oh my God. He does." She stood up from her chair slowly. "Are you telling me that Wiz has been watching me this whole time?"

"It's a strong possibility, and if I'm right, I'm pretty sure he's the one that got that footage of us in the backyard and leaked it."

"Damn!" Ms. Regina replied. "I can't believe this didn't cross my mind sooner."

"Yeah, I can't believe I didn't think of it either," I said. "I was so damn worried about Simone getting the locks changed that I completely forgot about all the other shit that fool could still have access to."

Shaking her head, Simone paced the floor. "I don't believe this. How could he do this to me?"

"I don't know," I shot back. "But I'm damn sure about to find out."

Simone stopped. "Wait a minute. Where are you going?"

"To get some answers."

The concern on her face was evident as she gripped tightly at her sides trying to process my response. But I didn't have time to put her mind at ease, and given what I had on my mind, I couldn't, even if I tried.

Strolling out of the office, I looked through my phone until I got to Kendrick's number.

He answered on the second ring. "Hey, bro. What's up?"

"I need you to do me a favor."

"Sure thing. What do you need?"

"Find out where Wiz is. I need to pay his ass a visit."

38

SIMONE

"Can't you go a little faster?" I told my mom as she weaved through traffic while trying to keep up with Legend.

He was several cars ahead of us, and his foot was definitely on the gas.

"If I go any faster, we're going to be wrapped around a tree," she spat. "Is that your objective this afternoon?"

I dropped my shoulders and fell back against the seat. "No, it's not. I just don't want Legend to do something that's going to land his ass in jail."

"Oh, trust me, I feel the same way. If it turns out that Wiz was the one behind all of this, the outcome of their conversation isn't going to be pretty."

"I know." I sighed. "But just the thought of Wiz being behind this is—"

"Sickening," my mother replied. "But it's not surprising at all. He's made it clear that he's not happy about the breakup."

"Yeah, but to stoop to this level? That's insane. I would never do something like this to him, and after all the years we spent together, I wouldn't think that he would want to do this to me either." I looked straight ahead. "Mama, Legend just turned."

"Yeah, I know. It looks like he's pulling into Fit Focus."

My eyes widened. "There's no way we can let him go into the damn fitness center. The last thing we need is him beating Wiz's ass with some weights."

"Don't worry. We won't."

We hurried into the parking lot.

As soon as my mother pulled into a space, I hopped out of the car and met Legend at his.

Noticing he was on a call, I remained still until he was finished, then tapped on his window, and said, "Legend, please leave."

"Simone, what are you doing here?"

"Trying to stop you."

"Well, you're wasting your time." He stepped out of the car and closed the door behind him.

I placed my hand against his chest to stop him. "You can't do this."

"Why the hell not? I should've beat his ass a long time ago."

"Legend—"

"Well, well, well, look at what we have here," Wiz said as he stepped out of the building, a smug grin plastered on his face. He dropped his gym bag and folded his arms over his chest. "A little birdy told me that one of your boys was calling around looking for me. Is that right?"

Returning the same grin, Legend lifted his head and shoved his hands into his pockets. "Yeah, motherfucker, we're looking for you."

"Okay, well, what can I help you with?"

Before Legend could respond, I stepped in front of him and turned to look Wiz in the eyes. "Did you leak that video of me and Legend?"

He tilted his head to the side. "Now what would make you think that?"

"Because you're the only other person that has access to my security cameras, and you've been on some bullshit since we broke up."

"Well, that's kind of what happens when you find out that the woman you've been with for years cheated on you."

My nostrils flared as I moved closer to him. "For the last fucking time...I didn't cheat on you. I did what we both agreed on."

"If that's what helps you sleep at night, then go right ahead and keep telling yourself that. But we both know the truth."

"Man, fuck this shit," Legend said as he forced himself around me and into Wiz's face. "Did your punk ass leak the fucking video or not?"

He shrugged. "What if I did? What are you going to do about it?"

Not giving it a second thought, Legend took his fist and smashed it into his face. Wiz stumbled back but quickly recovered and met him with a right hook of his own. But the exchange didn't seem to faze Legend.

Laughing, Legend slid the back of his hand over his mouth. "You punch like a bitch," he shouted. "If you're planning to take me out, you're going to have to come a lot harder than that."

"Stop it!" My mother called out while looking around to make sure no one was seeing what was going on.

But her words fell on deaf ears.

The fight was on, and given how hard they were going, someone was sure to walk out any minute.

Circling each other, they traded blow after blow. Blood dripped from a cut on Wiz's forehead, and bruises began to form on his face. The sound of the scuffle echoed through the lot as they both refused to back down.

Finally, Legend landed a hard punch, knocking Wiz to the ground.

A loud thud echoed against the pavement, prompting me to flinch.

Wiz didn't move, which I was thankful for. I needed this shit to be over.

But just as I let out a sigh of relief, Legend walked over to Wiz and lifted him from the ground by his shirt. "Bitch ass nigga, I hope you learned your lesson. Don't fuck with me, and don't fuck with Simone. Don't call her, don't text her...matter of fact, make today the last day you even think about her. If I find out that you've done otherwise, I'm going to come find your ass and remind you why you shouldn't have. Do I make myself clear?"

If Wiz responded, I definitely couldn't hear him, thanks to Kendrick speeding into the parking lot. He jumped out of the car and rushed over to Legend. "Damn! You fucked his ass up."

"Kendrick," I scolded. "You're not helping."

"My bad." He grabbed Legend, which prompted him to let Wiz fall to the ground. Still dumbfounded by the damage that had been done, he looked at Legend and said, "Come on, man. We need to get out of here before someone sees this shit."

"Yes, please," I said. "And where the hell is Cade?"

"Taking a break like I told him to," Legend said.

"A break? Are you serious?"

"Yep. I needed to take care of this shit without any interruptions."

Barely holding his head up, Wiz spit out blood, then looked at Legend. "Nigga fuck you. You can have her ass."

"Really?" I spat, disgusted by his lack of remorse. "Ten years and that's what you have to say?"

"Man, whatever. I knew we weren't right for each other anymore. I should've just moved the fuck on."

"Wow, you're unbelievable. You still think you're justified for the shit you pulled." Overwhelmed with anger and frustration, I clenched my fist and struck him as hard as I could, causing him to fall back one last time.

"What the fuck?" he shouted.

"Trust me, you deserve that and so much more," I told him. "Oh, and I hope when you saw that video of me having sex with Legend, it made your insides burn. I hope you saw every moment...and just in case you missed anything, let me fill you in. He does everything to me that you never did. He licks every part of my pussy like it's candy land, and he plays with it like it's all his." Tilting my head to the side, I let out a little giggle. "Shit, now that I think about it, it is all his, and after the way he beat your ass, I'm going to go ride his dick all night just to thank him." Smiling, I shot Wiz a wink and stuck up my middle finger.

I could see the venom spewing from his eyes, which gave me instant satisfaction. Although he hadn't outright admitted that he was the one behind the video, I knew it was him.

Disgusted by the sight of him, I shoved back the urge to give him another meeting with my fist. Instead, I made my way to Legend's car. He sat in the passenger seat while my mother and Kendrick stood near him.

"You okay?" my mother asked as she pressed her hands against my cheek.

"I'm fine."

"You sure?"

"Yeah. I just want to get out of here."

"Okay," she replied. "I'll take you home."

Standing, Legend said, "If you don't mind, I would like to take you home."

I cleared my throat, unsure if that was such a good idea. Even though I'd talked a good game in front of Wiz, I was still in a weird space. Not necessarily with Legend, but with myself. "Um..."

"Please, Simone. I just want to make sure you get home safe."

I shrugged. "Okay. Fine. But I'll drive."

"I'm good enough to drive. That fool's punches didn't do anything to me."

I moved in closer to Legend and looked him over. The bruises on his face weren't too bad. But I still wasn't comfortable with him driving.

"I'll drive," I insisted.

"Fine," he said then walked to the driver's side to open the door for me.

"Thank you."

He nodded, then watched as I slid inside.

While starting the car, I looked back at Wiz as he finally built up enough energy to stand. Shaking his head, he gave me a smirk, then grabbed his gym bag before slowly limping to his car.

I just stared, confused by what I ever saw in him.

In the past, I'd always seen glimpses of who Wiz was, but I never thought he would be that person with me.

It's funny how quickly people can switch up on you when things are no longer going their way. If I knew then what I knew now, I would have left his ass as just a memory from my teenage years. But then, I probably wouldn't have learned the lesson that I should've come to grips with a long time ago.

Pay attention to a person's actions. That will tell you how they truly feel about you.

39

SIMONE

"I'm shocked we were able to get out of there without anyone seeing you two fighting," I said as I walked over to the stool in front of my kitchen island to meet Legend. Easing between his legs, I pressed the ice-filled plastic bag against his cheek. "You two were really going at it."

"I know, and I apologize you had to see me act that way. But I hope you know that my actions were a direct result of knowing that he hurt you and then tried to play like it wasn't a big deal."

"Legend, you don't have to explain yourself to me. I know why you did what you did. Am I proud that things got physical between the two of you? No. But I also know that when it comes to protecting me, you'll do whatever it takes, and I appreciate you for that. I really do."

He nodded, then removed the bag of ice from his cheek. "A man that will stoop that low to hurt a woman that he claimed to love doesn't know shit about respect. He didn't know your worth, and he didn't care to know."

"Yeah, I see that now." I lowered my gaze and shook my head. "It's just crazy to think that I had so many blinders on when it came to him. I never thought he would've chosen to hurt me like that."

"He couldn't get past you sleeping with someone else, and I knew he wouldn't. Which is why I don't know why he ever mentioned a pass in the first place."

"That's because he thought he was the only one that would do it." Laughing, I said, "And like a dummy, I was about to fall for it."

Grabbing my hands, Legend pulled me close to him. "Yeah, you were. Then I gave you a taste of what it would be like if I tapped that ass one time."

I rolled my eyes. "Oh my God, that had nothing to do with it."

"Oh, really? So, you're saying that when I gave you a sneak peek of what else I could do to you, that didn't make your ass a little curious?"

Unable to hold back my smile, I turned away from him. I didn't need him to see the truth in my face. Knowing exactly what I was trying to do, he moved my face back toward him and looked me in the eyes. "Come on now, baby girl, you can tell me the truth. I mean, I already know, but it's so much better if I get to hear you say it."

Tilting my head to the side, I sucked my teeth. "Okay, fine. You did do a few things that made me want to know more."

"Oh yeah? Like what?"

I jerked my head back. "Legend, I'm not going there with you. You know what you did."

He nodded his head slowly. "Okay, fine. You don't have to tell me."

"Good."

Smiling, he tucked his bottom lip between his teeth, yanked me forward, then cupped my pussy with his hand.

I gasped, the feeling of his hand gliding back and forth forcing me into a trance.

With his lips right in front of mine, he whispered, "You don't have to say a single word. Like you said, I already know, which means I have no problem doing it again."

My eyes slid closed, unable to make my mouth push out anything other than a moan.

"Mmhmm," he whispered while still gliding over my pussy with one hand and grabbing my neck with the other. "Now, tell me that you love me."

I smiled, the inner workings of me pleased by the demanding tone of his voice, and the tightness of his grip. "I...I love you."

"And tell me that you know that I would never do anything to disrespect you?"

"I know that you would never do anything to disrespect me."

Grinning, he pressed his lips into mine and devoured me with his mouth. Time escaped us, and I could feel the throbbing between my legs as my body begged for more.

As if he could hear my insides speaking to him, he lowered himself until his face rested against the thin fabric that was covering my lower lips. "I just need to know one more thing," he said.

"What?"

"Are you ready to be with me for real?" he said. "I know that giving me an answer right now after everything that's happened is hard. But I think it's only because you're afraid to say it out loud. It's not because you don't know."

"Legend—"

"Hold on. I just want you to hear me out. I know that you gave a lot of years to a man that hurt you. I also know that there was a part of you that knew you two didn't belong together. I'm here to tell you why you felt that way. It's because your heart was meant for me. I want what you want. There's nothing to be confused about when it comes to us," he said and stood back up.

"Bottom line, this shit is real, and no matter how long you try to put it off, it's always going to come back around. Don't waste time trying to sort through feelings that have always been there. Whatever you need to work through, we can work through it together. Give us a chance. I know there's not a single part of you that will ever be disappointed."

I rested my hands against his face and held his gaze.

I needed to look deep into his eyes as I said what I had to say. "Legend...baby...no matter what you said to me right now, my answer was always going to be yes." Smiling, I wrapped my arms around his neck. "You've shown me what genuine love looks like. You've protected me while also respecting me. That means something to me, and I'm not willing to lose that...*ever*. So, yes, I'll be with you...today, tomorrow, and every day after that."

"Damn, you trying to make a brother cry?"

I laughed. "It's okay to cry, babe. I won't tell nobody."

Shaking his head, he reached into his pocket and grabbed his shades. "Nah, you're not about to have me looking like I'm soft."

I snatched them out of his hand. "What if I told you that seeing a man cry makes my pussy wet?"

He paused, then slid his hands into my pants to see just how serious I was. When his fingers met with the juices flowing from my swollen lips, his eyes widened. "Damn."

"Mmhmm."

Wasting no time, he dropped down to the floor and yanked my pants from my waist. As soon as his lips touched my flesh, I thought I was going to explode in his mouth. But I held it together, enjoying the warmth of his tongue as he slid in and out of me while brushing against my walls.

"Fuck, baby, fuck!"

He forced me around so that my back was against the island. Thankful for his attention to my weakness, I smiled and pressed my hand against the top of his head. I loved feeling him as he made continuous circles inside of me.

"Damn, this pussy is good," he mumbled.

I giggled, then pushed myself into him a little more to give him an even better taste.

He pressed his hands against my hips, then lifted to meet my gaze. "Now why are you playing with me like that?"

"What did I do?" I replied innocently.

He laughed, then picked me up from the floor and slung me over his shoulder. "I'm about to enjoy every minute of this."

"That makes two of us."

Letting out another laugh, he gave me a hard slap on the ass, then hurried up the stairs.

The rest of the night was everything I needed, and it wasn't just because of the sex. It was because I knew I was with the person that was made specifically for me. Even though I despised my ex with every fiber of my being, and I hated the bullshit he'd put me through. I'm grateful that his inability to give me what I needed brought me to the person who could.

Seven days later

Standing in the middle of Legend's dressing room, I pressed my hands against his chest and kissed his lips. "How are you feeling?"

"I'm feeling pretty good. Ready to hit the stage."

"Good. Mama sent me a video. It's a big crowd out there."

His phone went off, and I grabbed it from the table. "Oh, it's your grandmother."

"Cool. She's right on time." He pulled the cell from my hand

and put it on speaker. "Hey, Grandmother. Are you good out there? Did Ms. Regina get you a good seat?"

"She got me the perfect seat. I can't wait to see you boys perform. I'm still a little sad that it's the last time though."

"I know. But, hey, at least it's happening."

"That's true. I'm grateful for that."

"Me too," I chimed in.

"Hey pretty lady," she said, her smile beaming through the phone. "I hope you're not in there doing any funny business. I don't want you two in there holding up the show."

"No ma'am. There's no funny business going on. We're just talking."

"Mmhmm...that's just what you tell me.

Legend laughed. "Grandmother, she's telling the truth."

"Alright, I guess I believe you," she said. "You guys ready to say a prayer before hitting the stage?"

Just as she said that, my mother, Eden, Kendrick, and Teddy walked in.

"Hold on Grandmother, everyone just got in here." He waved for everyone to come closer. "Come on, we're about to pray."

They hurried over and grabbed each other's hands.

"We're ready," Teddy yelled toward the phone.

There was a few more seconds of silence, then Legend's grandmother said, "Lord, thank you for bringing everyone together today. Thank you for doing what needed to be done to make this happen. Thank you for seeing what was needed to heal the wounds that needed to be healed. If it wasn't for you, the blessings that we're witnessing take place in these individual's life wouldn't be happening. I pray that tonight you allow them to go out there and put their all on the stage. The fans love them, and I love them. Thank you for all your blessings. Amen."

"Amen," everyone said in unison.

"Um...can I add a little something to that prayer?" Legend chimed in.

"Go right ahead," his grandmother replied.

Gripping my hand a little tighter, he said, "I know we've all been through a rough time. So much has happened and so many things were said. Yet and still, we made it here." He took a deep breath, then looked at Teddy. "I hope things go well for you, and I hope you prove that you're stronger than the addiction that's trying to consume you."

Nodding, Teddy said, "Thank you. I appreciate that." He turned toward Eden. "I know I haven't always been fair to you, and I'm truly sorry for that. Despite the things I've said and done, you've still tried to keep a level head and hold out so I could be there for my child. I thank you for that."

"You're welcome," she replied.

Feeling the need to say something myself, I turned to face Legend and grabbed his other hand. Smiling, I looked him in his eyes. "Thank you so much for every moment you've given me. Thank you for making room for me in your world, and most importantly..." I paused and closed my eyes, trying to hold back the tears that were making their way to the surface. Clearing my throat, I pulled myself together and returned my gaze to his. "And most importantly, thank you for the bundle of joy that we will soon be able to call our own."

He looked me over with a confused expression, then pressed his hand against my stomach. "Wait a minute...are you saying—"

"I'm pregnant!" I blurted as I grabbed my cell and showed him a picture of the test that I took last night.

"Oh my God. Are you for real?"

"Yes, babe, I'm for real. We're going to have a baby."

He dropped to his knees and pressed his lips against my belly. "I'm about to be a father. You hear that, Grandmother?"

"I did. Congratulations you two."

"Congratulations," everyone screamed before pulling me into several hugs.

I couldn't stop the tears from falling down my face. Not only was I excited to be starting the family I'd always wanted, but I was even more excited to know that I was going to be starting it with the man who wanted to do the same with me.

Legend ended the call with his grandmother, then pulled me back toward him. "You know you just made me the happiest man on earth, right?"

"Did I, really?"

"Hell yeah," he shot back.

"Well, you've made me just as happy." I wrapped my arms around his neck, then teased his lips with the tip of my tongue.

He chuckled. "Baby, your mom's standing right next to us."

"Oh, my bad Mama. I forgot anyone else was in here."

"That's okay," she said before motioning for everyone to head to the door. "We'll give you two some time alone. Not too long though. The last act will be off stage soon, and you guys are up next."

"Okay. Thanks, Ms. Regina," Legend replied.

"No problem."

With my arms still around his neck, we watched as everyone strolled out of the dressing room.

Finally, alone, we stood still and just looked at each other.

"I can't believe this is real," Legend said.

"Me either. But I'm glad we're here."

He took a deep breath. "So how do you feel about flying to Vegas and becoming my wife tonight?"

"Tonight?"

"Yes, tonight."

"But what about our family?"

"Shit, they can hop on a plane and come too."

"Okay, but what about a wedding? I can't just get married and not have a wedding."

"We can do that whenever you want. But I don't want this night to end without making you my wife, and I don't want to bring our baby into this world before I do either," he said. "You deserve that and so much more."

I took a deep breath.

I was at a loss for words. Everything felt so surreal, but it also felt so right.

Grinning from ear to ear, I said, "Okay. Let's do it."

Pleased to hear my response, he pressed his hands against my face and kissed me until I couldn't do anything but giggle.

"Alright you two," my mother said as she stepped back into the dressing room. "Time to hit the stage."

Easing away from him, I tucked my bottom lip between my teeth and gripped his hand. "So, this is what finding your soulmate feels like, huh?"

"Sure is, baby girl."

"Hmm...well, I hope it stays like this forever."

"Trust me, it will."

THE END

So, what did you think? I truly hope you enjoyed Legend and Simone's story. If so, please let me know in your review and recommend it to a friend. Also, be on the lookout for what's next. If you've signed up for my mailing list or follow me on social media, you'll be the first to know. Details on the next page.

LET'S CONNECT

Join My Mailing List
www.ac-taylor.com

facebook.com/actaylortheauthor
instagram.com/actaylorbooks

ALSO BY A.C. TAYLOR

A Love Series:
A Love I Can't Control
A Love I Can't Hide
A Love I Can't Forget

Love Me Series:
Love Me When It Counts
Love Me When It Hurts
Love Me Or Lose Me

Let's Make Love Series:
Let's Make Love Tonight
You Should Still Be Mine

Everything Series:
Everything To Me
Everything I Need
Everything To Lose

Hightown Series:
Worth The Risk
Worth The Wait

Love Me Right Series:

Give Me You

Standalones:

Infinite Love

Anything Goes

Loving Sydnee Jones

Love Always, Nova Black

Something Real

The Only One

Far From Friends

Been About You

Made in the USA
Monee, IL
31 March 2025

14976777R00163